Billionaires Don't Like Nice Girls

Those Fabulous Jones Girls
Book One

M i a   C a l d w e l l

ISBN: 978-1523355907

*"From what we get, we can make a living;
what we give, however, makes a life."*
— *Arthur Ashe*

CHAPTER ONE

THE OPERATION HAD PROCEEDED as expected until Phae heard the distinctive crunch of feet stepping on gravel. She adjusted her head gear as she peered around the yard.

No night in the history of humankind could have been darker than this one. No moon graced the clear sky and the streetlights had been taken out by a robust burst of heat lightning.

Everything would have been perfect except her night vision monocle had gone blinky when she needed it most. Typical.

Phae impatiently tapped on the plastic casing, wishing for the hundredth time that she could afford something better.

The night scene flickered off and on in sickly shades of green. After one more tap on the side of the monocle, the yard finally came into steady, albeit blurry, view.

Phae scanned her surroundings but saw nothing unusual. Cautiously, she stepped to her left for a better view of the gravel driveway beside the house—nothing but Miss Eugenia's ancient Dodge.

Phae didn't doubt what she'd heard. In her experience, once she started doubting her senses she might as well pack it in and go home.

Trust your instincts, she told herself. The sound of shoes on gravel is unmistakable. No dog, cat or other furry animal could make that noise.

She waited it out. And then she finally saw him.

The man appeared silently from around the other side of the house. She couldn't discern any of his features, but she could tell that he was big ... scary big. When he looked directly at her, her heart began a fierce pounding even though he couldn't possibly see her.

8

Had she been discovered? Had she been heard going about her work? Impossible. Miss Eugenia lived alone, and judging from the way the man moved quietly and stealthily, Phae determined he must be an intruder.

Everything she had wanted to do this evening was now ruined, cancelled because of this large, menacing man. Damn.

She wondered what he planned to do, then decided it didn't matter. He was skulking where he shouldn't have skulked and one way or another she would stop him, his intentions be damned.

She formulated a plan. Her only weapon was a stun gun. Unfortunately, she'd never used it before, and since she'd bought it and the blinky night-vision monocle from the same company, she wasn't certain she should trust it.

Be creative and think fast, she thought as the man crept toward Miss Eugenia's back door.

Silently, Phae removed the pack from her waist and pulled out a long nylon cord. She slunk to a bird feeder and secured the rope to the base about a foot off the ground.

She then made her way down the yard to an ornate birdbath and secured the other end of the rope there.

The man had nearly reached the back door.

All she needed now was the brawny thug's attention. She smiled, picked up a dry twig and snapped it in half.

The man immediately stiffened. Come on, big guy, she thought.

As expected, the man moved in her direction. He approached her trip line.

Crouched low, muscles tensed, she waited. He was walking much too carefully to trip and fall, but she only needed him to drop his guard for a second, then he would be hers.

Distances were hard to estimate with the blurry monocle. He was close, maybe fifteen feet away. She took a deep, steadying breath. Five more feet and he would hit the rope.

Phae nearly gasped aloud when she heard a noisy thump to her right. She gritted her teeth when she turned and saw a big tomcat settle himself on the lid of Miss Eugenia's compost bin.

The stupid cat must have jumped off the fence, she thought, watching in frustration as the man soundlessly walked toward the bin.

She watched with surprise as the cat leapt off the bin, walked up to the man and let loose a gigantic meow before rubbing against his legs. The man jerked, then chuckled and bent down to pet the animal.

Huh. A burglar and an animal lover. People's morals often mystified Phae.

"You've given me a run for my money tonight, haven't you?" the man asked in a silken, deep voice.

Phae soundlessly pounded once on the soft grass beside her as she watched the man give the cat a final pat before turning toward the house. No twig snap would stop him this time, not with that cat around.

He was beside Miss Eugenia's t-shaped clothesline pole when Phae hopped up in desperation and dashed forward to gain the man's attention.

"Hey, buddy," she said in the lowest, most masculine bass she could muster.

Phae didn't know it, but she'd just changed the course of her life.

CHAPTER TWO

"GOOD MORNING, SUNSHINE," SYLVIE announced as she breezed into the beauty shop, the small bells over the door chiming wildly.

Shear Stylin' was clean and inviting as usual, its bright blue awning colorful in the morning light. The shop sat on a busy, quaint street in downtown Zeke's Bend, sandwiched between an antique (second hand) store and a small pharmacy that still had a soda fountain. For a small town, this was prime real estate.

Phae leaned over a sink and didn't glance up from the combs she'd been scrubbing. "You know I can't stand that happy-assed attitude this early in the morning."

"Ah, Phae. It's such a pleasure working with you. I mean, thanks to you, I get to be a Mary Poppins kind of person. With anyone else, well, I'd just be normal."

Phae didn't acknowledge the dig.

Sylvie hummed as she fluffed her short frosted-tipped hair in front of one of the large mirrors which covered most of one wall.

Phae leveled a long-suffering look at her. "Very funny. I get it. It's that 'Spoonful of Sugar' song from Mary Poppins. Ha-ha. Hilarious."

Sylvie grinned. "It helps the medicine go down, you know. Sugar, that is. It also helps you catch more flies."

"That's honey."

"Whatever." Sylvie fussed with her ample cleavage.

Phae loved her cousin, but thought she was far too girly. Sylvie was a curvy girl and took pride in every hill and valley of her voluptuous landscape. Her nails were always perfect, her hair styled, her makeup and clothes as much in fashion as she could afford.

"Your hair looks fine, as always. Quit torturing it," Phae said, not caring that she sounded grumpy as hell.

Sylvie sighed. "You're so picky about some things. Who cares if honey draws flies? But my hair? That's important!"

Phae rinsed the combs and let Sylvie rattle on. She'd heard this particular lecture a thousand times.

"After all," Sylvie continued, "our customers need to have confidence in my abilities and I can't think of a better way to reassure them than with my own appearance. You, that's a completely different thing. You worry about songs and flies, while your hair … well, I hate to be rude, but did you even pat that rats' nest down before you tied it up in a ponytail?"

Phae sensed she should have been offended to have her hair referred to as a rodent's lair. She finished rinsing the combs and dumped them into the nearby glass decanter.

"Well?" Sylvie asked, hands on her hips.

Phae glanced at herself in the mirror. Her hair did look awful. She turned her head to the side to get a better view of the lumpy bumps of black hair bunching behind the ponytail holder.

Okay, it stunk. She smiled. But she had no intention of admitting it.

"Whatever," she said, then began to fold the clean towels she'd dumped into the hydraulic chair earlier.

"Oh no, you don't." Sylvie marched over to Phae and grabbed the towel out of her hand. "Sit down and let me do something with this mess."

Phae reluctantly let Sylvie push her into the other chair, knowing from experience she'd never win this battle. "Fine. But don't do something too fru-fru with it."

She braced herself for Sylvie's chatter. Once that girl touched hair, no power in the world could stay the chitchat.

"You have such gorgeous hair." She began poking and picking and fluffing and pulling. "But it would be nicer if you'd spend a few minutes on it. And those nails—all short and unpainted. It's like you're not even a sister, cousin."

"Stereotypes, Sylvie," Phae warned. "Watch it."

Sylvie wasn't put off by the reprimand. "I think I should braid it, then you won't have to mess with it hardly at all. Ooh, yes, braids. Don't have time now, of course. How about this weekend?"

"I told you and told you, it hurts my head."

"What a baby. There's a price to pay for beauty."

"And I'm too broke to pay it."

Her cousin sighed, put out with Phae's lack of commitment. "Well, I'll do something with it so you don't frighten off business. How about a twist? That would be gorgeous and look so classy."

"I'm at work, not the grand opera."

"You're a difficult customer, Phae, and you know it. I'll figure out something." Sylvie smiled and batted her long eyelashes. "So I'm sitting at home last night waiting for Alan to call and tell me when he'd pick me up. He said he would and I believed him, like the idiot I am. I should have gone out with Neesa, but I didn't. I waited all night and the jerk never called or answered my texts. I mean, he's a chiropractor. Shouldn't a doctor be honorable and trustworthy?"

Since Sylvie had stopped separating Phae's hair, Phae assumed an answer was required. "Yes?" She hoped that was the right answer. Phae didn't like Alan, never had, and wished Sylvie would blow him off. She knew better than to say it, though.

"Right," Sylvie said. "I don't get men … what they're thinking, I mean. They say these things and don't realize it's important. Or maybe they get together and brag about how many women they've got waiting for calls every night. But that's not what I wanted to tell you. While I was waiting, Neesa called and told me that ever since the Clip and Dip did the Janson wedding … you know how that worried me, and I was right because Neesa said that she overheard the Janson twins talking about how great their hair looked at the wedding and ... I tell you, we're going to lose business over this thing and I don't know what we're going to ..."

Phae closed her eyes and tried to ignore Sylvie's worrying. She tried to be sensitive because of Sylvie's tough upbringing, her father abandoning her family when Sylvie was so young.

Still, it was hard to keep a level head when Sylvie was always terrified they were on the verge of financial disaster. Sylvie's worries sometimes made Phae question her decision to take Sylvie on as a partner. Still, she had a way with hair. She cut hair with an abandon and easy skill that Phae envied.

Phae worked in a meticulous manner, or at least she tried. Somehow, though, her styles didn't come out as well as she'd thought they should. Good thing she had so much family in Zeke's Bend to take pity on her and bring her their business or she probably really would have gone broke.

"Are you asleep? Are you listening to me?" Sylvie asked.

Phae opened her eyes. "I didn't sleep well last night. And yes, I heard. We're two days away from homelessness. Got it."

Sylvie smoothed her palms over Phae's hair. "Okay, we're done. I just need some product to control the frizzy fly-aways."

Phae swiveled and jumped out of the chair. The last thing she needed was helmet head. "Think of those fly-aways as tendrils. My first appointment will be here any second and I've still got to fold the towels. Thanks for fixing me up."

Sylvie shrugged. "You're hopeless, cousin. So who's on tap first this morning?"

"Miss Eugenia."

Sylvie startled Phae by laughing. "Oh, that's too good! I can't wait until she gets here. She'll give us the real scoop. First thing this morning Neesa called me and told me the news. Last night—"

The jingling of bells interrupted her story as Miss Eugenia entered the shop. Phae looked sharply at Sylvie to squelch her story.

Phae knew where this one was going … straight in the direction of Miss Eugenia's backyard garden.

Phae had spent most of the night lying awake, mentally re-running her encounter with the burglar.

Phae smiled at the tiny, white-haired lady. "Good morning, Miss Eugenia. What a lovely blue blouse you have on today. Come have a seat. I'm ready for you."

Miss Eugenia didn't return Phae's smile, but she did seat herself. "It's not a good morning, dear, though that's not your fault."

"I heard all about it, Miss Eugenia. How are you holding up?" Sylvie asked with far too much twinkle in her eyes.

"My dear, I'm at my wit's end." She sighed loudly. "But it's Kent that I'm most worried about. The poor boy. Look what I've done to him. I feel terrible, Lord is my witness, I truly do."

"But Miss Eugenia," Sylvie said, "it's not your fault. It's that Captain Nice Guy. Sure, he's done a lot of good things, but this time he messed up."

I didn't mess up, Phae thought. What were they talking about? And what happened to Miss Eugenia's nephew, Kent?

Miss Eugenia frowned harder, doubling the wrinkles on her brow. "Captain who?"

"You know," Sylvie said while settling herself into the other hydraulic chair. "That pretend superhero guy who's been going around town doing all those good deeds. The newspaper has started calling him Captain Nice Guy. Ha-ha!"

"Oh him. He's been around a long time," Miss Eugenia said. "I'd forgotten that's what they've been calling him lately. I'm very old. You'll know what it's like one day. Last night, the police called him the perpetrator."

Perpetrator? What did she mean by that?

All three women looked toward the door as the tinkling bells proclaimed another patron. Neesa, another cousin and unofficial best friend to both Sylvie and Phae, strolled into the shop.

Neesa, Sylvie and Phae were all cousins of an age, twenty-six-ish, and had grown up together in Zeke's Bend with the rest of the massive Jones family. The small, quaint town of 5,000 had been founded by one of the Jones' ancestors.

In the mid-1800s, Zeke Jones had been a trapper and trader and settled at a bend in the Elk River during the off season to sell his goods to river travelers. Zeke got married eventually, had a family, more people moved in to the area, and eventually, it became a town.

Phae loved Zeke's Bend, having returned there from Chicago when life in the city didn't work out after college. Coming home had seemed like failure at first, but now, she realized this was always where she'd been meant to be: surrounded by friends and family.

"Neesa!" Sylvie jumped out of the chair. "Sit down. Miss Eugenia is telling us all about what happened last night."

Neesa gave Miss Eugenia a sympathetic smile while seating herself. "How is Kent doing this morning?"

The older lady's eyes glistened with unshed tears. "The doctor said he'll recover, but it will take some time. You should see him. It's terrible. I blame myself. He would have been okay if I hadn't been such a ninny about that garden. And you know how I worry about his health. He never complains, mind you. Insists he's the very picture of health, brave thing. But I can see he's actually a very sickly boy."

Sylvie and Neesa nodded seriously while Phae clenched her hands tightly behind her back. Something awful must have happened. Did the burglar escape and attack Kent? How could that have happened? She'd tied the robber securely.

"Don't blame yourself," Sylvie said. "If that Captain Nice Guy hadn't been out minding other people's business, everything would have been all right."

Neesa murmured her assent.

Miss Eugenia shook her head as vigorously as her eighty-two years allowed. "No, I can't blame him. He's helped many people around here and I can't find it in myself to condemn him. He obviously thought he was doing a good deed. No, it's all my fault. My dear Kent was beaten to unconsciousness because I overreacted."

Phae kept her voice as calm as she could. "Maybe you could clarify this for me, Miss Eugenia. Exactly what happened? Did someone attack your nephew?"

Tears glistened once again in the elderly lady's eyes. "I'm sorry dear. I didn't realize you didn't know. This Captain Nice Guy attacked my dear Kent last night. He smashed him over the head then tied him up like an animal to my old laundry line pole. It was dreadful. Then he called the police and told them my poor Kent was a criminal ... Phae, you look ... Sylvie, get a chair and some smelling salts. Fast! I think she's going to faint."

PHAE TRIED TO KEEP HER balance while Sylvie yanked a chair over and shoved Phae into it.

"Smelling salts, Sylvie! Quickly!" Miss Eugenia demanded.

Sylvie lightly slapped Phae's cheeks. "It's not 1880. We don't have smelling salts laying around."

Neesa looked closely into Phae's face. "She looks ashen around the mouth. She hasn't fainted, though. I don't think all that slapping is necessary, Sylvie."

Phae heard nothing. She told herself that none of the story could be true. She refused to consider the idea that she could make such a mistake. And yet, the man skulking around Miss Eugenia's house hadn't been a burglar. Unbelievable. The nearly unconscious man she'd tied to the post had been the sickly nephew, Kent.

But what was this about bashing him on the head? She'd done no such thing.

Neesa's voice penetrated Phae's mental haze. "Look, her eyes are coming back into focus. Seriously, Sylvie, quit slapping her. How is she supposed to talk with you smacking her around like that?"

"I think it's helping," Sylvie said.

Phae grabbed Sylvie's hands and pushed them away. "Stop it! My cheeks are on fire."

"Oh my goodness," Miss Eugenia said. "You gave us quite a scare. Poor, sweet girl. I didn't mean to distress you so badly. I didn't realize you cared so much for my poor Kent. You've never met, have you? I've told you so much about him over the years that you probably feel like you know him, though. Forgive me. Poor, sweet girl. A sensitive soul."

Phae wondered if maybe she should be doing a little slapping herself. "No, honestly, I'm fine. I didn't eat any breakfast. I'm fine now."

Neesa frowned. "Sylvie, run back into her apartment and get her something to eat."

Phae began to protest but Sylvie had already raced away, gone through the back door. Phae returned her attention to the elderly lady.

"So," she said to Miss Eugenia, "someone hit your nephew on the head?"

"Oh yes. Bashed him right on the forehead. Poor Kent could have been killed."

Phae tried to settle this version of events with what had actually happened. It didn't add up. She contemplated her next question.

Sylvie returned with a cold hot dog on a piece of white bread. She thrust it into Phae's hands. "Eat it. It's repulsive, but it's all I could find in that wasteland you call a fridge."

In order to keep up her cover story, Phae took a big bite.

Sylvie grimaced. "That is so gross."

"Get over it," Phae grumbled, her mouth still full. It wasn't so bad. Sylvie was a food snob.

"Let the poor woman eat," Neesa said.

Phae nodded. "I wanna know about the nephew."

Sylvie pulled a chair beside Phae. "Captain Nice Guy snuck into Miss Eugenia's back yard last night, apparently to replant the garden that those hooligans ran their bikes through a couple days ago. He didn't finish, though, and left all these unplanted flowers behind. Anyway, Miss Eugenia had been worried about those hooligans destroying her garden and so she called her nephew to come stay with her and protect her for a few days …"

"Actually," Miss Eugenia interrupted, "he was coming anyway to spend some time with me. And I didn't ask him to come. He was concerned about me and my safety, so he flew in from Phoenix a few days early."

Sylvie winked at Phae. "Right. Anyway, Captain Nice Guy must not be as well-informed as we've thought. He didn't know Kent was there. So, last night, Kent told the police that he couldn't sleep and that he heard a noise in the back yard. He went outside to investigate and found a cat and figured that was what had made the noise. On his way back into the house—"

Miss Eugenia broke in. "And that's when Captain Nice Guy smashed poor Kent on the head and tied him to my laundry pole. It's all my fault. I should have had those poles taken out years ago. Poor Kent. You should see him. He looks simply dreadful."

Phae grimaced. She hadn't hit anyone. Was Kent lying? "He said that the captain hit him? For sure?"

"Yes."

Sylvie turned her back on Miss Eugenia and grinned slyly at Phae. "That's one side of the story. I heard that Kent told the police that he'd started to go back into the house when someone said something like, 'Hey you!' He nearly had a heart attack as I hear it. He turned around fast and BAM! He smashed his head on the cross bar of the laundry line pole."

Neesa hid a grin behind her hand when Miss Eugenia sniffed loudly. Phae was simply relieved that Kent had told the truth after all.

Sylvie continued her version of events. "Kent said the next thing he realized, he was tied to the pole and this guy was kind of laughing at him, saying it served him right, and that the police would be there soon to take care of him." Sylvie couldn't contain herself any longer and burst out laughing.

Neesa joined her.

"Oh, hush, you two," Miss Eugenia scolded with an offended look. "Kent invented all that to protect the real villain, that Captain man. Kent can't know what actually happened. He's befuddled from the blow. It nearly killed him, I tell you, though he won't admit it. You simply would not believe the trouble I had making him stay in bed today. I blame myself, though, no one else. Not even the captain. He was trying to help, I'm sure. But he should be more careful about who he whacks on the head and ties up. He should be thankful that Kent covered for him by making up that other story."

Sylvie stifled more laughter and headed over to where Neesa was waiting to get her hair washed.

Sylvie lowered the back of the chair. "I heard all that really happened is Kent got a bump on his head."

"That's what I heard, too," Neesa added quickly before Sylvie turned on the water.

Miss Eugenia raised her chin. "I throw my hands up on the lot of you. This town is filled with gossips who can't get their stories straight. Laugh all you want, but I know the truth of the matter."

Phae could see she was getting wound up but knew no way to stop it.

Miss Eugenia continued. "And what am I going to do about my garden? That captain may do some good deeds for folks, but he's a terrible gardener. You should see it. The two rows he planted are all crooked and some of the plants are nearly sideways in the ground. It was very dark last night, granted, and he should probably do his good deeds during the day. But still, is he blind or something?"

Phae winced, once again cursing her lousy night-vision gear. Without thinking, she blurted, "I'll take care of it, Miss Eugenia. How about this weekend?"

Sylvie and Neesa looked shocked. Though Miss Eugenia was a kind old lady, no one volunteered to spend time with her. "Such a sweet girl," Miss Eugenia said. "So concerned. You nearly fainted when I told you about what happened to poor Kent, didn't you? You're so sweet to offer, Phae."

"Actually, the fainting thing was because I hadn't eaten. I'm fine. Let's do your hair."

"Don't be so modest. You're a concerned human being and you care about others. When you come, you'll meet Kent. I'm sure you'll get along fabulously. Now, about my hair. I want a set. I can't be away from poor Kent for too long. He never has been very healthy. Have I mentioned that? I'm afraid this recent to-do might cause him a setback. You don't suppose you could come plant my garden tomorrow afternoon, do you? It would be so nice if Kent had a visitor during his convalescence. I'll help him come outside so he can keep you company while you work."

Phae struggled to keep from grinning at the idea of the frail lady helping anyone get anywhere. She couldn't figure out how Miss Eugenia got herself around and about. "Sure. I'll be there tomorrow."

Sylvie patted Neesa's hair with a towel. "Are you matchmaking, Miss Eugenia?"

She waved her hand. "I honestly hadn't given it any thought." She gave Phae a critical look-over. "Phae's a lovely girl, but too independent for my Kent. He needs someone to take care of him and pamper him. Maybe someone who's a nurse. I don't know if I've mentioned it, but Kent's not very well."

Phae spritzed down Miss Eugenia's baby-fine hair and began to roll it. Only half-listening to Miss Eugenia's chatter, she nodded off and on. She told herself not to think about what had happened to Kent. She also avoided considering what criminal charges she might face if she were discovered.

Having no children herself, Miss Eugenia doted on her only nephew, boring everyone in town with her endless bragging about him. She said Kent was the owner of some big shot software company out in Phoenix. She even went so far as to claim the guy was a billionaire. Phae had nearly snorted out loud the first time she heard that one.

A billionaire. Sure he was. She supposed Kent might be moderately successful, and she couldn't blame Miss Eugenia for being proud of him, but she didn't believe a quarter of the old lady's stories.

As for who Kent actually was, he was probably a sniveling narcissist thanks to the elderly lady's overbearing devotion. She imagined him at that very moment gathering all the manpower his supposed wealth could muster to wreak revenge on Captain Nice Guy.

Ridiculous. He was probably like every other small business owner Phae knew: struggling to keep their doors open and living hand-to-mouth.

This morning had not turned out as she'd expected. She had thought that, once again, everyone in town would hail Captain Nice Guy as a great hero. Instead, he was a laughingstock to some and a villain to others. Damn.

How could she have made such a stupid mistake? Funny thing, though. For such a sickly man, Kent appeared to be awfully large and muscular. And he was really heavy when she shoved him up against the pole.

Maybe she needed to work out more.

She'd have to reschedule three appointments the next day in order to spend a long afternoon with a chatterbox lady and a sickly, wheezy computer nerd. Great.

She hoped her lousy night vision monocle would like its new home in the landfill.

CHAPTER THREE

PHAE RELUCTANTLY KNOCKED ON Miss Eugenia's front door. Maybe she'd get lucky and if she clicked her heels together, the afternoon would be over. Or she'd disappear. Or Miss Eugenia wouldn't answer the door. Or—

Miss Eugenia opened the door.

"Phae, dear, come in. I'm all ready for you. I know you're busy, so we'll go on out to the back yard. Unless you'd like some pie first. Would you like some pie? No, well, I have plenty if you'd like a slice. Rhubarb. And sweet potato. And peach. And blueberry. And, oh I can't remember them all. Everyone has been so kind, sending over treats to succor poor Kent during his convalescence. Follow me, dear. Right through here."

Last night, Phae had had a terrible nightmare. She'd been stuck in Miss Eugenia's parlor sipping a lukewarm, bottomless cup of tea as the elderly woman recited the family history of every person in Zeke's Bend. Garden implements floated by, an inch out of reach. Whenever Phae tried to grab one, it disappeared, and Miss Eugenia would make her eat another cookie. Pasty-faced, skinny Kent reclined on the sofa cackling like a maniac. "I'll get that Captain Nice Guy," he screeched.

She'd woken and sat up straight, her brow damp from sweat. Dumbass nightmare.

While her visit today wasn't likely to turn into a wonderful outing, it had to be better than her nightmare.

"Here we go, dear," Miss Eugenia said. "Out the back door. Watch that step. It always takes me by surprise." She rambled on about how long she'd been living in the house (forty years) and how her father left it to her, and how it was a good thing because she was an old maid and a poor, retired school teacher.

"I never much liked children," Miss Eugenia added, saying her first interesting thing of the visit. "Kent is the only child I ever liked. And now he's all grown up."

She pointed to the rear of her large yard. "There's my garden, dear. Come along. You should have seen how lovely my flowers were before those ruffians tore it up. I'm not sure how these new plants will fare since it's already June. Look at that. Terrible sight, isn't it?"

Phae frowned as she took in the sloppy, crooked rows of wilting plants. "Captain Nice Guy isn't much of a gardener, is he?"

"It'll take some work to get it back in shape. But you're young and strong. I'm sure you'll do a fine job."

Phae nodded, wondering morosely how long the replanting would take. She pasted a smile on her face while Miss Eugenia pointed out where the tools could be found and other information she thought Phae required, like who had built the tool shed and how she was afraid of spiders and how the mealy worms got her roses, etc.

Phae grabbed some tools out of the shed then kneeled down to get started.

The elderly lady settled into a nearby lawn chair. "I'm glad it turned off cool and cloudy today. The weatherman said it will be unseasonably cool for the next couple days. It's a front from Canada. Or maybe Alaska. Do we get fronts from Alaska? You should have worn gloves, dear. You have to protect your pretty hands if you don't want callouses. And you don't, by the way. It's not ladylike, my mother always said. I think there's some gloves in the shed. Go fetch them. Right. There you go. A lady must protect her hands. I'm not sure why, but that's what everyone says, so there must be truth to it."

Screw the gloves, Phae thought, digging around in the cobwebby shed, wishing she had earplugs instead.

"Can you find them, Phae? Ah, I see. They're large, aren't they? They'll work, though. They probably belong to Kent. Oh … Kent. What's happening to me? I forgot all about him. He's still in bed. I'll be back shortly. Carry on without me."

Phae watched Miss Eugenia speed across the lawn. For all her complaints, the woman had her spry moments. The plants lifted easily out of the loose soil. She could probably finish the job in a few hours. She glanced at her watch. If she managed to avoid a dinner invitation, she'd be home by six. Phae sped up her digging and soon lost herself in the work. She jerked when she heard the bang of the screen door. She looked up. And her mouth dropped open.

MISS EUGENIA, TINY LADY THAT she was, plodded slowly across the lawn, a giant man draped around her. Phae hid her grin behind the back of her gloved hand.

She couldn't see Kent's face because he'd lowered his head, obviously in an attempt to better hear Miss Eugenia's admonitions to take care and walk slower. He'd bent himself nearly in half in order to wrap both his arms around Miss Eugenia's thin shoulders.

His aunt had one hand on his waist while the other hand fluttered about to emphasize her warnings. Kent's rear end bobbed up and down with each mincing step.

They looked like they were involved in the most bizarre hug Phae had ever seen.

"Be careful, Kent. It's only a few more steps. You can do it. Almost there. Be careful. There's the chair behind her. Not too fast! You might get dizzy. There … there … there. Ahh." Miss Eugenia beamed triumphantly.

"We made it," she burbled. "I knew we would. Now you sit and rest. I know it was a terrible trip. Oh. This is Phae Jones. She's the one who kindly offered to replant my garden. Phae, this is my darling nephew—"

Miss Eugenia gasped then rushed to Phae's side. "Oh, my poor dear. Look, Kent ... tears! Oh, don't cry, Phae. He'll be fine, eventually. Truly. He's just weak. See, Kent? Didn't I tell you how compassionate she is?"

Phae fought to control herself but was losing the battle. Every second she held in the laughter, more tears streamed down her cheeks. She tried to take a deep, steadying breath but only tiny spurts of air would enter her spasmodic windpipe.

Wiping her face with the delicate handkerchief that Miss Eugenia gave her, Phae realized that to outsiders she probably looked like she was having a grief fit. This insight only made the situation funnier.

"Oh, Kent!" Miss Eugenia cried. "Her face is a funny color. I bet it's the heat stroke. Is it hot enough for that? I don't know. I'll get a cool cloth anyway. And some lemonade." She patted Phae's shoulder. "Lemonade fixes everything. I'll be right back."

Phae clamped her hand over her mouth until the little lady disappeared into the house. Then she collapsed onto the ground and cut loose, laughing.

The more she thought about it, the funnier it got. She indulged herself until her hilarity subsided into a giggle, then pulled herself into a seated position and realized she'd been hearing a deep, rumbling chuckle.

She looked at Kent.

He sat reclined back in the lawn chair, hands clasped behind his head and legs stretched out straight. He was nothing like she'd imagined.

He had thick black hair, so shiny it nearly shimmered blue like a blackbird's wing. He had a handsome Roman nose, straight and long. A square jaw. Unblemished tanned, beach bum skin. Beautiful, twinkling blue eyes. The only imperfection on that face was the blue and green lump on his wide forehead.

He was a powerfully handsome man, with the kind of hard body a woman dreams about while taking a bubble bath. His biceps bulged in perfect definition. And his chest ... mmm ...

"I take it I didn't fool you with my cripple act," Kent said in the deepest, richest bass voice she'd ever heard. It was mesmerizing.

Phae blinked. "Huh?"

"I said I was unable to fool you. How tall are you?"

"Fool me? I don't think so. Tall?"

Kent smiled then repeated himself, slowly. "How ... tall ... are ... you?"

His tone snapped Phae to attention. "Five-eight, smart guy."

Kent smiled on.

"Why do you want to know how tall I am? And that's what I meant when I said 'tall' the way I did," Phae said.

"Pardon me. I misunderstood. I thought maybe your heat stroke had left you giddy, disoriented perhaps."

Phae grinned. "I'm feeling better now, thank you. So about the tall question ..."

Kent lowered his arms and leaned forward. "I like curious women. I asked about your height because my aunt is playing matchmaker and once she has her mind set on something, you might as well go along with it. Since I'm a tall man, the first requirement you must meet is height."

"I see. And do I pass?"

His brow furrowed. "We've got about a seven inch difference. Not insurmountable. You'll do on that count."

"Are you implying that I have deficiencies elsewhere?"

"You're worse for the wear from all that crying, and your eyes are more red than brown right now. And that hair. Did you even brush it before you pulled it back?"

"Your aunt has told me a lot about you, but she didn't mention that you're a rude jerk."

"Ah! Impertinent. I like that. But those delicate female sensibilities will never do. You'll have to learn to be less sensitive about your shortcomings if you're going to improve yourself. Still, for all that, you have a nice shape. Why don't you stand up so I can get a better look?"

"I don't need that kind of scrutiny from a puny, sickly invalid like you. Perhaps you'd like to judge my feet instead?" She waved a foot in the air. "Too big? Too wide? Too small? Too narrow?"

"They're okay, but what I really like is the way your muscles flex when you move your foot like that. And those white shorts. They show off your long, golden-brown legs to perfection."

Phae dropped her leg. "My golden-brown legs?"

"That's right. Your skin glows, in case you haven't noticed. I've noticed. And however much they emphasize your lovely skin, I have to question the practicality of wearing white shorts while gardening. You're not very sensible, are you?"

"I'll have you know that—"

"Yoo-hoo!" Miss Eugenia called.

Phae and Kent turned toward the house.

"I've got to run a quick errand. Mrs. Tate has had a setback."

"I'll drive you," Kent said, making to stand up.

"Good heavens, no! Stay right there, silly boy. Keep an eye on him while I'm gone, Phae. He refuses to heed the danger of his injuries. And Kent, don't move from that chair until I return."

They called their goodbyes and the back door closed behind the elderly do-gooder.

"Miss Eugenia to the rescue," Phae said, returning to her planting.

"It seems that Mrs. Tate's distress takes precedence over your grief-induced heat stroke."

"Damn. I was going to get lemonade. Still, she has her priorities in the right order." Phae pushed a marigold into the hole she'd dug.

"So," Kent continued, kicked back and relaxed into his chair again, "when you dress up for a night on the town, do you wear sequined dresses? I can't stand those things. I like what you women call little black dresses. You know, the super short kind. With thin straps that remind me of lingerie."

"I don't own any fancy dresses. In case you haven't noticed, Zeke's Bend doesn't have any overpriced restaurants or nightclubs or anything else like that. And you can quit with the quiz. Miss Eugenia isn't trying to get us together."

"She's not? Then why are you here?"

Phae held up her gloved hands. "The garden? This thing where I'm sticking plants in the ground."

"That? It's a ruse." He waved a dismissive hand in the air. "My aunt planned it all out. Last night I had to listen to her describe you for hours and hours. You certainly have a lengthy list of accomplishments."

"And probably not one of them is true," Phae said, pushing an escaped tendril of long, curly hair away from her face. "Anyway, it's only fair. We've had to listen to stories about you for oh, I don't know, forever."

Kent groaned, a low seductive rumble that made Phae's stomach flutter. "Tell me the bad news. I can only imagine what she's been saying."

"Nothing awful. She's proud of your successes. You own a software company, right?"

"Personal security apps. So, about you again. I've been told you have a degree from an Ivy League college out east, something to do with business. You used your fine education to become a hairdresser here where you grew up. Is hairdressing an artistic calling or are you not interested in competing in the big world?"

"What?" Phae stared at his gloating, though handsome face, his teasing truly annoying her for the first time. "You'd better back off, buddy. I like this town and I'm not going to listen to an uptight computer geek insult it, or me, for that matter. You've been riding a fine line during this whole conversation and now you've veered off course—"

"I'm not trying to insult you or your town, though I can't say the same for you. Computer geek's a little harsh. Besides, I like this town. When I was a kid, I used to spend my summers here with Aunt Eugenia. She didn't let me out of her sight, or this yard much, either, but I've always liked it."

Phae gave him an indifferent nod then resumed her digging. Out of the corner of her eye, she saw him leisurely cross his legs.

"No apology for the geek crack?" He sighed dramatically. "So you hold a grudge, too. Unfortunate. We'll have to work on that if we don't want to disappoint my aunt and her matchmaking efforts. First, you have to learn to forgive. It's not easy, I know, but I can give you lessons. Second, you need to learn how to live up to your potential. I can help there, too. But you're going to—"

"Hold it right there. Before you get carried away solving my problems, listen up. I'm here to plant this garden. I repeat … the garden. Miss Eugenia is not playing matchmaker for us."

Phae had a wicked thought. "Actually, Mr. Kent Big Shot Holmes, Miss Eugenia informed me that I am far too independent for someone like you. She said you need a more motherly kind of woman who will take care of you because you're so sickly. She was right. Look at you. Pale and puny. You need a nurse, not a girlfriend." She smiled to herself as she stabbed the small spade into the ground.

"I see," he said, his eyes twinkling more than ever. "That's that, I guess. I don't gainsay my aunt. You know, I'd rather grown to like you, in spite of your shortcomings. It's a pity, but I guess it can't be helped." He stood. "I suppose I might as well help you with the garden."

"Don't over-stress yourself. I'd hate for you to have a setback. Miss Eugenia would skin me alive and she'd have to haul you back inside. Doubt I'd survive another scene like that." She grinned at the memory.

Kent knelt beside her and began digging. "I'll be fine. Keep a lookout for Aunt Eugenia. If she catches me doing this I'll probably have to go to the hospital for another x-ray."

"I take it that bump on your forehead has already been x-rayed once?"

"Yeah. She wanted an MRI, too, but the doctor managed to get her to see reason eventually. I love my aunt, but sometimes …"

"No need to explain. By the way, I'm sorry about what happened to you the other night. With Captain Nice Guy, I mean."

Kent nodded. "Thanks. But it's not your fault. And I'll live."

They worked together in silence for a few minutes. Phae surreptitiously watched Kent's large, capable hands gently cover a plant's roots. Why was it so sexy when a big strong man was tender with something small and delicate? Too bad he had to ruin it when he began talking again.

"So tell me about this Captain Nice Guy," Kent said. "Something other than the obvious part about him being a lousy gardener."

"I don't know much about him. Nobody does."

"How long has he been running around helping people?"

"Nobody knows."

"What sort of things has he done?"

Phae picked at the roots of the daisy she held. "Lots of little things. Nothing important."

"One of the deputies told me that the captain stopped a robbery at a convenience store last year."

"I think he simply called the police. I'm not sure."

"When did everyone start calling him Captain Nice Guy?"

Phae nearly groaned. She hated the name. "Local newspaper. Somebody used it in a letter to the editor I think. Don't know."

Kent had a bemused expression. "You're awfully uncertain on this subject. I feel like we're playing twenty questions. Are the goings-on of this guy a secret or something?"

"No, I don't pay much attention to him, that's all. I think it's kind of silly, the way people gossip about him. I say leave him alone and let him do his thing."

"I think it's fascinating, myself. Although I've got to admit that since my run-in with him, I've worried about what might happen if he got too carried away. What happened to me was likely an accident, and he didn't actually harm me, but still, this guy sneaks around town in the middle of the night. Anything could happen."

Phae found herself affronted by the suggestion that she might be incompetent. "I don't think so. He doesn't get involved with rough stuff."

"You mean he hasn't so far, which isn't to say that he won't at some point in the future."

"I don't think he would."

"We'll see eventually. By the way, I understand no one has ever gotten a good look at him?"

"Nope. Never."

"Then how does everyone know Captain Nice Guy isn't actually Captain Nice Girl?"

Phae stiffened, then quickly shoved another plant into the loose soil.

CHAPTER FOUR

"YOU GONNA EAT THAT, PHAE?"

Phae pushed her plate toward Sylvie, who happily snatched up the remaining crinkly fries.

"I've got to stop eating these big lunches," Phae said while eyeing her half-eaten burger and fries. "It costs too much, and it's too much food. I'm having a salad at home tomorrow, Sylvie, so don't tempt me again."

"Nobody said you had to order the deluxe fat special, you know. Look at me. I'm eating a salad." She ate a fry drenched in ketchup and swallowed quickly. "You don't have to eat at home to eat healthy."

"I can't order healthy food when I eat out. And I can't leave food on my plate, either." Phae grabbed another fry and began to munch.

"Just because you paid for it, doesn't mean you have to eat it. Practice some self-discipline. Put the fry down."

Phae shook her head.

"The fry. Put it down." She pointed her fork at Phae. "I don't want to have to poke you."

"Don't act righteous. I know you're not trying to save me from the fries. You want all of them for yourself."

Sylvie grinned charmingly. "It can be both things at once, you know. They aren't mutually exclusive."

"Okay, tough girl with the scary fork. You win. Take it with you when we leave. You can use it to keep me out of here tomorrow."

"Actually, I think you should come here every day. You need to get out more, be social, see people and be seen."

"I work in a beauty shop. All I do all day long is see people. And talk to people. And listen to people. And put up with people and—"

"Okay, I didn't mean people. I meant men. Men never come into the shop and when they do, it's only to pick up their wives or girlfriends."

"Look around this place. How many people are in here? Maybe thirty? And yes, most of them are men, but if they're not married, they're related. Leave it alone and let me handle my own love life."

Sylvie shrugged and raised her hands in surrender. "Okay, already. Tomorrow we'll eat salads at the shop. Hey, wait a minute. Who's that?"

Phae turned toward the door. Her heart stopped for a moment when she recognized Kent Holmes. He looked even more handsome than she remembered in a snug knit shirt and casual slacks.

She reminded herself to act naturally. After the way she'd bolted from Miss Eugenia's garden the other day, Kent must think her either foolish or shifty.

Phae took a deep breath, smiled and waved.

"Oh my God, you know him," Sylvie said. "Does that mean you have dibs? He's gorgeous. He's coming over here. He's hot."

"I know. Calm down. And anyway, you should be thinking about Dr. Alan."

"Doctor who? Oh, right. He's not really a doctor, you know. He's a chiropractor," she hissed.

"Shh. And I don't have dibs. Well, maybe, I don't know." Phae took a sip of water.

Kent strolled up in all his manly glory, impossibly tall in the cafe. "Hi, mind if I join you?" he asked in his wonderfully deep voice.

Phae waved to a chair. "Please do."

The women avidly watched him sit down, imagining the motions of the muscles under his pants.

"Where's your ponytail?" he asked with a smile.

"Sylvie took pity on me and did my hair today. Sylvie, this is Miss Eugenia's puny, sickly nephew Kent Holmes. As you can see, he's not well, so don't be too witty or charming. We don't want to wear him out."

Kent grinned at Phae and raised a perfectly shaped brow. "I haven't seen you in five excruciatingly long days and this is how you greet me? Have some pity, woman." He looked at Sylvie. "It's nice to meet you. My aunt tells me you work with Phae. My condolences."

Phae rolled her eyes at Sylvie's girlish giggle. "Don't egg him on, Sylvie. He's impossible to stop once he gets started."

Sylvie batted her eyelashes at Kent. "I can't imagine why any lady would ever want to stop you from getting anything you wanted."

"You need to take lessons from your partner, Phae. She knows how to talk to a man," he teased. "You should have seen how rude your cousin was the other day, Sylvie. We were having a nice conversation and the next thing you know—whoosh—she was gone, ranting about some class she was missing. I don't know what I could have said that set her off like that. I had to finish the garden by myself. And my aunt is giving her all the glory." He shot Phae a handsome sideways glance. "How tall are you, Sylvie?"

Phae snorted and crossed her arms over her chest.

Sylvie answered sweetly, "I'm five-four. And how tall are you?"

"Don't encourage him," Phae said. "He's socially awkward and asks odd things."

Kent leaned back in his chair and slowly perused Phae. "And you, I'm sure, are the most accomplished socialite in Zeke's Bend. I can tell by your clothes, the jeans that couldn't be a day over ten years old. And there's that big, frayed rip on the knee. You ripped it intentionally, I'm sure, so the guys can get tantalizing glimpses of your lovely knee cap."

He was interrupted briefly while he ordered some coffee from the waitress.

"And that baggy t-shirt," he continued when the waitress was gone, "it's a prime example of feminine wiles. By concealing yourself under loose clothes, you leave it up to a man's imagination to picture your shape. Far better than revealing yourself in something like a low-cut blouse. And crossing your arms over your chest only adds fuel to the fire."

He winked at Sylvie. "The true finishing touch to this vamp is her lack of make-up. Take notes, Sylvie. By not enhancing her features with cosmetics, she's telling the world that she's bold and free. There's nothing men like better than a bold, free woman."

"Okay, Tim Gunn, that's enough," Phae said with a disdainful little smile. "Maybe I was wrong when I called you socially awkward. You're more like socially demented."

"How do you work with her, Sylvie?" Kent asked, but looked only at Phae. "She's so cantankerous I'm surprised she doesn't run off all your customers."

"She's an acquired taste," Sylvie answered.

"Hmm. I could see that," Kent said, suggestive speculation in his tone.

The waitress returned with his coffee and he thanked her. "See, Phae? I can be polite when no one's provoking me."

Phae unfolded her arms. "Me provoke you? Puh-lease. I can hardly get a word in edgewise."

Sylvie scooted her chair back and stood. "All right, you two. I'm leaving. No, don't ask me to stay. I have an appointment in five minutes anyway. What about you, Phae?"

"She's going to be late," Kent said, raising an eyebrow as he looked at Phae.

She smiled lazily and returned his stare. "Tell Meg I'll be late, please, Sylvie."

Kent grinned. "Actually, Phae's going to have to cancel that appointment."

"Cancel my appointment, Sylvie," Phae said.

"Good grief," Sylvie muttered as she walked away. "I've never seen anything like that in my entire life."

Kent and Phae inspected one another through lidded eyes.

"I think she sensed our attraction to each other," Kent said.

"Who said I'm attracted to you?"

"I assumed. Why else would you cancel an appointment? I doubt it's something you normally do."

"How do you know what I normally do? I cancelled three appointments to replant your aunt's garden, so don't get a big head."

"You're not very dedicated to your career are you?"

"Right now," she said, "I'm dedicated to convincing a certain socially demented man that he is the provoker and I am the provokee."

He sipped his coffee. "I wish you luck, particularly since I'm certain that provokee isn't a word."

Phae watched him purse his sexy lips as he gently blew on his coffee. Sipping coffee shouldn't have been erotic, but with this guy, it was. When he swallowed, she swallowed.

"Ho! What do we have here?" a voice boomed from above them.

Although she was disappointed to be interrupted from studying Kent's lips, she smiled at the burly middle-aged man standing beside the table. She said hello and reluctantly introduced Kent to her Uncle Leon.

"Well, then," Leon said in his usual loud voice. "So you're Genia's nephew. Didn't I see you in here yesterday? How's that head of yours holding up, boy? All I see is a little bruise. Buck up and tell that aunt of yours to quit bending everybody's ears about how you're dying."

Kent shook his head. "I'm not fighting her. She's too tough for me. Why don't you go over to the house and tell her yourself? I'm sure she's home. Or at least she was when I snuck out the back door an hour ago. Sneaking around has been the story of my life lately."

"Ho, ho, boy. This old rabbit's foot I carry is real powerful, but not powerful enough to protect me from your aunt. I know better than to tangle with Genia. I figured since you're family she'd take it easy on ya."

"Then you're living in a fantasy world, sir."

Leon laughed and slapped Kent on the shoulder. "Yep, you're okay, boy … for a billionaire. Ha-ha! That was the best one ever, Genia going around telling everyone how you've got a billion dollars! Why didn't she go on and say you're a trillionaire, or a goo-goo-gagillionaire. Ha-ha!"

Kent chuckled. "Aunt Eugenia. She's a caution."

Leon laughed some more then glanced at Phae. "So how do you know our girl here?"

"I met her the other day when she replanted Aunt Eugenia's garden."

"Don't get any ideas about her, if you know what I'm saying. Yeah, she's good-looking enough and she's got a good heart, but when it comes to men, she's mean, boy. Real mean. She doesn't take no pity on a man, I hear, and seen some of it myself. She'll tear ya down and leave ya whimperin' before you can count to ten."

Kent glanced in question at the glowering Phae.

"She doesn't care about a man's ego," Leon continued, settling into his blustering tale, rocking back and forth on the balls of his big feet. "And she's too darned independent. We gave up years ago on the hopes of her marryin' and settlin' down. When my mother died, she left all her money to Phae so she'd be taken care of in her old age. The rest of us were okay with that, we're all that sure about our Phae. Why, one time this fellow took a liking to her and we all had high hopes that maybe somebody could handle her, but she knocked him down a peg or—"

"I'd like to knock you off, Uncle Leon," Phae broke in. "I thought you said you were in a hurry to get back to work."

"Did I? Oh, all right, girl. Don't get mean on me." He winked at Phae and gave Kent a hearty handshaking. "Well, as they say, hardware waits for no man. I'd best get back to the store. See you around, boy. Be careful that aunt of yours doesn't catch you AWOL."

Phae and Kent watched his retreating bear-like figure.

"Well, that was a new one," Kent said.

Phae winced. She needed to have a talk with her uncle about his opinions. "He's a little eccentric. Also, he doesn't know what he's talking about."

Kent blinked in wonderment. "Do you mean to tell me that hardware *will* wait for a man?"

Phae grinned. "You know what I mean."

"Don't look now, but I think we're getting more visitors." Kent motioned toward three teenage boys nearing the table.

Phae sighed. Family. She had way too much of it in Zeke's Bend.

"Hi there, cuz," said the tallest of the three, Jackson. "Whatcha doin?"

Phae introduced Jackson, Tonio and Neptune. They were fourteen years old, cousins, good-looking kids and about the biggest scoundrels in the entire Jones family. Good thing they were likable or everyone might have worried more over them.

Tonio had a mischievous gleam in his eye. "You don't need to tell us who this guy is. We've heard all about him."

"That's right," Neptune added. "So, Kent, you run into any poles lately?"

The three boys burst into laughter. Kent smiled.

Phae leveled a scolding look at them. "Get out of here, you jokers. Don't you have a lawn to mow or something?"

"We're just having some fun, Phae. Don't get all mean on us," Jackson said, cowering in fake fear.

"So Kent," Tonio said, "we heard what Uncle Leon was telling you and—"

"Heck, people on the sidewalk heard him," Neptune said.

"Uncle Leon's right, you know," Jackson continued. "Phae sends all the men running. We like her okay, but she can be pretty mean when she gets going. If you thought that pole was hard, wait until you butt heads with Phae."

The boys roared in glee, Phae got half out of her chair. The scoundrels ran out of the cafe, still laughing like hyenas.

"My family is loaded with comedians," Phae said.

"And this cafe is filled with your family," Kent said. "How many more can I expect?"

"No telling. Half the town is related to me in some way or other. You do know, don't you, that it was an ancestor of mine who founded this town, Zeke Jones."

"I didn't know. So I'm sitting with local royalty, am I?"

"That's right. And I'll appreciate it if you bow next time before you speak to me."

"Warning heard."

"But not heeded, I bet."

"So who was Zeke Jones?"

Phae liked to tell the story of her family in Zeke's Bend. It was part of the connection she felt to the town and the people in it. "He was a trapper and trader. He'd winter in the hills and in the summer he'd sell his furs out of a little trading post he set up on a bend in the Elk River. Did a decent business with the river traffic they had back then."

"Eventually, he got married and had lots of children," she continued, "and they settled the area. It's a great place to live, so it grew into an actual town. And now you see it, heavily over-populated with Zeke Jones' descendants, like me."

"You speak about it like you own the place, in a good way."

"I guess so. It feels like it belongs to me, small and podunky though it might be."

"I wouldn't call it podunky," he said. "Oh, looks like more Joneses are coming our way."

Phae glanced in the direction he was looking. "Two of my great aunts, Charmaine and Chelly. They're sweet. They'll probably flutter around you and pat your head. Hope we don't run into Great-Great-Great-Aunt Elfleda. She's ninety-six and still going strong. Sees through people like they're screen doors."

Kent groaned. "Exactly how much family do you have in this town?"

"Let me put it this way—don't say anything bad about anyone in Zeke's Bend. We're practically all connected in one way or another."

"I'm beginning to see why you're so mean and crotchety."

"I'm not mean and crotchety. I simply tell it like I see it."

"Too bad," Kent said with an exaggerated forlorn expression on his face. "It so happens that I like mean, crotchety women. Now introduce me to your aunts."

Thirty minutes later, Phae signed with relief as the last of her relatives left the cafe. She'd endured three more aunts, a great-uncle, two cousins and two second-cousins.

Every one of them had enlightened Kent about Phae's lack of womanliness. One of her aunts had even gone so far as to apologize to Kent for Phae's rudeness, adding that even if Phae hadn't been rude yet, she most certainly would be, and she hoped he'd accept a general Jones family apology in advance.

It had been an embarrassing thirty minutes, but Phae raised her chin. Much of what had been said was true, and if it sent Kent running, then good riddance.

Oh, but she'd miss him. Especially those strong, thick arms that she hadn't gotten the opportunity to touch. And the silky, raven black hair. She wouldn't mind running her fingers through it.

"Was that all of them?" Kent asked. "Your whole family?"

"Not even close. Today was a slow day. One of my cousins owns this cafe."

"So, have you ever added all of them up? And don't include the far-fetched ones like second cousins twice removed."

"I've never counted," Phae replied. "My grandpa had twelve brothers and sisters, and my dad has ten brothers and sisters. Some of the older ones have died, and not everyone stayed in Zeke's Bend, though most did and had their own big families. Now their children have grown up and had children. Oh, I don't know. A couple hundred probably, not counting all the connections through marriage."

Phae laughed at his aghast expression. "Calm down, Kent. Zeke's Bend has around 5,000 people in it. I was only joking about us being half the population."

"Yeah, but when you start thinking about it, really thinking about how many people you're related to by marriage, and other extensions like step-siblings and so on, the numbers get staggering. I didn't know you came from such a long line of overactive breeders."

42

"Breeders." Phae rolled her eyes. "What a word. Funny thing is though, I don't have any brothers or sisters. And my parents moved to Boston when Dad retired from the Post Office."

"No siblings for me, either. Other than my parents, my only other relative is Aunt Eugenia. She's my father's sister."

"Were you lonely growing up?"

"Not really. My parents traveled and were often away from home, but we had a lot of servants and I had a wonderful nanny."

"So you were a rich little boy. Sounds lonely, though, being without your parents."

Kent paused for a second. "It might sound strange, but it wasn't that bad. And when my parents were home, they were really home. They spent time with me. Why did your parents move to Boston?"

"Mom told Dad that she'd been putting up with his crazy relatives her entire adult life and she wanted to spend her dotage with her own crazy relatives in Boston."

Kent smiled. "I think I'd like your mother."

"Yeah, she's great. They come back several times a year for visits."

"They sound like kind people."

Phae nodded.

For the first time, the conversation stalled and they sat in awkward silence, the earlier carefree behavior crunched under the weight of too much family.

Phae finally broke the silence. "I've got to get back to work. I can't believe I cancelled an appointment for a crummy family reunion."

"Don't go yet, Phae. I, um, well, I was hoping that we could get together some time. You know, a date. We'll do anything you like. What do you like to do?"

Phae's heart leapt in her chest.

CHAPTER FIVE

KENT WATCHED PHAE'S FACE closely, trying to judge her reaction. She didn't reveal much, but that was true of her in general.

"You mean my family hasn't scared you off?" she asked, her big brown eyes sparkling magnificently.

He shook his head. "I form my own opinions of people. So what do you think? A movie? Is there anywhere we can go that's not overrun with your relatives?"

"No. Not in this town, anyway. Besides, I don't date. There's all this pressure to be perfect. As you might have already guessed, I'm not very good at being perfect."

"I hadn't noticed."

"Anyway, the Zeke's Bend Fair is this weekend. Sylvie roped me into working a booth. Maybe I'll see you there?"

"Just tell me when."

"I'll be there every night. Oh no! There's my cousin, James. He's the sheriff, by the way. I'm leaving. See ya!" She snatched up her purse and headed for the door.

Kent grabbed her arm as she passed by him. "I'll see you Friday night, Phae. And wear those white shorts again, would you? I'd like to see more of those beautiful legs than a tiny peek through a hole in your jeans."

Phae mumbled something unintelligible, tossed some bills on the table then sped out of the cafe with only a passing nod at her cousin, James.

Kent watched her go, satisfied that he'd flustered her, and admiring her rear view as much as he admired the front.

He'd been struck by her since the moment he saw her fighting not to laugh in his aunt's garden. In the days since, he hadn't been able to get her off his mind.

Her fawn skin had glowed with golden undertones in the sunlight, and escaping tendrils of spiraling deep brown tresses framed her face in shimmers. And those kissable lips, high-cut cheekbones and sparkling dark eyes would have turned any man's head. What a beauty.

And her body, toned and firm yet rounded in all the right places. Legs that stretched forever. High perky breasts that would fit in his big hands … well … without doubt, Kent considered Phae Jones the most beautiful woman he'd ever seen.

And the fact that she was so clueless about her beauty made her even sexier. How the woman was still single was an unsolvable mystery.

He was pulled from his reverie when James walked up to his table.

"James," Kent said, "have a seat."

The stocky man sat in Phae's vacated chair. "Sparkin' my cousin, are ya?"

"I'm trying. I made a complete ass of myself, though. You should have heard the bumbling way I asked her out."

"Did she accept?"

"Kind of. I'm supposed to meet her at the fair this weekend. How fun is that? It's like I'm a teenager again. A date at the fair."

James motioned to the waitress, pointing at Kent's coffee cup and then to himself. "I know you've got a thick skin, but I'm not sure it's thick enough if Phae's gonna be in the picture. She's—"

"Don't bother. I've heard it all. I think half your family paraded by today. Phae was full up with it, which is why she ran out of here when she saw you. Thanks a lot for that, by the way."

"Doesn't she know we've been friends since you were a tadpole?"

"Enough with the hillbilly act, already. And no, I didn't get a chance to tell her."

Kent and James thanked the waitress for the hot coffee.

Kent picked up his cup. "You always said you had a lot of family in this town, but I never realized exactly how many."

"Yeah, well, we had more important things to talk about when we were kids, like how big a slingshot needs to be if you want to shoot yourself to the moon."

The men smiled in remembrance as they sipped their steaming coffee.

"I miss those old days sometimes," Kent said. "We've grown apart over the years, but I still think of you as the best friend I ever had."

James tugged at his belt. "You've been busy running that big company of yours, friend."

"And you've been protecting the citizens of Zeke's Bend."

James cleared his throat. "So, I take it some of my kin gave you an earful about Phae today?"

James never changed, Kent thought. Even as a child, James used a gruff facade to mask his kind nature. Kent, however, spoke his feelings as soon as he felt them, a trait that had gotten him into all kinds of trouble as a child and sometimes even now as a full-grown man in his thirties.

He grinned. "I don't know what to believe, James. Phae is exciting and intelligent from what I've seen, but your family tells me she's a man-eating shrew."

"Man-eating shrew?" James chuckled. "They were giving you a hard time. She's not that bad. Phae speaks her mind and that doesn't sit too well with the men who come sniffing around her. She didn't used to be that way, though. Before she went off to college and got that job in Chicago, she was soft-hearted as anything and the biggest pushover you've ever met."

"I can't imagine her ever being a pushover."

"She still is, most of the time, though you wouldn't know it unless you look past her crusty surface. I think it's good that she's learned how to say no, and if she makes a few people upset because she says what she thinks, well, that's their problem, not hers."

Kent raised an eyebrow. "Why is she working as a beautician when she's got a degree in business?"

"She doesn't have any old degree. She graduated from Harvard Business School."

Kent nearly choked on his coffee. "Are you serious?"

"Yep. Everyone was real proud of her. She graduated top of her class and got a big time job with a corporation in Chicago. From what I heard, she was doing well. Then a few years back, she suddenly moved back home. Signed up at a beauty college in Rollinsburg and after she got her license, opened her shop."

"What happened in Chicago?"

"She's never really said. Just says she missed home. I don't think she ever told anyone except Grandma Jones. Word was that Grandma Jones had the biggest fit you've ever seen. I heard the argument nearly took the roof off her house. I don't know who won, but Grandma wouldn't talk about it with anyone. And of course, neither did Phae."

Kent silently wondered at James' cavalier attitude. "So you still don't know what happened in Chicago, after all this time?"

"Nope. Phae keeps to herself. Sylvie and Neesa drag her out and about every so often, but mostly Phae is a homebody. She takes defense and martial arts classes over in Rollinsburg, though. Last I heard, she was working on her black belt. She could have it by now. Anything else you want to know, you ask her."

Kent decided he would do that. He loved a good mystery, especially when those mysteries came packaged as nicely as Phae Jones.

"Those classes must be what keeps her in such great shape," he said. "You know I'm a leg and butt man, and I've got to tell you that your cousin has both for days and days. When I first saw those stems of hers the other day, I thought I'd—"

"Stems? Good one, Frank Sinatra. Anyway, I may be your friend, but you've gotta remember she's my cousin, and one of my favorites at that. Since her dad moved to Boston, all us Jones men have gotten protective of her. She needs a man to look out for her, so watch your tongue."

Kent raised his arms in the air and said in a drawl, "I'll go peaceful, Sheriff. Don't start a-shootin' at me."

James squinted. "You keep your hormones under control, and we'll get along fine."

"Does Phae know she needs the Jones men to look after her?"

"Don't tell her I said that. She thinks she doesn't need anyone or anything. She won't even come to family reunions. Says she sees everybody all year long and doesn't see the point of it."

James chuckled lightly, then added, "I gotta admit, I kind of agree with her. You ought to see these reunions. Hundreds of kids crawling everywhere, everyone talking and yelling at the same time. Gives me a headache. I'd stay at home like Phae, but Mama would rip my ears off if I did."

"Sounds wonderful to me," Kent said. "I always thought it would be great to have a big family."

James snorted. "Sometimes I'd like a rest from mine, but I guess I'm mostly thankful." He paused and began to buff his badge with a napkin. "You know, you could help me out a little. If you married Phae, that'd be one less person I'd have to worry about and you'd have that big family you always wanted."

"I've only seen the woman twice, James. We're not ready for the altar quite yet."

The sheriff gave his badge one last stroke then looked up at Kent. "Just makin' suggestions. Besides, you owe me. Aren't I the one who rescued you the other night?"

Kent had reached his limit on laundry pole jokes. "Don't get on that again. I've heard every lame joke there is about it. I do have some pride, you know."

"You're right, my friend. I apologize."

Kent saw the teasing glint in James' eyes and knew he was full of it. "So, what, exactly, is the fine police force around here doing to catch this Captain Nice Guy?"

"Why would we catch him? He's done a lot of good things for folks."

"I know, and I guess that's okay, but you can't have a vigilante running around righting the world's wrongs without anyone to double-check his verdicts. I'd think you'd see that after what happened to me. It may have worked out in the end, but what if he'd had a gun?"

"Nah. the other night was a fluke. It's never happened before. The guy is careful and never tries to do my job for me."

James looked solemnly at Kent and spoke in a low voice so he wouldn't be overheard by the other diners in the cafe. "Once, about a year and a half ago, I got a call at the office from a man who wouldn't identify himself. He said there was a house over on tenth street that was being used as a meth lab. He gave the address and hung up. I checked it out, to be on the safe side, and sure enough, the caller was right. I got to make one of the biggest drug busts in county history."

"It was Captain Nice Guy who made that call," James continued. "He didn't interfere and he didn't take the law into his own hands. I'm telling you, he's careful."

"How do you know it was him?"

"He uses an electronic voice disguiser when he calls. He's reported numerous things using it."

Kent toyed with the glass salt shaker on the table, fidgety and unwilling to drop his opinion. "What else has this guy done?"

"Little things mostly, like replacing stolen bicycles and finding lost dogs, though it's hard to say for sure. He's been at it longer than the public knows. Who could say?"

"I'd think that would make you nervous. This guy sounds like he could cause trouble for you if he switched loyalties. After all, nobody's seen him, so he must be good at slipping in and out of places unseen."

James grinned. "You're getting a little carried away, don't you think? What do you think the man's been up to all this time? Practicing for a future career as a cat burglar?"

"Okay, you're probably right. But something about it doesn't sit right with me. Do you have any guesses who he might be?"

"I have my suspicions, along with everybody else in this town. Guessing who Captain Nice Guy is has become one of our favorite games."

For several moments, Kent considered what James had told him. What made a person slink around at night doing good deeds for others? Why not simply be up front about it and take the deserved credit?

Kent couldn't understand why the man had made everything so secretive. It didn't make sense. Something else was going on here, and Kent wanted to be the one to discover it.

"How do you know," he asked James, "that the Captain is a man? He could be a woman."

James burst out laughing. "A woman? You've got to be joking. What kind of woman would do the stuff this guy does? Oh yeah, I can see it—some woman out on the prowl, looking for criminals. I wonder if she paints her nails while she's on stakeout."

Kent scowled.

James slapped his thigh and hooted even louder. "You've been watching too many movies, friend."

Kent ignored him. We'll see, my friend, Kent thought as he shoved the salt shaker back into the shiny metal napkin holder.

The waitress walked up and offered to refill their cups. Kent declined.

"I've got to get home before Aunt Eugenia finds out I'm gone," Kent said. "I've already pushed my luck."

"You'd better hurry. I don't want her finding you with me. She'll accuse me of being a bad influence again. Remember when she did that?"

"As I recall, you spread trash all over her back yard and made me play in it."

James wasn't impressed. "Don't start. You know it was you who threw that trash everywhere because you wanted to pretend we were on a treasure hunt. Best treasure I found was a half-eaten cupcake covered in grass clippings."

"Hey, that was an ancient offering to Pharaoh Tut."

"You were a bossy kid. Imaginative, though," James said with a grin.

"I wasn't all that bossy."

"Hell you weren't. You'd get full of yourself and start bossing me around like I was one of those servants you had back at your folks' mansion. I'd have to take you down a peg or two every now and then to remind you what's what."

"You're exaggerating. I wasn't that bad. And anyway, I've outgrown it."

James cocked an eyebrow. "Sure you have. Anyway, here's a warning. Don't try bossing Phae around, not if you don't want to be taken down a dozen pegs at a whack."

Kent tossed some money on the table and rose from his chair. "James, your cousin can take me anywhere she wants. And now I'm getting out of here before you start attacking all my other faults. Not that I have many."

The two men chuckled as Kent walked away.

Before Kent reached the door, James called out. "Hey there, Luke. Did I ever tell you I've known that fellow by the door there just about forever? Yep, we were buds every summer when he visited his aunt."

Kent opened the door and almost managed to slip away before hearing James' punch line.

"Yep," James called, "I knew that fellow a looooong time before he got all famous for knocking himself silly on laundry poles."

The cafe patrons hooted.

As he shut the door on their catcalls, he wondered if he'd ever live that one down. Probably not.

CHAPTER SIX

PHAE STOOD IN FRONT OF the small booth and inspected the growing crowd. She glanced at her watch. It was nearly seven-thirty. She peered around the fairgrounds once again.

"I can't imagine who you're looking for," Neesa said, fussing with a pink crepe paper bow affixed to the front counter.

"I'm not looking for anyone. I'm impatient to get home." She sighed and turned to Sylvie. "Honestly, you can't have a kissing booth in this day and age. There's too many diseases."

"I'm doing all the kissing, so I don't see what your problem is." Sylvie strolled up and plopped down on a metal stool behind the counter, smiling at the passersby and batting her eyelashes.

"My problem is that we aren't doing any business," Phae said, leaning against the counter.

"Quit that!" Neesa interjected. "You're mashing my decorations. And stop griping. She's only kissing on the cheek." She propped her hands on her hips. "And if we aren't doing any business, it's your fault. You're supposed to be the barker. So get on out there and bark, sister. Bark, bark, bark."

"I'm not some damned dog," Phae mumbled as she shuffled to the front of the booth. "But fine, I'll do it."

She couldn't believe she'd agreed to do this stupid thing. In a bored, weary voice, she called out, "Hear ye, hear ye. Gather around."

People swarmed past, paying her no attention.

She rolled her eyes and waved sloppily. "Buy a kiss from the pretty lady. Sure, it's only a kiss on the cheek, but you can't be too careful these days. Guaranteed mono-free."

"Psst!" Neesa hissed at her. "We don't make guarantees. We don't need legal issues."

"Hey, I resent that," Sylvie said. "I don't have mono!"

52

"Whatever," Phae said and called out into the crowd. "Probably mono-free, mostly, but not guaranteed for legal reasons. Come on. Buy a kiss from the pretty, loony girl. Only a dollar. Support the Zeke's Bend Animal Shelter."

Neesa laughed. "That's the worst barking I've heard in my whole life. You could at least look at the people while you're talking to them."

Phae shrugged.

Sylvie smoothed her hair. "You're out of sorts because you-know-who isn't here."

"I'm not looking for him." Phae stepped out of the stream of traffic and leaned against the support post again.

"I said to quit doing that." Neesa scowled as harshly as her angelic face would allow. "You're gonna tear the place down. Here, take my stool. And quit lying. It's bad for your soul."

Phae toyed with the tail of her long braid. "My soul's perfectly fine, thank you."

Neesa began retying a squashed paper flower. "We know you're looking for Kent. I caught a glimpse of him the other day. What woman wouldn't be looking? He's fine as hell. And I hear he's a billionaire."

"He's not a billionaire," Phae said. "You know how Miss Eugenia exaggerates."

"Guy who looks like that, he doesn't need money," Sylvie said.

"But it doesn't hurt," Neesa added with a knowing grin.

Sylvie waved and flirted at a likely-looking older man who walked on by without stopping. She sighed. "You know you've got it bad, Phae. And what's wrong with that? I've never seen you act the way you did at the diner. You wouldn't have believed it, Neesa. They practically sizzled together. And Phae was all like, 'Cancel my appointment, Sylvie,' just because he said so. It was like, 'Bam!' and 'Boom!' and they were looking at each other like they were gonna take a bite out of something that shouldn't be bitten in a public place."

Sylvie and Neesa laughed at Phae's disgruntled expression.

"He'll be here," Neesa said, shooing Phae back into the crowd. "Go on now. Put a little spirit into your pitch. Sylvie will do her sexy pout she's always practicing in her selfies."

"I don't have a sexy pout," Sylvie said.

This time Neesa and Phae laughed.

Phae stepped in front of the gaudy, pink-streamer-covered booth and scanned the crowd. Still no Kent. Where was he?

"Hear ye, hear ye," she began with no more spirit than before. "Buy a kiss from the pretty lady. Chapped lips? No problem. Step right up. Fever blisters? Yeah, you'd better move it along. This so isn't right. But buy a kiss anyway. Only a dollar. I mean, what's a dollar these days? Come on—"

Phae stopped short as a pair of strong hands grasped her shoulders and spun her around. Her startled gaze locked onto Kent's clear, blue eyes.

"I never can resist a good sales pitch," he said, his rumbly bass voice making Phae shiver.

Kent lowered his head slowly and gently touched his lips to hers. She closed her eyes at the feel of his warm breath.

One of his hands glided to the back of her neck while the other lowered to her waist, pulling her securely against the length of his hard body. His heart pounded as rapidly as her own.

The sensations were overpowering and she opened her eyes.

"We'd better make this quick," Kent whispered huskily against her lips. "Or I'm going to embarrass us both."

Unthinking, Phae brought her arms up around his neck as he deepened the kiss. His lips slid with silken softness against her own. So this is heaven, she thought hazily. His tongue lightly touched her upper lip.

"Okay you two, that's enough," said a brusque male voice, unmistakably belonging to her cousin, James.

Phae and Kent broke apart.

"I didn't see you there," Phae said stiffly to her uniformed cousin.

She relaxed when Kent smiled and took her hand into his own.

"You're kissing the wrong person," Sylvie called to them. "She's the barker. I'm the kisser."

"Sorry. Honest mistake," Kent said. "I got swept up in her rousing marketing."

Sylvie snorted. "It's still gonna cost you a dollar."

Kent released Phae's hand and lazily removed his wallet from his back pocket. He extracted a bill and tossed it onto the booth's counter.

Neesa snatched it up and shook her head. "I can't make change for a hundred."

Kent grabbed up Phae's hand again. "Keep it. That was no one dollar kiss."

Phae found herself inexplicably tongue-tied. Sylvie and Neesa had no such problems.

"Oh, that's sooo romantic," Sylvie gushed.

"Yeah, that's pretty good. I'm Neesa, by the way, Phae's cousin. Are you a billionaire?"

Phae came crashing back down to earth. "Neesa! For God's sake."

James gave Kent a wary look. "You can't buy my cousin, you know."

"I'd think she'd want more than a hundred bucks," Kent said, laughing.

James harrumphed. "Regardless, no more of these public displays. I've got order to maintain. I'm closing down your booth, you three. It's a health nuisance."

"What?" came the outraged responses from the three women.

Hands on hips, Phae, Neesa and Sylvie advanced on the blustering sheriff.

"I don't know who you think you are, but—"

"Listen up, buddy, you can't order us—"

"Why are you being such a dick—"

Kent stood back, amusement lifting one side of his mouth, while James tried to hold off his outraged relatives.

"Okay, okay," he said. "It's not because of health issues. Here's the thing. I need you two, Neesa and Sylvie, to follow these other two around and keep an eye on them. Make sure they don't get into any trouble."

"Since when are you my keeper, James? Ignore him. He's being obnoxious," Phae said.

"Kent may be my friend, but that doesn't mean I'm going to give him free rein with you," James said.

Phae turned to Kent. "You're friends with James?"

"I didn't get the chance to tell you the other day. I met him—"

"What the hell do you mean, 'free rein?'" Neesa broke in. "Phae isn't a horse, James, you jackass."

"Hold up there," James said. "Watch what you call me. I'm the sheriff, after all. Respect the position. And I don't see why you have a problem protecting your cousin, Neesa."

Kent turned his attention to James. "What do you think I'm going to do to her, exactly? Kidnap her?"

"I've known you too long, my friend, and heard too many stories about your conquests. This is your first date and I want to make sure it's done properly."

Phae glowered at James. "Kent and I aren't on a date. And what's gotten into you? I'm a full-grown, twenty-eight-year-old woman. If you think for one minute I'll let you tell me how to run my life, then you're in for a big surprise. The more I think about it the madder I get. Men! I ought to—"

"Simmer down, Phae," James interrupted. "Don't get worked up. I know I can trust you. It's the company you're keeping that I'm not so sure about."

"Look what you've done," Kent said with a sigh. "She's ready to explode. I had her all softened up with that kiss and now you've blown it and made her mad."

He pulled out his wallet and tossed another bill onto the counter. "You're costing me a fortune, woman," Kent said, tugging Phae into his arms.

She pushed against his chest. "Have I fallen into a time warp where you've all turned into cave men?"

"You tell him, Phae," James said.

"Don't listen to him, Phae," Sylvie said. "Kiss Kent. I don't want to have to give back all this money. Think about the poor shelter animals."

Neesa snorted. "Right. The animals. The hell with that. These two big animals are acting like Phae's a piece of meat to fight over. Tell 'em where to get off, cuz."

"Hit him with a karate chop," James said.

Phae briefly considered the suggestion, then made the mistake of getting caught in Kent's smoldering gaze. Before she could stop herself, she threw her arms around his neck and pulled him toward her.

Their lips crushed together in a searing kiss. She soared when his arms tightened around her.

She vaguely heard James and Neesa arguing in the background, but she couldn't be bothered to make out the words.

To her disappointment, Kent released his hold and gently drew back.

His hot breath sent shivers through her as he whispered, "I don't want to let you go, but James is starting to attract a crowd with his cursing."

Phae gathered her wits. She was stunned she'd given into his manhandling. Forcefully, she shoved him away.

An elderly man tottered up beside her, holding out a dollar bill. "I'll have one of those, please," he said with a happy, toothless smile.

"Oh, that's just great. I'm not the kisser," Phae snapped, gesturing to Sylvie with her thumb. "See what she'll do for you."

The man shrugged and headed to the booth.

"Let that be a lesson to you, Mr. Tyrannosaurus Rex." Phae wagged her finger in Kent's surprised face. "I hope you'll remember this the next time you try to force yourself on some unsuspecting woman."

"Are you implying you weren't affected by our kiss?"

"I think that's what she's telling you, friend," James said with a satisfied smile.

"Hey! All I get is a kiss on the cheek?" the elderly man cried behind them. "That's false advertising!"

Kent studied Phae closely. A slow grin crossed his face. She squinted, wondering what he'd seen. Probably that she was full of it.

"You're absolutely correct, Phae," Kent said. "I've learned my lesson. I hope you'll allow me to make it up to you. Shall we venture to the snack shack and stuff ourselves with carnival junk food?" He held out his arm in a courtly gesture.

Phae did what any woman would do when confronted with a caveman too charming and sexy for his own good: she graciously accepted his invitation. "Fine. Let's go." Okay, perhaps not so graciously, but accepted nonetheless.

"Come on, Neesa. We're up," James said.

"Neesa? What's he saying?" Phae asked.

"Sorry, he talked me into helping him follow you around," she answered, then leaned in beside Phae and whispered, "The plan is to follow you until I can find a way to distract James long enough so you and Kent can slip away. Now act pissy with me so he won't be suspicious."

Phae crossed her arms over her chest. "Traitor. I can't believe you'd side with him."

"I only want the best for you," Neesa said.

"Arrest that old coot!" Sylvie cried out. "He didn't pay up—it's a kiss and dash!"

They swiveled and saw the old man hobbling away at top speed, which wasn't very fast at all. He kept looking behind him to see if anyone was chasing him and nearly ran into a trash can.

"False advertising!" the old man yelled and shook his fist in the air.

"Seriously, what's the point of having my cousin be sheriff if you're not going to arrest people who rip me off?" Sylvie complained.

Phae took Kent's arm. "Shall we go before this gets any weirder?"

"Please," he said, and led her away.

"Come on, Neesa," James said, falling in behind the pair.

Neesa hopped up beside him, leaving a complaining Sylvie behind.

"Oh, sure. Go off and have fun while I slave away by myself, saving the little cats and dogs!" Sylvie called.

Her complaints went unheeded, and the foursome quickly disappeared into the crowd.

CHAPTER SEVEN

THIRTY MINUTES, TWO SODAS and two greasy funnel cakes later, Phae and Kent strolled together to the gaming booths. They pointedly ignored their escorts, James and Neesa, who had been arguing steadily about whether James might or might not be a sexist pig.

Phae glanced over her shoulder. "I'm afraid we're going to be stuck with them all night."

Kent said in a weary tone, "I tried to lose him before I found your booth, but I obviously didn't have any luck. We can try to sneak away when it gets dark."

"Almost eight. It won't be dark for another hour. Neesa said she'd try to distract him so we can get away, but she's not having any luck either."

"While we wait, how about I win you a prize at one of these booths? If I scored some fuzzy dice for you, would you reward me?"

She'd jump into his arms for a cheap plastic whistle, Phae thought. "Let me think. Hmm. I believe the appropriate reward for that prize is a handshake."

The late evening sunlight made Kent's black hair sparkle. "You wound me. Your family was right. You have no regard for the male ego."

"Do all men obsess about this ego business? What's the deal with that?"

"It's a secret that all men swear never to reveal to a woman."

Phae smiled sweetly. "But you'll tell me, won't you?"

"Nope. Last time I checked, and trust me, it wasn't but a few seconds ago, you were all woman."

They stopped beside a shooting gallery where Kent leisurely surveyed Phae from head to heel. "While we're on the subject of the mysteries of the genders, why don't you tell me why you didn't wear your white shorts?"

"I didn't have a chance to do laundry."

"Mmhm. I'm sure that's what happened."

"You didn't actually expect me to wear them just because you told me to, did you?"

"Actually, no. I like these blue shorts you've got on. Aren't they a little tighter than the white ones?"

Phae inspected her fingernails. "I don't think so."

"Maybe they look tighter because your shirt isn't so long. I like it, by the way. You look good in pink and it shows off your assets far better than those baggy t-shirts I've seen you wear."

"If you're trying to get a rise out of me, it's working."

"Why would I deliberately provoke a beautiful woman like yourself?"

"Because you're a sexist pig?"

"Phae! You wound me. Has it occurred to you that maybe I'm just a run-of-the-mill horndog?"

She laughed and swatted his arm. "Shut up."

"Maybe I like to get you wound up so I can see that evil glint in your eyes when you're mad," he said.

"In other words, you think I'm beautiful when I'm angry. I hate to tell you this, Romeo, but that's trite."

"I didn't say it made you beautiful. Actually your skin gets kind of puffy, and your nostrils flare all crazy, and your face kind of scrunches in on itself. It's not very attractive. If it weren't for that wicked glint of yours, I'd recommend reserving your anger for your most private moments."

"It's a good thing I can tell you're teasing, Kent Holmes, or I might punch you in your washboard stomach."

Neesa's voice rang out behind them. "I challenge you to a duel!"

Phae and Kent turned to the other pair.

James' hands were raised. "Calm down, Neesa. All I said was that I'd win you a prize if you'd quit nagging me."

"You called me childish! And by saying I was nagging, you mean I'm a shrew."

James dropped his hands. "If the shoe fits, cuz."

Neesa spun and beckoned to Phae. "Get over here, sister. You and I are gonna kick these Flintstone brothers' asses."

"What did I do?" Kent asked.

"You were born a man."

Kent shrugged. "Can't argue with that, I guess. What kind of duel are we talking about?"

"A gaming booth duel," Neesa answered.

Kent snorted. "Fine, but you two wouldn't stand a chance against James and me."

Phae sauntered over to Neesa's side. "Us little weaklings against two big strong fellows like you? We'd annihilate you."

"I didn't mean to insult you, Phae," Kent said. "It's just that James and I used to do well at these fairs when we were kids. We spent hours practicing at home."

Neesa poked Phae in the ribs with her elbow. "Yeah, well, it's been a long, *long* time since you two guys were kids. Way longer than us."

Phae leveled a disdainful look at the two men. "Can't you imagine them way, way back then? They probably strutted around like they owned the midway."

"I'm sure you're right," Neesa added. "I mean, that's how they're acting right now, so why should they have been any different back then?"

"What's it gonna be, boys? Are you going to accept the challenge or are you going to beg off like a couple of chickens?" Phae grinned when she saw a muscle twitch in Kent's cheek.

"I ought to wring your neck, James," Kent grumbled. "All I wanted was a pleasant evening with a beautiful woman, but because you've got the diplomacy skills of a rabid rhino, I'm going to be forced to trounce Phae in this ridiculous contest. That's not good news for my love life."

Before Phae could respond, James said, "Good. You haven't known her long enough to have a love life." He glanced at Neesa. "I accept your challenge, child. But you said this was a duel, so I get to pick my second. I pick Phae."

Phae smiled at Kent's astonishment.

"What do you mean you pick Phae?" Kent asked.

At the same time, Neesa said, "You can't have her."

"It's a duel. I can pick who I want," James said.

Kent frowned. "What the hell? I'm better at these games than you are, and you're throwing me over for Phae."

Phae held up her hands for peace. "Okay, everybody. That's enough. It's going to be the women against the men and that's that. No, James, don't argue. Neesa and I are going to show you two who the weaker sex is. Tell them the rules, Neesa."

James groaned but stopped short when Kent glared at him.

Neesa squared her shoulders. "All right, boys. Listen up. We'll play one round each at eight different booths. James will go first, then me, then Kent, and lastly Phae. Each team will take turns picking the booth and whoever picks the booth, pays. Understand? Good. When we're finished, we'll put all the prizes in two piles and whoever has the biggest pile wins the challenge. Agreed?"

They all agreed.

"Since I made the challenge," Neesa said, "you can pick first."

Kent cocked an eyebrow. "Right here. The gun shoot."

"Fine by me," she said casually, but thinking 'oh yeah' inside.

James scowled. "I don't think that's a good choice."

"For crying out loud, you're a cop, James!" Kent said.

James shrugged. "Yeah, and I'm sure I could beat you hands down, but Phae—"

Phae quickly interrupted. "You're up first, James."

Kent yanked out his wallet and slapped some bills on the counter. "Go, James. Have some confidence. Buck up."

"Buck up?" James grabbed up an air rifle and pumped it vigorously, the carnie giving him a hard look.

The rules of the booth were ten shots per play. The smaller the target, the bigger the prize. There were ten tiny ducks spinning on a wheel, and if a shooter managed to hit all ten, they won the grand prize, a giant stuffed dog propped on the highest shelf.

James aimed carefully and ended up hitting eight out of ten shots, not attempting to hit the spinning ducks. He selected the largest prize offered him, a hand-sized teddy bear.

Neesa only hit six of the larger targets, and hung her head as she accepted her prize, a key chain.

"Guess that explains why the coyotes keep getting the chickens out on your farm, Neesa," James teased.

Neesa raised her nose in the air. "I don't know that it's coyotes getting them."

"Neesa has a farm that she runs all by herself," Phae told Kent proudly. "She grows all these organic vegetables and stuff for fancy restaurants."

Kent looked impressed. "That would be hard work for a single woman, I'd think."

"And she moonlights as a security guard at the college in Rollinsburg," Phae added. "You don't go around messing with Jones women, Kent. You might as well throw in the towel right now and save yourself some embarrassment."

Kent smirked. "Nice try. You're not going to rattle me. Give me that rifle. I'm going for the little ducks. Wish me luck."

"Don't do it," James said. "You'll never hit that little thing ten times in a row, not the way it's jerking around."

"It's nice that you've got confidence in me," Kent drawled.

"Go for it!" Neesa cheered, winking at Phae.

Phae admired the way Kent's biceps flexed as he pumped then sighted the rifle. He turned to the side, his stomach muscles rippling under the fine lawn of his shirt.

She had more than enough time to enjoy his physique. He took forever to aim his shots. By the time he finished shooting, she was tapping her foot in annoyance.

"I got six out of ten ducks. What do I win?" Kent asked.

The worker dug under the counter and extracted a pair of fuzzy dice.

Kent dangled them in front of Phae. "Not bad. Your turn, my lady. Shall I show you how to pump the rifle?"

Phae waved him aside. "How's my hair holding up, Neesa?" She lightly patted the back of her long braid.

"It's perfect."

"Are you sure? You know how I hate to shoot guns if my hair isn't perfect."

"Women," Kent muttered. "Hurry up, Phae. We haven't got all night."

"Hard to believe you would rush me after you took like three hours to take ten shots."

James nudged Kent. "Ignore her. She's trying to rattle you."

Phae shrugged, pretending that wasn't exactly what she'd been trying to do. She turned to the man behind the counter. "Do you have ten rifles back there?"

"Sorry. Only got six."

"Then let me see them."

"What do you think you're doing?" Kent snapped.

"You said you wanted me to hurry," she replied as she rapidly inspected the rifles. "This one's no good," she said, returning it to the worker. "And reset the spinning duck wheel, please."

In quick succession, she pumped air into the five remaining guns then laid them neatly on the countertop.

"Do it, Phae," Neesa called.

Phae carefully eyed the spinning ducks. It had been many years since she'd played this game. She took a deep breath. No problem. It'd come back to her. Muscle memory, like riding a bike.

One after the other, she raised the rifles to her shoulder, sighted and pulled the trigger. Then she re-pumped the guns and five more times she aimed and fired.

All the little ducks lay flat behind the spinning wheel.

Neesa cheered loudly, jumping up and down as Phae pointed to the gigantic, four-foot-tall yellow dog.

Phae took the stuffed animal from the flabbergasted carnie then turned to face an equally flabbergasted Kent.

"After the contest, I'll give him to you, Kent," she said. "I hope you know how to thank me appropriately."

CHAPTER EIGHT

"THAT WAS AMAZING," KENT SAID, glancing at James. "I see why you wanted her to be your partner."

James puffed out his barrel chest. "Tried to tell you. She knows all the tricks. An uncle on her mother's side owns a carnival and taught her how to win these games. We've tried to get her to share her secrets, but she says her uncle made her promise not to tell."

"I see," Kent said. "So you're cheating."

"I'm not cheating," Phae said. "It takes skill to do what I did."

"Maybe, but by knowing what you do, you've got an unfair advantage."

Neesa waggled a finger at him. "You're jealous that she's better than you."

"That's easy for you to say. She's on your side. What you did was pick a ringer to settle your ridiculous argument with James."

"Ridiculous argument?" Neesa's voice raised in pitch, surprising Phae since Neesa was usually so easy-going. "Hey, you don't have anything to complain about. You said you and James used to win a lot and that you practiced. So all three of you are good at this stuff and I'm not. I'm Phae's handicap, and that makes this an even contest. Now quit acting like a baby and get on with it."

Phae stared at her angry cousin, wide-eyed. "Damn, someone ate their Wheaties this morning. He's kind of right about the cheating, though. There are tricks to some of these games if you want to beat them."

"Yeah," James said. "One year she was barred from the fair for winning too much."

"And most of it I won for someone else," Phae said. "I didn't hear you complaining back then when I was only twelve and you were eighteen, begging me to win a gaudy necklace so you could give it to a twit you wanted to impress."

James grinned. "That girl was kind of a twit."

Kent ignored James and said to Phae, "So what are we going to do now that you've admitted you're cheating?"

"I said you were kind of right about it, that there are tricks to help."

"I don't think that's what you said, but semantics aside, we need to level the field somehow."

"I won't tell you my secrets," Phae said. "I'd never break my promise to my uncle. This is all kind of dumb, anyway. Let's forget the whole thing."

"No!" the other three exclaimed in unison.

"I can't believe this," Phae said. "Fine. There are a lot of games that are new since I was a kid. Like that water thing over there and the electronic gizmo that's making all those pinging sounds. We'll stick to games my uncle didn't teach me about and that should make it fair for everyone. How's that?"

The two men grumbled, looked questioningly at one another, then nodded their affirmation.

"Finally," Neesa said. "Let's go! We pick the duck pond next."

"We do?" asked Phae. "But that's just a game of luck."

"I know." She lowered her voice and whispered to Phae. "I'm going to get Sylvie to help us pick. You know how she claims to be psychic."

"Please. She's about as psychic as my big toe."

"Yeah, well, I say it's worth a shot."

They walked off into the crowd, the two men so disgusted with the duck pond selection that they looked ready to bolt. Phae decided this alone was a good enough reason for Neesa to have picked the game.

She didn't want to admit it, but Phae wanted to win this contest. She wished she weren't so competitive, but she simply couldn't help it.

In the past, she'd run off men with this type of behavior. She knew the smart thing would have been to play dumb at the shooting gallery. Instead, she'd allowed herself to react to Kent's gibes and gave her best Annie Oakley impression.

What had it gotten her? Or more importantly, what had it cost? So far, Kent was still hanging around. But for how long?

She had a friend in high school who had all the boys traipsing after her as if she were a goddess. Phae used to watch her in amazement, because, frankly, this friend wasn't a great beauty or anything. But the men thought she was gorgeous. Why?

After watching the girl for a while, Phae learned her secret: she played the helpless little female act. She was all fluttery lashes and compliments and carrying on about how strong and great the guys were. "Ooh, I wish I could do that as good as you do," was a constant refrain.

Phae used to watch her coo and gush until she was so revolted she couldn't take it anymore. That friend of hers was terrifically intelligent, extremely capable and had a biting wit. But she didn't show a moment of any of it to the guys she dated.

And she dated A LOT of guys.

Phae hadn't dated hardly anyone the past few years, and she hadn't been out with anyone more than twice. It seemed the more independent and outspoken she became, the more time she spent without the company of the opposite sex.

Now here she was with the hottest man she'd ever known, and she'd been drawn into a contest that could ruin everything. Her old friend from high school would have never let this happen.

As Phae, Neesa, Kent and James moved from game to game, Phae discovered that Kent was as competitive as she was. He was determined to beat her, and no matter how hard she tried to squelch the feelings, she wanted to beat him every bit as badly.

A large crowd, filled mostly with members of the Jones family, began to follow them around. They were a boisterous cheering section, and a distraction, but at least they helped carry all of the competitors' loot.

The scene at each booth grew increasingly rowdy as the spectators took sides and placed bets on the outcomes. Phae watched Kent as he teased and joked with everyone, but she could see how seriously he concentrated whenever it was his turn to play.

This man was used to winning, and he hated to lose.

By the time they completed seven rounds, full dark had fallen.

Bright lights flashed colorfully while the delicious smells of popcorn and cotton candy wafted on the night-cooled breeze. A cacophony of music from the amusement rides couldn't completely overpower the shrieks and squeals of the thrill-seeking riders. Farther away, one could hear the muffled applause of the audience attending the judging in the fair barns.

But on the midway, few people noticed these other sights, smells and sounds. On the midway, everyone's attention was firmly on two large piles of stuffed animals, plastic trinkets and cheap appliances.

The crowd circled the piles. tightly packed adults jostled for a view while children crawled around, under and over their elders to catch their own glimpses of the tantalizing goodies.

Phae stood aside while the adults argued over which pile was largest.

Sylvie sidled up and shouted, "Our pile is bigger than theirs!"

"I don't know. They look pretty even to me. And what do you mean 'ours?'"

"Hey, I contributed at the duck pond. We kicked their asses there."

Phae had to admit it was true. Sylvie had told Phae and Neesa which ducks to pick, and they'd actually been good ones. They got lucky, she told herself. Sylvie would be crowing about her psychic ability for weeks, though, and Phae had to ask herself if the win was worth it.

Nearby, James argued hotly with his mother. Kent stood relaxed in the midst of the pandemonium, his thumbs tucked loosely into the pockets of his trousers, an amused expression on his handsome face.

Phae began to fear they'd never finish the challenge when Uncle Leon and Aunt Meg pushed their way into the center of the circle, calling for everyone to quiet down. They were both forceful, strong-minded people, and Phae was confident they could bring some order to the situation.

"I said simmer down," Uncle Leon shouted.

Aunt Meg pointed at James. "Especially you, young man. You're the sheriff, now get yourself together, apologize to your mother and act respectable."

Phae and several others in the crowd chuckled when James immediately snapped to attention and asked his mother to forgive him.

He somewhat spoiled the effect, however, when he mumbled, "My own mother and she's siding with the enemy."

Most of the Jones clan was split on gender lines in this contest.

Uncle Leon and Aunt Meg declared they'd be referees in the final round and everyone agreed to obey their verdicts. They surveyed the two piles of cheap prizes, murmuring to one another and looking dutifully official.

After several minutes of contemplation, Meg turned to Phae and asked, "What's the next game?"

"The basketball booth," Neesa answered before Phae had a chance.

Phae frowned. She hated that game. And it was rigged. "No, not that one."

"Yeah, yeah, everyone knows that one's rigged." Neesa looked out over the crowd and raised her voice so everyone could hear. "We all know the basketball game is extra hard to win, right? Because of all the stuff they do. The ball is smaller than regulation and the rim is barely big enough for it. And the backboard is tilted wonky. And sometimes they have hidden springs where the rim attaches to the backboard so the ball won't bounce into the basket like normal."

Phae was impressed. "Did you know about all that?" she asked Kent and James.

They agreed they had.

"Basketball it is, then," Neesa said.

So be it, thought Phae.

Uncle Leon and Aunt Meg whispered to each other then Leon raised his hands for silence.

"We've made our decision," Meg said. "These two piles are equal."

The crowd erupted in dissent.

Leon plucked a whistle from a prize pile and blew hard, the shrill sound quickly quelling the mayhem.

"The decision is final," he said in his booming voice. "And if any of you yay-hoos want to argue about it, then do it somewhere else. Now listen to my wife."

Meg smiled at her husband. "Okay, so how many shots do you get for your money at the basketball booth?"

"Three," several people called.

"Okay, then each of the four competitors will take their three shots. Whichever team makes the most shots, wins."

The crowd burst into chatter and surged to the basketball booth, dragging Phae, Neesa, Kent and James, and their piles of prizes, along with it.

Phae paid the man behind the counter since it was her turn. He handed a basketball to James.

Several men called out encouragement while several women did a decent bit of smack talk.

"I hate basketball," James muttered as he squinted in concentration.

He shot. He missed.

Phae glanced at Kent. He stood near James, calmly reassuring his friend.

James missed his second shot but made his third.

Neesa stepped up to the counter. Phae had a pretty good idea how this one would go.

Taking her time, Neesa aimed carefully. Everyone cheered heartily as Neesa sunk all three balls, one after the other.

She sauntered over to James and tossed her prize to him, a large plush basketball. "I still got it. Didn't win a state championship for nothing, old man."

"Yeah, yeah, yeah," he said. "But have you noticed how tall Kent is? I'm thinking he may have played some b-ball back in his school years, too."

The smug expression dropped from Neesa's face as she turned to watch Kent belly up to the counter.

"Give me three balls," Kent said to the attendant.

"Oh no," Neesa groaned.

Phae could only shake her head and smile.

In a gracefully fluid motion, Kent launched the balls into the air. One, two, three. Nothing but net.

The crowd roared its appreciation. Kent threw his prize to them like he was a golfer who'd won the U.S. Open.

Phae clapped loudly as she walked up beside him. "Impressive jump shot you've got."

He looked down at her, his eyes and expression unreadable. "Thanks. It's all up to you now."

Phae turned and took the ball that the booth attendant held out to her.

Neesa slipped up next to her. "You can do it, Phae. Just two baskets and we win!"

"Yeah, I know. By the way, great job of distracting James so Kent and I could slip away quietly."

"I'll concede my plan may have gotten a little out of hand. Beat their asses anyway. Come on now."

Uncle Leon's voice rang out from behind. "I'm rubbin' my rabbit's foot, Phae-girl, so you can't miss. You can do it! I've got five bucks riding on you."

James peered out into the crowd. "Hey! What are you doing rubbing your rabbit's foot for the women! We men have to stick together. And you're my uncle too. And the judge!"

"Sorry, my boy," Leon said, "but your Aunt Meg stole my wallet and made the decision without me."

Some people in the crowd hooted and hollered.

"Damn, thanks for the support, Uncle Leon," Phae called without turning around.

"Ow!" Leon cried. "Don't go beatin' on me, wife. Phae'll do fine."

Phae mentally upgraded Meg to most-favored aunt status.

She blocked out the rowdy crowd. It's a stupid game, she told herself. Then she shot the ball.

It fell through the hoop.

Phae nodded in relief. Only one more, she chanted silently.

She grabbed up a ball, aimed and shot. The ball spun around the rim several times then rolled out over the edge. She'd missed.

CHAPTER NINE

THE CALLS OF THE HORDE penetrated Phae's concentration.

She heard Sylvie and Neesa chanting, "You can do it. You can do it. You can do it."

Phae hadn't been this nervous since ... she couldn't remember. She briefly considered chucking the next ball and missing deliberately. Kent would probably be pacified if she did.

But no. She didn't care about his reaction, not if beating him in a friendly competition made him dislike her. She'd be better off without him.

She took a deep breath and picked up the basketball. Don't think, she told herself. Shoot it already. She arced the ball into the air.

Everyone held their breath as the ball sailed toward the basket. It hit the back of the rim which propelled it into the front of the metal hoop. The ball banged back against the rear of the rim again. Then, swoosh! The ball dived through the basket.

Phae barely had time to register her victory before the onlookers surrounded her. The women in the crowd cheered so loudly that Phae thought her eardrums might burst.

To her astonishment, her dainty widowed aunts, Charmaine and Chelly, gave one another snappy fist bumps.

Someone grabbed Phae's wrist and began pulling her through the swarm. So many people were crushed against her, it took several moments to figure out that it was Kent dragging her away.

At the edge of the crowd, Phae tried to yank her arm away. Kent only tightened his grip and began walking more quickly. Phae resisted.

"Stop it," Kent hissed. "We've got to get out of here while the getting's good."

Startled by his vehemence, Phae allowed him to lead her away from the crowd. Then she noticed the big stuffed yellow dog tucked under his free arm and the fuzzy dice dangling from his fingers. Somehow, during all that craziness, he'd managed to retrieve those particular two prizes. This could prove interesting.

They were both jogging by the time they reached the end of the midway. Kent slowed his pace once they'd left the fairgrounds behind.

"Where are we going?" Phae asked.

"A little farther away from all these lights."

"Why?"

"Shh!" Kent quickly glanced behind him.

She glanced back, too, but saw no one pursuing them. "You're making me feel like we're escaping prison or something."

"In a way we are, if you can call a sheriff a warden."

When he led her into a grove of tall trees, Kent finally released her hand. Though the night was clear and the moon glowed softly, it was shadowy under the canopy of leafy branches.

She took a few moments to catch her breath, a situation caused as much by her excitement as physical exertion.

She knew where they were. The rise of land hid the lights of the carnival but she could still plainly hear the music and other carnival sounds, and the scents of sugar and funnel cakes, caramel and grease floated past in breezy puffs.

Kent's shadow was large, and though he stood less than ten feet away, she couldn't see his face clearly. She could see, however, that he'd dropped the dog and dice onto the ground.

"Why have you brought me here?" she asked, though she knew the answer.

"Come here," he said crisply, the deep bass of his voice making Phae tremble slightly, but not from fear.

Phae feared no man; she knew she could defend herself. And something about Kent made her trust him, though she couldn't put her finger on what it was, exactly. She simply knew he'd never hurt her, physically, anyway.

She stepped forward slowly. She clearly heard his rough, ragged breathing and stopped less than a foot away from him.

The manly lines of his face appeared harsh in the faint moonlight filtering through the leaves. She didn't flinch when he raised his hand to her face. With a feathery touch, he skimmed his fingertips down her cheek.

His touch strayed to her sensitive neck then into the base of her loose braid as he pulled her closer. "You're so beautiful, Phae. I've got to—"

He kissed her then, a searing, powerful kiss, his lips slanting across hers and claiming what he wanted. He probed with his hot tongue and she opened for him, letting him claim what he wanted there, as well.

She wrapped her arms around his waist and locked her hands at the base of his spine. He held her head and turned her how he wanted, drinking from her like she held intoxicating nectar.

And she tasted him, too. He was sweet, like the cakes they'd been eating, and fresh and clean, and there was no way she'd ever get enough of it.

Her breasts smashed against his chest and her nipples went rock hard. Down low, something inside her turned over. Desire, long lying dormant within her, was waking up at last. And it was starved for attention.

Kent jerked away and inhaled sharply. "I've got to stop."

Phae's eyes popped open. "What? Why?"

He rubbed his chest against hers, then released her head and stepped backward. "Because your nipples are hard and you've got me so worked up I'm afraid I won't be able to stop myself from tearing your clothes off and throwing you to the ground."

"Um, okay. The tearing part might be a problem because I won't have anything to wear. But I have no objection to getting naked the normal way."

He groaned, leaned against a tree and slowly slid downward until he sat at the base of it. "Don't come near me. Knowing that you want me makes it worse."

"I don't get you."

"Would you please sit down or something? You're too tempting standing like that. You don't know what your sexy legs do to me."

She blew out a breath and sat under a nearby tree. "I can't believe this is happening. I'm alone in the woods with a man tease. It's just my luck."

"You're quite a woman, Phae Jones. Even when I think it's not possible, you find a way to make me smile."

"Great, I make you smile. If you would tell me what I need to do to get you to do more than that, my life would be complete."

"Make James disappear," he answered. "That's what we need. You do realize that he's undoubtedly looking for us already?"

She silently cursed her cousin. "Damn. You're right. I didn't think about him. So why did you drag me out here if you knew James would be behind us?"

"I lost my head. When I saw you standing there with that basketball, so calm and collected while everyone around you was going nuts and then you made the shot … it was incredible. I had no idea basketball could be so hot. I wish you could have seen yourself."

Phae's stomach tightened.

"I wanted to be alone with you," he continued. "So I grabbed you and ran. You were so beautiful in the moonlight, but I had to stop. When you and I make love, and don't think for one second that we won't, we're going to do it right. Not like this, in the dark, scrambling around like teenagers whose parents might come home at any second."

His voice dropped deeper. "When you and I make love, I want plenty of light so I can see that gorgeous body of yours. And I want lots of time so I can taste every last inch of you before I—"

"You could still taste me."

"Oh God," Kent groaned. "You're killing me. We don't have much time, damn it."

"Sometimes, when you're ready, fast can be good. Fast can be better than good if—"

She never got the chance to finish. Kent rose in a flash and loomed over her in another instant.

"Do you mean it?" he asked, or more like, growled. "I can taste you?"

She swallowed hard. "Hell yes."

HE LANDED ON HIS KNEES in front of her and without preamble, reached out and unbuttoned her shorts. Yanking down the zipper, he tugged on the waistband. She lifted herself up to help.

He took her panties with her shorts, and in an instant, she was bare to him from the waist down. He spread her knees and looked at her most private place.

"I wish I had a flashlight," he said, stroking his fingers over her inner thighs and around her sex.

Phae was glad he didn't, while at the same time excited that he wanted one.

"I can't hold back," he said, and dipped his head between her legs.

She gasped as his tongue flicked over her labia then dove between her folds. He murmured in pleasure.

He wrapped his hands around her thighs. She reached down and tangled her fingers in his thick hair, pulling him closer.

His tongue teased up and down her slit. With gently pinching fingers, he spread her open and pulled back to look at her.

"You're so damned beautiful," he said. "So hot. I want to—" and he bent his head down and bit lightly on her pussy lips, nibbling up one side and down the other.

Phae squirmed and moaned his name. Yes, that was it. It was perfect. Touch me. Lick me. Squeeze me. Take me.

He tugged on her nipple, making it harder than ever. His hand slipped under her shirt and pulled up her bra to reveal her swollen breast. He squeezed her and made her push against him for more.

She was swept away. She pulled his hair and didn't mind what sounds she made. It was good. So good. Do that more. Do it more. Lick me there. Pinch me here.

Then his tongue dipped deeper inside her and she thrust her hips upward. His thumb rolled over her clit and sent sparks shooting from her womb all the way to the top of her head and down to the tips of her toes.

"Mmm, baby, you taste so good," came the muffled sounds as he worked his magic between her legs.

She felt a pressure building inside her, a burgeoning fullness, a throbbing ache that demanded release. Already? Was she on the verge of coming already?

Then he pushed two fingers inside her, twisting his way in, exploring her, scissoring inside. His tongue moved up to her clit, the center point of her world at that moment, and flicked her sensitive nub.

She wanted to stay this way forever, but she was climbing too fast. She couldn't stop it, couldn't hold back. It had been so long. So very long.

He rolled his hot, hard tongue over and over her, around and around, up and down, setting a solid rhythm that complimented the push and pull of his fingers.

Phae threw back her head and saw the stars peeking through the leafy canopy. Then she let herself go wherever Kent wanted to take her.

"Come for me, Phae," she thought she heard him say. "Come for me."

She thrust herself against him, abandoning herself to this onslaught of pleasure, pleasure like she'd never known. She couldn't control the pressure any longer.

It erupted inside her, electric bolts of glorious release shooting from inside out. It passed in wave after wave, curling her toes and arching her back. She cried out, yes, yes, yes, again and again, without being much aware of it.

All she knew was that there was a man doing things to her that she'd never felt before. And this was heaven, this was the great unknown.

He worked her clit and pussy until the last of her orgasm died away, then he licked and stroked her gently until she came down the rest of the way. She lay limp and stunned as tiny aftershocks shivered inside her every few seconds.

Phae hardly registered that Kent was putting her shorts back on her until he needed her to lift her hips so he could pull them up.

She pushed the shorts away. "What are you doing?"

"Getting you dressed," he said. "Believe me, I don't want to, but we've pushed our luck far enough."

"I want more. Come on. Let's risk it." Phae was positively daring right then. She didn't care what might happen. It felt too good to be stopping. "And you're left hanging."

He smiled at her, his teeth white in the moonlight. "Baby, I've been hanging practically since the first moment I saw you. At least now I've had a taste."

"It's only been a week."

"What?"

She pushed his hands away and buttoned her shorts. "Since we met. A week."

"Is that all? Huh." He moved beside her and sat. "Then I guess that's another good reason for us to keep our distance tonight."

"Who are you trying to convince? Me or you?" Phae fixed her bra and shirt.

"Definitely me."

Neither of them spoke for several minutes. Phae finally relaxed under Kent's silken touch stroking the outside of her thigh. Intermittent puffs of breeze cooled her heated face.

The leaves rustled gently and added a soothing rhythm to the distant fair sounds. She grew strangely happy. Okay, so there wouldn't be any lovemaking tonight, but she'd had a hell of an orgasm all the same, and she'd learned that the man she desired, desired her in return.

She glanced at his still, shadowy form. "So, I guess you're okay with me beating you back at the carnival."

"It was a fluke."

She heard the smile in his voice. "I see. And you're not the least bit mad at me."

"Don't see why I should be. James and I talked it over before that last round and decided to let you and Neesa win. We figured there wouldn't be any living with either one of you if you lost."

"Uh-huh. I could have sworn that you genuinely wanted to win. You must be incredible actors. The way you threw that basketball into the crowd was a masterful touch. I'm impressed."

"Thanks. I did it all for you."

Phae ran her fingers down his muscular arm. "It's kind of weird talking to you in the dark. You seem mysterious. I can see you, kind of, but not all the details."

"I'm hurting, because I can't have ... you know what I can't have. And I'm trying to get comfortable on this lumpy ground, but I'm smiling because your leg feels like silk. So why don't you tell me about yourself? When we're not together, I think of all these questions I want to ask, but then when you're around, I never seem to ask them."

"I bet Miss Eugenia and James have told you everything about me already."

"I can't trust what my aunt tells me and James wouldn't tell me much. I know you grew up here, but that you went to Harvard and worked briefly in Chicago before coming back here and setting up shop as a hairdresser. Not much to go on. Why don't we start with you telling my why you left Chicago?"

"It's personal," Phae said sharply.

"After what we just did, what could be more personal than that?"

Phae didn't want to think about what happened in Chicago. She was happy and wanted to stay that way. "I left. End of story."

"I heard you had a great future ahead of you."

"I think I've still got a great future ahead of me."

"I didn't mean anything by it," he said.

"Not everyone wants the same things, Mr. Entrepreneur, so-called billionaire," she said, hoping to throw him off track.

"Where did you work?"

She sighed. "If you've got to know, then fine. I left because of politics. I couldn't handle it. You wouldn't believe all the backstabbing that goes on in big companies like that."

"Where did you work?"

"In marketing at Fullerton."

Kent whistled. "Wow. You really were in the big leagues."

"I don't know how big your company is, Kent, but Fullerton is beyond huge. They employ tens of thousands of people in the U.S. alone. Their world-wide figures are even more staggering since most of their production is carried out in third world countries. When people talk about gigantic, faceless corporations, they're talking about Fullerton."

Phae took a deep breath and continued. "I couldn't handle it. The constant pressure to be perfect and you couldn't trust anyone. I hated it. There was no point in being miserable the rest of my life, so I left. And that's all there is to tell."

"You could have gone to work for a smaller company."

She shook her head vehemently. "No. I didn't want to. I still don't. I like it here. It's safe."

"Safe? That's an interesting choice of words."

"Just an expression."

"I don't think so. What are you holding back?"

"Don't read so much into it," she said. "Are you so bored in your present occupation that you've decided to branch out into psychology?"

Kent finally must have sensed her wishes because he answered, "I'm far from bored. In fact, business is so good at my company it's driving me crazy. I've decided to sell it."

Phae was surprised. "Why would you sell it if it's doing well?"

"That's easy. It's all in the details. When I started, I had a partner. He was supposed to handle the business side and I was going to write the software. It took longer to become profitable than he was ready for, so when he wanted out, I didn't stop him."

"I've heard Miss Eugenia talk about him like he was evil incarnate."

Kent laughed lightly. "Hardly. He simply lost faith, and he's paid for it. About six months after he left, my latest app took off and I haven't had a dud since. Only problem is, the bigger the company gets, the less time I get to spend doing what I love—creating the apps."

"Why don't you hire a manager?" Phae asked.

"I thought about it, but I'm unwilling to put my trust into someone I don't know well, who might blow everything or rob the company blind. So, while I haven't enjoyed it, I've learned what I needed to learn to run the business side of things. And it's gone well."

"That's impressive," Phae said.

"Someone more knowledgeable could have done better, I'm sure. Anyway, not long ago, I walked into my office one morning and turned on my computer. I needed to review a financial report before I met with accounting, but I couldn't find the file. Because I couldn't remember the exact name, the computer's search turned up an enormous list of possibilities. As I scrolled and all those file names flew by, it struck me that not a single file had any connection to programming. It was all management reports, financial records, advertising contracts and so on. You get the picture."

"Yeah."

Kent continued. "Somewhere along the road to becoming successful, I'd forgotten why I started the company to begin with. I had too many commitments to do much more than check in with what the creative team was doing without doing any of the real work. I've been feeling more and more dissatisfied ever since. So I think I'm done with it. I'm going to sell."

"That's a huge decision."

"Yes and no. I've had an offer from a good company that I think will do right by it, so I don't have worries on that front. I'm flying out to Phoenix tomorrow to meet with my people then on Sunday I'll fly to San Diego for a Monday meeting with the potential buyers. It's possible that the next time you see me I'll be a free man."

"And when will that be?" Phae tried not to sound disappointed that he was leaving so soon.

"Probably Wednesday. Will you miss me?"

"I'm not going to answer that. You're conceited enough as it is."

"You said you wanted me."

"That's the sort of thing I'm talking about. You think you know all the answers."

"Only where you're concerned."

He pushed himself up off the ground and held out his hand. She grabbed it and he helped pull her up.

He twirled her into his arms and whispered in her ear. "I know that if I kissed you right now, you'd do anything I asked you."

She opened her mouth to give him a snappy reply, but stopped short when she heard someone yelling Kent's name.

"Oh, thrill," she said. "I think it's James."

"The man has radar," Kent said, bending down to pick up the stuffed dog and dice from the ground.

"I take it we're leaving?"

James' voice had gotten louder, then receded.

"I think he's going away," she said.

"Yeah, well, we'd better move anyway. He's my best friend and I'd like to keep it that way. I can't understand why he's being so overprotective of you, though he did kind of warn me the other day at the cafe."

"He's not my keeper, no matter what he thinks," Phae said.

Kent shrugged. "He's stubborn. What do you say we go ride the Ferris wheel and eat some cotton candy or whatever else your heart desires?"

Phae firmly grasped the hand he offered and they began the stroll back to the fairgrounds.

"You know," Kent said, "we started off talking about you, then I got sidetracked talking about selling my company and we never got back to you."

"I don't mind it. What's next for you after the sale? Early retirement?"

"I don't know yet. Maybe games this time. Not bloody games. Smart games that challenge kids and adults both. Something like that."

"Fascinating. Tell me more."

"No, Phae. That won't work. I want to know … what's your favorite color?"

"Blue, like your eyes. What's yours?"

"Brown of course, like your eyes. What's your favorite food?"

"I have too many favorites to pick. You?"

"Lasagna," he answered quickly. "Do you like it?"

"Love it," she said.

"Good. When I get back from San Diego, I'll come over to your place and cook lasagna for you on one condition."

"What's that?"

"You have to leave your hair down. I want to see it down and untamed."

"Hmm. I might do it."

"I love your honesty. It's a deal," he said. He gently raised her hand to his lips and kissed her palm. "We need to think of a story to tell James when we get back."

Phae mumbled a reply but didn't listen to what he said. She was too busy mulling over his comment about her honesty.

She hadn't been completely truthful about what happened in Chicago. And she certainly hadn't told him about being Captain Nice Guy. He wouldn't be pleased about that particular bit of information.

She didn't want to think about it. It was too soon to worry about confessions and the future.

"Phae? Are you listening? I said we should tell James that we were at the ag barns."

"Right," she answered quickly. "Ag barns."

She admired Kent's handsome profile as they stepped back into the lights of the carnival. She left her worries behind, in the darkness.

CHAPTER TEN

KENT CHECKED HIS SPEED AS he neared the city limits of Zeke's Bend. He stifled a yawn. It was nearly two o'clock in the morning.

He probably shouldn't have rushed his return from San Diego, but the meeting with the buyers had lasted nearly two days longer than he'd expected and he'd been impatient to return home to Phae.

He'd called her on Wednesday to tell her that he'd see her Friday. She'd been strangely distant on the phone, not her usual sassy self. He'd texted her, too, but her responses were terse. She said she didn't like texting.

He flattered himself by assuming that she was only disappointed by his delay, but truthfully, he guessed her reserve had been caused by second-guessing what had happened between them at the fair.

It had been hard to focus on the details of the sale because he'd kept daydreaming about Phae under the trees, dappled moonlight playing on her satiny skin.

It was as if he could still see, taste, touch and smell her. And hear her gentle moans when he made her come.

Damn. He was hard again. The woman had put some kind of spell on him. They hadn't known one another long, or spent much time together, but he knew a winner when he saw one. And he wasn't about to let this particular winner go.

While Kent's career lay grounded in modern science and technology, his heart and mind remained open to a more mystical side of life. He believed in love at first sight.

His own parents were perfect examples that instantaneous love could happen, and more importantly, could last. They'd been married for over thirty-seven years, yet had only known one another for a month when they sealed their union.

Kent wanted what his parents had, and he'd been waiting for his perfect woman his entire adult life.

Just when he thought he'd never find her, Phae Jones had appeared. In his eyes, she embodied perfection. Beauty, brains and wit with a fiery, passionate side. And she was proud, confident, lusty. Oh hell yes. Lusty.

Her honesty about her attraction to him worked like an aphrodisiac. He didn't like coy women, or those who were out of touch with their physicality. He liked women who knew what they wanted, and he especially liked that Phae wanted him.

He could barely concentrate on the road when he recalled the way Phae had responded to him at the fair.

As he drove down the quiet streets of Zeke's Bend, he contemplated dropping by Phae's apartment. He glanced at the gift box on the passenger seat. He could use the present as an excuse to see her.

No, it was late, and she had undoubtedly gone to bed hours ago. He shouldn't wake her.

He grinned as he wondered what her response would be to his gift. He'd searched through more than a few boutiques in San Diego looking for the consummate little black dress. The box held the sexy fruit of his labors.

He laid his plans. Tomorrow morning he would drop by Phae's shop and give her the present. She'd probably put up a fuss about him trying to clothe her, but Kent had confidence he could goad her into wearing the dress.

And hey, if the dress was a little too small, he couldn't be blamed. After all, he was a man, and what did men know about dress sizes? His deep, throaty chuckle rumbled in the quiet car.

He pictured himself hand-feeding her a bite of lasagna. Maybe a drop of sauce would drip off the fork onto her luscious cleavage which would undoubtedly be spilling over the top of the oh-so-little black dress.

He'd be less than a gentleman if he didn't clean up his mess. But wait. Where had his napkin gone? Oh well, when faced with life's little challenges, one must improvise. His tongue could clean up the spill quite nicely.

He wore a wicked grin. Maybe Phae hadn't gone to bed yet. He could drive by quickly and see if her lights were on. He turned the car down the next street, in the direction of Phae's home.

He was less than two blocks away and had been wondering if Phae owned a pair of high heels when, out of the corner of his eye, he noticed some shaking bushes over to his left. It was a windless night. He slowed to a near crawl.

Less than six feet away from the porch of a fine old house, the bushes fronted the sidewalk which ran the length of the residential street. A streetlight adequately lit the scene, but the depths of the shrubbery remained in shadows.

He stopped the car and waited a few moments. Nothing moved. It had probably been an animal.

He eased his foot onto the accelerator. Then he saw it. A man. Dressed all in black, including a stocking cap.

The back of his body was illuminated for a split second as he leapt gracefully from behind the bushes then disappeared into the shadows at the side of the house. Kent briefly considered chasing the man, but knew it would be pointless.

He'd just seen the elusive Captain Nice Guy.

He couldn't believe his luck. And he had no doubt whatsoever that the man he'd seen was indeed Captain Nice Guy and not a burglar.

The man had a bulky belt around his waist, probably filled with the tricks of his do-gooder trade. A town the size of Zeke's Bend wouldn't attract someone the caliber of a pro cat burglar.

Kent drove away rapidly, desperately hoping that Phae would be awake so he could share what he'd seen. And James. He'd have to tell

James tomorrow. The sheriff would be thrilled to get a description of the man, even if that description was basic at best.

Kent recalled what he'd seen to burn it into his memory.

The man had been average to shorter than average in height. He wore a black stocking cap with some kind of strap around it. His long-sleeved shirt and pants were also black. He was thin and had leapt with panther-like agility. Kent had been unable to make out his face.

Kent turned into the alley that ran behind Phae's shop, knowing her apartment was in the rear of the building.

He drove past slowly. All was dark, her lights off. He'd have to wait until tomorrow to tell his story. The little black dress would have to wait as well.

He was half-amused to find himself disappointed. And he liked that Phae was the first person he wanted to tell. He pulled out of the alley and headed toward his aunt's house.

Captain Nice Guy. He'd spotted him. The brief scene of the man's leap replayed itself over and over in his mind.

He'd nearly reached his aunt's house when he sensed that something he'd seen wasn't quite right. The more he thought about it, the more the leaping man seemed familiar.

Something in the picture jogged his memory, but he didn't know what it was.

He pulled into Miss Eugenia's driveway and was pleased to see that she'd left the porch light on for him. Kent had called her from San Diego to tell her that he'd be getting back late and she'd been so excited about his return that he felt guilty for not visiting more often.

He turned off the car and sat quietly. Captain Nice Guy. Something familiar. What could it be?

He closed his eyes and froze the mental image of the leaping man. Nothing seemed out of the ordinary. Black cap. Thin.

Very long legs, especially for a man.

The pants had stretched taut across his butt as he jumped—Kent inhaled sharply and his eyes flew open.

It couldn't be.

He shook his head. He had to be wrong. The idea was ridiculous. And yet, hadn't he kept his mind open to the possibility that Captain Nice Guy might be a woman?

Yes, a woman. Any woman other than Phae Jones. Not her.

Think logically, he told himself. What were the facts?

There truly weren't any facts other than a lusciously rounded ass. Did men's asses look like that? He didn't know; he'd never looked.

He recalled his encounter with the do-gooder in Miss Eugenia's garden. There was a floral scent surrounding his attacker when Kent was tied up. At the time, he thought it must be from the flowers in the garden.

Phae wore a floral perfume at the fair. Were the two scents the same? He couldn't be certain. His memory of the events on that embarrassing night in his aunt's back yard was clouded by being nearly unconscious at the time.

What had the captain said to him? "Hey you." No, that wasn't it. "Hey buddy." That was it. Buddy.

Phae had called him buddy numerous times. He'd noticed because she'd called both him and James buddy when she was getting angry. It was a common word, though. Circumstantial evidence at best.

In fact, all the evidence Kent could muster against Phae hardly stood a chance of being considered circumstantial.

He flashed on an image of Phae gracefully shooting the basketball at the fair and on her fluidly jogging out of Miss Eugenia's garden the first day he met her.

They'd been talking about Captain Nice Guy. Kent had said he might be a woman. Phae had raced away like her fine ass was on fire.

Kent reached for the keys still hanging in the ignition.

KENT TURNED OFF HIS HEADLIGHTS when he pulled into the alley behind Phae's shop. He drove slowly in the moonlight and switched off the motor before getting too close to her driveway. He coasted to a halt.

Kent thought the vein in his forehead might pop wide open when he saw Phae's lights were on.

He warned himself to remain calm and not condemn her out of hand. She could be awake for any number of reasons. He picked up the present sitting on the passenger's seat.

He walked up to her place and knocked gently. He heard feet crossing the floor.

"Who is it" Phae called through the door.

He tried to sound casual. "It's Kent. Can I come in?"

"Kent?" She sounded surprised. The porch light came on. "Wait a sec. I need to get some clothes on."

He heard her running away. While he waited, he stepped back a few yards and surveyed the building.

It only had one story and wasn't particularly wide, though it was deep, with the shop in front and the apartment in back. The apartment had to be small. He disliked the idea of her living there; she deserved to live in a palace, not in a cubby hole in a building that, at best, could be considered past its prime.

But the paint was in good shape and the tiny yard was well-kept. Certainly the store front on the other side was in good repair and looked as nice as the rest of the businesses on the quaint street. He would have expected nothing less from Phae.

He frowned. She certainly was taking her time. Surely all she needed to do was throw on a robe ... unless she had on her Captain Nice Guy gear.

If Phae were guilty, she probably wouldn't have had enough time to return home and change clothes in the ten minutes or so since he'd seen her, or since he'd seen someone he hoped wasn't her.

He waited impatiently. The minutes seemed interminably long. Finally, he heard her approaching. She opened the door.

Phae barely glanced at Kent as she motioned for him to enter. "Sorry it took so long. Come on in."

When Kent saw her standing there in a long terrycloth robe, he felt certain his suspicions had been correct. "Thanks."

He glanced around the minuscule living room. An empty doorway opened onto a darkened hallway on the left and another empty doorway on the right side of the facing wall opened onto a small kitchen.

Only a few pieces of furniture filled the living room. An old, lumpy-looking sofa stretched the length of one wall and an easy chair with faded brown upholstery sat beside the door. No pictures hung on the walls. In fact, the decor could best be described as extremely sparse.

The top of the coffee table was empty, marred by numerous scratches in the finish. A circular rag rug covered the center of the slightly warped wooden floor. Everything was old but scrupulously clean.

The only object of beauty in the room was a magnificent mahogany china cabinet that graced the wall to his right, so tall it nearly touched the ceiling. The beveled glass in the doors and the brass hardware shined defiantly in the dreary room. The piece was obviously a valuable antique. Its glistening wooden shelves were as barren as the beat-up coffee table.

Phae had been living here for how long … three years? And the room looked as if she'd just moved in and hadn't yet finished unpacking. Kent's stomach clenched.

Phae gestured toward the china cabinet. "Grandma Jones left it to me."

Kent nodded.

"I know what you're thinking."

"No, you don't."

"Yeah, I do," she said, staring forthrightly into his eyes. "You're thinking that I'm a poor pitiful woman who doesn't have enough money to decorate her home. You're thinking that life must be hard for me, living like this."

Kent was uncomfortable under her gaze. "Not exactly."

"Don't feel sorry for me. I have money. Grandma Jones saw to that and I make a decent living from my business. I prefer to keep things simple."

"I think you've taken simple to a whole other level."

Phae sat down in the brown chair, demurely holding her robe closed over her knees. "You sound like everybody else who has ever been here. I'm used to it. Sit down if you want. The sofa hasn't bitten anyone in a long time."

Kent sat down and was surprised to find it wasn't as uncomfortable as it looked.

"Is the rest of your apartment this … spare?" he asked.

"Pretty much. Except the extra bedroom. That's where I've got my exercise equipment."

"I find it hard to believe this place is big enough to have two bedrooms."

"Don't push it, Kent. Forget about my house and tell me why you're here. It's almost three a.m."

He didn't want to make her angry, so he dropped the subject of her odd apartment. "I drove in from the airport and thought I'd swing by your place on the chance that you'd still be awake. And you were. I'm surprised."

Phae covered her mouth, coughed lightly then said, "I'd gotten up to get a snack."

Kent thought she looked uneasy and too alert to have recently awakened. "Lucky for me." He set the wrapped present on the coffee table. "I wanted to give you this."

"You might have given it to me at a more decent hour," she said while reaching for the gift.

The way her beautiful brown eyes sparkled told him she was pleased, which in turn, pleased him. "I couldn't wait until tomorrow."

Phae carefully lifted the lid and placed it back on the table. Her hand rested on the tissue paper. With her other hand, she negligently pushed back a shining lock of hair that had escaped from her loose ponytail.

She smiled at him. "Give me a hint."

"Nope. See for yourself."

She pulled back the paper and lifted out the dress. Holding it up by the thin straps, she cocked her head sideways and her finely shaped brows drew together. "What is it? A leg warmer?"

"No. It's a little black dress."

"You're kidding." She continued to inspect the garment.

He leaned forward and took the dress. He'd thought she'd be reticent about wearing it, but this was ridiculous.

He grasped the sides of the dress and pulled. "See? It only looks tiny. It stretches."

Phae grinned and retrieved the dress. She slid her hands inside and stretched the garment. "From what I can see, it doesn't stretch far enough."

"Try it on and see."

"Um, it's not only too narrow, it's too short."

"No it's not. Women in cities wear this type of dress all the time."

"Yeah, on street corners."

Kent frowned. "It's not that revealing. You're out here in the country and not aware of what's in fashion."

To his surprise, Phae smiled. "I get it. This is a joke." She tossed the dress back in the box. "Good one. I actually thought you were serious for a second."

"I am serious about it." Kent tried to think of a way to persuade her to try it on. He gave her his best wistful look. "I hoped you'd wear it when I fix dinner for you. I thought a new dress would make the evening more special. I suppose the dress might be a *little* small, but I didn't know your size and had to guess. At least try it on."

Phae's brows lowered. "No way. I don't dress like a tramp for anyone. Especially not someone who thinks he can manipulate me so easily."

"I don't know what I was thinking. Nothing's ever easy with you, is it? Never mind. I didn't mean to offend you. I hope you won't cancel our dinner because of this misunderstanding."

She shook her head slowly. "No. I won't cancel. But I won't wear that dress, either." She covered her mouth and yawned. "It's late, and you should go now."

He rose from the sofa. "Guess I'll see you tomorrow night then. Is six too early?"

"Not tomorrow," she said quickly, too quickly in Kent's opinion.

"Why not?"

"I have plans. A class. I take a martial arts class in Rollinsburg."

She was lying. He knew it. She'd lifted her chin the tiniest fraction when she spoke. It was exactly what she'd done at the fair last week when she tried to save face by telling him that their kiss hadn't affected her.

"Oh," he said. "But we were at the fair last Friday and you didn't have a class then."

Her chin tilted upward. "I cancelled," she said smoothly as she opened the door for him. "That's why I need to go tomorrow. I shouldn't cancel two weeks in a row."

"Then I guess we'll have to make it Saturday."

"Sounds great. Call me and tell me what I need to buy," she said with a genuine-looking smile.

"No. I'll get it. Do you have enough cookware in there for me to cook the lasagna?"

She looked thoughtful. "Probably not."

"I'll bring what I need, then."

He studied her, standing tall and proud in her dumpy little apartment. She was magnificent, but he reminded himself, she was also hiding something.

"See you Saturday at six," he said gruffly as he walked out the door.

"I'm looking forward to it."

He raised his hand in a curt gesture of farewell and headed to his car. He heard her softly close the door.

As he drove back to his aunt's house, he thought of how Phae had lied about taking a class Friday night. Although he didn't have any actual proof that she was Captain Nice Guy, she certainly hadn't given him any reason to think she wasn't.

One way or another, he intended to uncover the truth. He'd be watching her tomorrow night. That much was certain.

"Your lies just earned you a shadow, Phae Jones," he vowed.

CHAPTER ELEVEN

PHAE WAITED UNTIL SHE COULD no longer hear Kent's engine before she breathed easily. He'd seemed upset when he left, but she didn't know why. Her refusal to try on the dress seemed the probable cause, but she didn't think that was it.

She glanced around the living room. She'd ignored everyone's admonishments about her monkish style of life, but seeing her home through Kent's eyes had been different.

He'd been shaken by the place, and his reaction affected her in a way no one else's had. Suddenly, she could see how shabby the furniture truly was.

She walked to the easy chair and ran her hand over the worn upholstery. When she moved into this apartment nearly three years ago, she couldn't afford new furniture so she'd raided her parents' storage shed and found the chair, sofa, coffee table and even the old rag rug.

It seemed in fine enough condition back then. Besides, these were furnishings from her childhood. How could she be expected to see them as they actually were?

She sank into the chair. She'd been so nervous the past week, thinking and rethinking about what had happened between her and Kent at the fair. She'd gone on a cleaning binge to distract herself.

Her living room didn't look this bare a week ago. In her cleaning frenzy, she'd thrown away magazines, old paperback books and anything else for which she couldn't find a future use. She'd done the same in the other rooms of the apartment.

Still, she hadn't dragged all that many bags out to the dumpster. Maybe her mother was right and Phae should buy some pictures and knick-knacks to brighten up the place.

102

No. She wouldn't do it. She liked her apartment this way. It was too tiny to clutter up with junk, and the less stuff in it, the bigger the place felt. She refused to destroy her well-being to placate a man.

She picked up the little black dress. She smiled wryly as she surveyed the scrap of stretchy fabric. It was hard to believe that he actually thought she'd wear the thing. If she wore it out in public, she'd get arrested for public indecency.

As she picked and pulled at the thing, she doubted she could even get it over her head let alone the rest of her body. When was the last time she'd worn something sexy? Chicago, probably. That was how long ago it had been.

The morning she'd left the city, she'd so desperately wanted to destroy all evidence of her life in Chicago that, except for a few pairs of jeans and a couple of sweaters, she'd given all her clothing to Goodwill.

When Grandma Jones died, she'd had to purchase a dress for the funeral, and it remained the only nice piece of clothing hanging in her closet.

Phae tossed Kent's ridiculous gift back into the box. She should throw the thing away. She gathered it all up and stomped to the kitchen.

The box was halfway into the trash can before she stopped herself. The dress had probably cost a fortune, and besides, Kent had given it to her, so she should save it if for no other reason than a sentimental one. She retrieved the dress then discarded the box.

By the time Phae entered her bedroom and flipped on the light, she'd managed to convince herself that she should at least try on the thing before condemning it to a long, light-deprived life in her closet.

There was no way it would fit, she reminded herself. Over the head or over the hips? She wrestled with the garment. Definitely over the head.

She yanked and jerked and stretched the dress, then yanked and jerked and stretched some more. Finally, with a loud grunt, she pulled it down over her hips.

Trying to push more of her bosom into the top cups, she stepped in front of the bureau mirror. She stopped cold. Her hands dropped to her sides.

Was that woman in the mirror really her?

She ran to her exercise room, snatched up her small stepper bench, then returned to her bedroom. Standing on the bench, she could better see her whole body.

She looked incredible, if she did say so herself. Her legs were sleek and long, her stomach flat under the stretchy fabric, her hips softly rounded, and her waist was smaller than she remembered.

Her defined, yet feminine shoulders were accented nicely by the thin spaghetti straps. And talk about cleavage. The dress was so tight across her chest that it looked like she'd spill out if she took a deep breath.

When had this happened? She hadn't looked this good in Chicago. She used to avoid any type of clingy fabric, but not because of her weight. In fact, she weighed about ten pounds more now than she did then.

Muscle tone. That was the difference. Back then, she'd been working seventy to eighty hours a week at Fullerton and had no time to even think about exercising.

It was unbelievable. She hadn't paid attention to how she looked the past several years. During all those hours she'd spent working out, she'd worried more about strength and endurance than appearances.

Had Kent seen this under her baggy clothes?

She smiled tentatively into the mirror. Maybe she actually would wear this dress for him on Saturday. She'd need to get some decent heels. She'd also have to ask Sylvie what to do about panties since all Phae owned were the regular kind and the lines of the pair she was wearing clearly showed under the tight dress.

She wondered if that was why some women wore that torturous thong underwear. She'd bought a pair once in Chicago but had been so aghast at how she'd looked that—

"What am I doing?" she asked her reflection.

She scowled into the mirror, wondering if she'd gone temporarily insane. She'd been acting like those women in those cereal commercials she sometimes saw on television while she was exercising.

How many times had she laughed at those women preening before their mirrors? And now, here she was doing it herself.

She hopped off the bench and began to jerkily undress.

She'd looked like a bimbo, she said to herself as she rolled the dress up over her chest. And she'd only been surprised to see herself in something so outrageously provocative and that was why she'd acted so vain.

Phae threw the dress haphazardly over a hanger and shoved it into the back of the closet. She'd keep the dress, but only because Kent gave it to her.

She noticed the clock on her bedside table as she picked up her nightgown from the bed. It was past three-thirty in the morning. She quickly redressed, scooped up the stepper bench, and nearly ran to the spare bedroom.

Kent was fast becoming a nuisance in her well-ordered life, albeit a handsome, sexy nuisance. She wound her way through the various pieces of exercise equipment and yanked open the closet door.

She pulled out the pile of clothing and gear she'd hidden earlier. Tossing the mess onto the nearby weight bench, she sat and began to sort through the pile.

As she swiftly sorted and cleaned, she thought about Kent. He'd created what she'd come to think of as a sexual fog which completely enveloped her senses whenever he was nearby. It even happened once over the phone.

She couldn't stop remembering what they'd done in that grove of trees at the fair. Her skin warmed at how she'd blatantly propositioned him, and not just once.

As the days passed, she'd become more and more embarrassed. It wasn't like her to proposition men, or to be embarrassed for that matter.

By the time Kent had called this past Wednesday, she'd convinced herself that she'd never be able to face him again, and that he must think of her as a desperate, sexually starved pity-case. But then his deep, sultry voice had flowed through the speakers and she was lost in the Kent fog again.

She knew she needed to make a decision about her relationship with him, and soon. She was certain that their dinner on Saturday would lead to other, more sensual pleasures. Was that what she wanted?

Her body shrieked yes. She'd never experienced such overwhelming passion in her twenty-eight years. But her heart and mind knew that she and Kent were moving too quickly.

She needed to learn more about him. And he needed to learn more about her. And more than anything else, she needed to detach herself from the boggling confusion of intense physical desire.

She stacked the gear neatly on the top shelf of the closet then retired to her bedroom. As she switched off her bedside lamp and settled under the covers, she told herself to quit making herself crazy about Kent.

If he attempted to seduce her Saturday night, she knew she would never be able to find the strength to stop him. And if he didn't, well, damn, that'd be the worst outcome. Regardless, she had to leave the problem up to fate.

In the morning, she had a long day in front of her and working in the beauty shop was merely the beginning. She decided that she'd take a long nap after work since she needed to wait until late to make her rounds.

Then there was the special project she had planned for the night. It was probably one of the most complicated and important things she'd ever tried to do. She fervently hoped she'd be successful.

As she fell asleep, her last thought was of Kent, and wondering why he hadn't kissed her before he left.

KENT PUSHED THE LIGHT BUTTON on his watch. It was almost eleven thirty. He'd been crouched behind the reeking dumpster for over an hour and a half, his only company the tree frogs and cicadas singing wildly in the darkness.

Something needed to happen soon before his nasal passages became permanently damaged by the noxious fumes he was breathing, made all the worse by the hot, muggy night.

He tensed when he saw the lights go out in Phae's apartment. Finally.

The minutes passed slowly as he waited. He began to relax, thinking she'd simply gone to bed. She hadn't lied to him. She wasn't Captain Nice Guy. She was still his perfect woman.

Then her door opened.

There she was, nearly unrecognizable under a coating of thick black face paint, slinking out the door. Though some wispy clouds occasionally obscured the moonlight, he could clearly tell that the woman walking stealthily along the fence line was Phae.

She was camouflaged in solid black from head to toe. She even wore the stocking cap he'd noted the previous night. It must be ungodly uncomfortable to wear such a thing in summer.

Damn. There was no getting around it now.

Phae Jones was Captain Nice Guy.

He could hardly believe it, and felt numb.

As she crossed the alley and disappeared between two buildings, the corner streetlight illuminated her sufficiently for Kent to see that she wasn't wearing a stocking cap after all. She had braided her thick hair and wrapped it around the top of her head. He wondered if the strange strap on her head held the hairdo in place.

He crept from behind the dumpster and followed her into the shadows.

Her lithe body moved swiftly and silently through the darkness. Although Kent moved as rapidly and as quietly as he could, he found it difficult to keep her within sight. He'd barely traveled two blocks when he lost her.

He hid behind a telephone pole and scanned the long row of houses. She'd disappeared. He ran behind the nearest house, hoping to gain a long view down the back yards.

He'd only taken two steps into the yard when he heard a low, menacing growl from a dark corner. Great. A dog. Slowly, Kent retreated. When the dog burst into frenzied, deafening barks, Kent turned and ran.

He went full-out for a good block before he glanced over his shoulder and saw that the dog wasn't pursuing him. Ducking behind an overgrown forsythia bush, he attempted to calm his racing heartbeat.

The dog must have been penned or tied, he realized. He hadn't been able to see it in the dark, but if its bark bore any relation to its size, then it must have been a monster.

When his heartbeat returned to normal and the dog quit barking, Kent resumed his search for Phae. After wandering down the next street, trying to stay cloaked in shadows, he realized that the search was pointless. He should return to her house and wait for her to come home.

A second later, less than five houses down from where he stood, he saw Phae cross the street. Bingo. He loped after her.

He was chasing her down a residential street when she stopped by a car parked on the curb in front of a small house. He slipped behind a massive oak tree to watch her.

Phae crouched down to open the car door, reached inside then noiselessly shut the door again. She dashed to the front porch of the small house, opened and closed the mailbox, then slipped back into the shadows at the side of the street.

Kent raced to the porch to see what she'd left. He reached into the mailbox and pulled out a set of car keys. Shaking his head, he lowered the keys back into the box then set out after Phae again.

As they traveled farther and farther from Phae's apartment, Kent watched her repeat her act with car keys several times. He wondered how all these people would find their keys in the morning.

She must be crazy, he thought, or at least woefully misinformed about the rate of car theft in Zeke's Bend. If people left their keys in their cars, then there probably wasn't much to worry about. If there were, people would lock their cars at night on their own. They didn't need a night-time do-gooder to do it for them.

Kent thought he'd lost her again when she disappeared along the fence between two houses. He hastened after her, but when he cleared the side of the house, he found himself in an enclosed back yard, and Phae was nowhere in sight. Carefully, he searched the yard. Nothing.

He ran back to the street and barely stopped in time to prevent her from seeing him. She was creeping out the front door of a house on the other side of the fence. How had she gotten over there? And what was she doing inside?

When Phae moved on down the street, Kent checked the door of the house she'd exited. It was locked. He began to wish he'd brought along a notepad so that he could write down all the questions he wanted to ask her.

He couldn't help but be amused a short while later when Phae carefully rolled away a kid's bicycle from behind a car. There was no question about her motives in that one.

He became confused again, however, when he watched her remove something from her belt and attach it to the bike. After Phae left the scene, he investigated.

Taped to the handlebars was a note with a sucker glued to it. He could barely read the typed words in the moonlight:

Please remember to put your bike away at night.
Your parents would be very sad if they accidentally
ran over it in their car.
Love, your Secret Friend.

Kent wasn't surprised when, a few minutes later, he investigated a different bike Phae had fiddled with and found another note. This bike hadn't been carelessly left behind a car. The note read:

Good job! You put your bike away.
You should be very proud of yourself.
Love, your Secret Friend.

Instead of a sucker, this note had a chocolate bar glued to it. Kent frowned in annoyance. How did she know this kid didn't have allergies or diabetes?

He continued to follow Phae on what he could only term "her rounds." Unused to the stifling humidity, he found it difficult to maintain Phae's pace. He lost sight of her several times, but she always appeared again, sometimes half a block or more away from where he'd last seen her.

She traversed a route that wound up and down and around what must have been half the streets of Zeke's Bend. Her good deeds consisted mostly of checking locks on doors and windows.

At one house, he watched in irritation as she lugged three big trash cans to the curb. He could only assume that she'd done this so the homeowner wouldn't miss pickup. Important work indeed, Kent thought.

Steadily, though circuitously, they made their way toward the outskirts of the town. Phae had no particular destination that Kent could discern, so he was surprised when she picked up speed, stopping at fewer and fewer houses until at last, Kent had to jog to keep up with her.

In no time, his shirt was soaked with sweat. He felt like he was racing through a rain forest as he tried to inhale the heavy, moisture-laden air.

They soon left Zeke's Bend behind. Kent could barely see Phae in the moonlight as she loped silently through the undergrowth alongside the deserted country road. She leapt and bounded and covered ground at a steady pace.

Kent opted to run on the road itself since it was easier, and he couldn't travel as quickly and quietly through the underbrush as Phae. Twice, he had to dive into the ditch to avoid being seen by passing cars.

Kent cursed when Phae veered into the dense woods at the side of the road. He had no idea how he could find her in the nearly complete darkness under the trees, but he trudged behind her nonetheless. At this point, what option did he have?

CHAPTER TWELVE

DRY LEAVES AND TWIGS CRACKLED loudly under Kent's heavy feet, forcing him to attempt a tiptoe through the forest. He clearly heard Phae ahead of him, loud enough to be heard over the shrill calls of bugs and frogs, making it easy for him to follow. She must have let down her guard since this area appeared to be devoid of human life.

Fanning his heavy, wet shirt, Kent came to the edge of the woods, stopping behind a tree to scout ahead for Phae.

The tree line broke on the top of a low hill overlooking a paved road which fronted a small lighted building. Kent heard the faint strains of country music.

A large sign stood in the parking lot. He squinted to read it: Trapper's Tavern. He knew where he was now. He'd been there a few times with James in the past. If he remembered correctly, it was several miles outside of town. Running in the dark had made it seem much farther.

He kept looking for Phae as he picked off the debris he'd accumulated during his forest jaunt. He snarled as he pulled small twigs and leaves from his hair and clothing. And stick-tights. Oh, how he hated stick-tights.

A small piece of paper clung tenaciously to his knee. Lifting a corner of the paper, he was disgusted by what he saw as he peeled it away from his jeans. Gum. He must have picked it up during one of his ignominious dives into the ditch.

He flicked the scrap of paper away and steadfastly ignored the gooey mess that remained on his knee. Phae was going to have a lot to make up for, he thought darkly. And gum was just the beginning.

Out of the corner of his eye, he saw someone moving in the parking lot. He stared closely at the vehicles parked in front of the building. The interior light came on in an old pickup truck. Phae leaned inside the vehicle and the hood popped up.

Kent could only watch and wonder as she raised the hood and bent over the engine.

He muttered softly, "Phae Jones, if I've run all this way to watch you give somebody a free oil change, so help me ..."

She reached inside the engine, then after a few seconds, stood up straight and lowered the hood quietly. Kent inhaled sharply when the tavern door swung open.

The soft light from inside the bar silhouetted the outline of a stocky man big enough to nearly fill the doorway. He lurched drunkenly into the parking lot.

Where had Phae gone? He couldn't see her now.

Another, smaller man exited the building. He trotted after the man who was making a bumbling attempt to enter one of the parked cars.

Kent heard their voices but couldn't make out the individual words. The smaller man pulled the drunken man to a different car, then shoved him into the passenger seat.

Kent didn't relax until the smaller man got into the car and drove away, tail lights fading into the distance. He watched Phae reappear magically from around the side of the tavern and run spryly across the parking lot. Once on the other side of the road, she stopped on the side of the ditch nearest Kent and hunkered down into the undergrowth.

He couldn't guess what she was waiting for, but he took advantage of the time by sitting down and resting. He checked his watch. It was shortly before two a.m. The bar would be closing soon.

Minutes later, the strains of music filtering out of the tavern abruptly ceased. Two more men left the building then drove off in a beat-up truck. Three vehicles remained in the parking lot, including the one Phae had tampered with.

Her dark figure remained immobile in the bushes as two more men left the now dark and noiseless tavern. One of the men locked the front door while the other man walked in less than a straight line to the old truck.

He'd reached for the door handle when the other man called something to him that Kent couldn't understand.

Part of the obviously inebriated man's shouted reply was clear. "I'm not in any hurry to get home to …" then it faded away.

The man's voice sounded familiar.

Kent watched in disgust as the sober man got into his jeep and drove away. The drunken man collapsed into the driver's seat of the truck, not bothering to close the door behind him.

When the man turned his head to the side, Kent recognized him in the glow of the cab light. Phae's Uncle Leon.

This was an interesting turn of events.

A faint clicking sound coming from the truck was soon overwhelmed by Leon bursting out into a loud string of curse words. He stumbled out of the cab and pulled up the hood.

Kent smiled. Phae had disabled her uncle's truck. Leon wouldn't be driving anywhere tonight. She'd finally done a good deed that made sense.

Cursing wildly, Leon fumbled with the engine, the beam from his flashlight bobbing haphazardly in the darkness. With a cry of disgust, he slammed down the hood then stomped his way back into the cab of the truck.

Kent watched him pick up what looked like a bottle and began to drink from it. More beer, perhaps? More beer was the last thing he needed.

Leon quickly finished the drink and flung the bottle into the bed of the truck, then attempted once more to start his truck.

All the while, Phae couched unmoving in the bushes below Kent.

Before long, Leon's swearing began to die down. Less than ten minutes had elapsed when he slowly slumped over the steering wheel and slid to his side across the seat.

"Finally," Kent whispered. Leon had passed out. Maybe now Kent could go home.

His wish did not come true. He watched in surprise as Phae eased herself out of the undergrowth and padded across the paved road toward the tavern's parking lot.

What did she think she was doing? Leon could wake at any moment and Kent didn't want to think about what might happen if Leon saw a mysterious midnight ninja poking around his pick-up truck.

Kent exploded out of the forest and rushed down the slope. He was battling his way through the roadside bushes when he noticed Phae standing less than five feet in front of him.

She whispered angrily. "Be quiet! If you wake him up and ruin my plans I'll never forgive you. Now sit down and be quiet until I come back."

Kent watched in stunned (and outraged) silence as Phae crossed to the parking lot and her uncle's truck. Something wasn't right, he thought as she popped up the hood. She hadn't acted surprised to see him.

Why wasn't she surprised?

Phae lowered the hood then crept by the sleeping man, gently shutting the door as she passed. She briefly reached into the truck bed before running toward Kent.

She shoved a beer bottle into one of the many pouches on her belt as she approached him.

"Let's get out of here," she said softly before jogging away.

Kent reacted slowly to her command. Certain facts begun combining into a startling conclusion: somehow, and he had no idea how, Phae had been aware that he'd been trailing her. There was no other explanation which could explain her reaction to his discovery. She was a cool-headed type, but she couldn't be *that* cool.

How the hell had she known? And why was she heading away from town? To continue with this absurd outing?

He'd had enough of Captain Nice Guy for one night.

He raced after her, quickly overtaking her. Grabbing her around the waist and lifting her, he slung her over his shoulder and began tromping toward the woods.

It was time to go home and let the question and answer session begin.

"Put me down!" Phae hissed.

He ignored her. He was in charge now.

"I can make you put me down, you know," Phae said calmly.

"I know you've got a black belt, but I don't care. If you want to get away, you'll have to hurt me. And I'm willing to bet that a woman who leaves cutesy notes on kids' bikes won't want to maim me."

She sighed. "I don't have a black belt. Do you have any idea how long it takes to get one of those? If it's legit, anyway. But I don't study that kind. And what makes you think you can carry me all the way back to town, assuming that's where we're headed?" Her tone was laced with sugary sweetness and she wrapped her arms around his torso.

He bristled. She had no right to be so infuriatingly chipper. He grunted his reply.

Phae plucked at his damp shirt. "I've got a small canteen in my belt. If you put me down, I'll let you have a drink. Doesn't that sound good?"

He lowered his head and continued his march through the forest.

"You know, Kent, you might get a hernia. Think about it. You'd be laid up for days, weeks maybe. Miss Eugenia would be so thrilled, she'd have a happy fit. You wouldn't want to give your aunt a fit."

Kent refused to react to her taunts.

"Just put me down," she continued. "We'll go get my car and drive home with air conditioning. Then we'll talk about this whole thing in comfort. Come on. Let's get my car."

"Your car is out here?"

"Of course. That's where I was heading when you snatched me up like Bigfoot."

Kent told himself not to be stubborn. He had nothing to prove, and besides, the way he felt at that moment, the sooner he got back to Phae's apartment, the better. He turned around and headed for the road.

"I'm glad you're being reasonable," she said. "But could you slow down a little? All this bouncing is making me nauseous."

Kent clenched his jaw and slowed his pace. Phae remained mercifully silent until they reached the roadside and he shoved her off his shoulder.

She landed with a muffled thump on her butt. She stood and brushed herself off. "Thanks a lot, buddy. You're a real tough guy, you know that?"

She stalked down the road like a cat that had been sprayed with a water hose.

Kent shrugged and followed her. He hadn't meant to dump her like that, but damned if he'd apologize.

True to her word, her car was about two hundred yards down the road in a dilapidated, deserted barn. The car was covered in a pile of moldering hay, leaves and branches. He helped her pull the mess onto the barn floor.

When they finished, Kent demanded that Phae give him the keys. She sighed then reached into a pocket on her belt and handed them over.

He cranked up the a/c then slowly drove them out onto the road, fearing that the barn might collapse around them before they could get out. They soon passed Trapper's Tavern, Leon still sleeping soundly in the parking lot.

Kent attempted to sound calm when he asked, "How long did you know I was following you?"

Phae turned her head away and looked out the passenger window. "If I tell you, you're going to yell at me."

"I'll risk it."

She turned toward him. "Before I say anything else, let me say that you did a good job for your first try. I'm certain I didn't do half as well when I started."

"Are you placating me? Don't."

"Fine. Since you asked, I knew almost immediately. I'd gone about a block or so when I realized someone was following me. I circled around and snuck up behind you. When I saw it was you, I didn't know what to do. And then you went and got that dog all worked up. You sure did shoot out of there and race down the street."

He heard amusement in her tone and had to suppress his annoyance. "Don't push it."

"Sorry. The same thing has happened to me more than once. Hey, slow down." She leaned forward and pointed at the road ahead. "Is that a dog up there in the ditch?"

Kent slowed the car and looked. Sure enough, a small brown dog was digging around in the underbrush.

"I know that dog. Stop," Phae said as they neared the animal.

"No more good deeds tonight, Phae. We're going to your apartment."

"If you don't stop this car immediately, I'll jump out." She opened the door.

He slammed on the brakes, grabbed her by the arm and pulled her toward him. "Are you crazy? You could get yourself killed!"

Phae yanked her arm away and leaped out of the car. She turned around and leaned down to where Kent could see her hard, camouflaged features in the glow of the dome light.

Her voice was low and harsh. "Never touch me like that again. It hurt and I won't allow it to happen again. Do you understand me?"

He flinched. Damn. He hadn't realized he'd grabbed her too hard. "I didn't mean to hurt you. I was upset. You could have fallen under the wheels of the car."

The harsh lines of her face didn't soften much. "Just don't do it again."

She turned and called to the dog in the ditch.

Kent realized he needed to calm the hell down. His frustration had been growing steadily all night. He breathed deeply as he listened to Phae cajole the reticent animal.

She picked up the dog and got back into the car. "It won't take but a few moments to drop her off at her house, I promise."

He eyed the little brown, furry dog. It yapped loudly and struggled in Phae's arms.

"Shh, Frisky. It's only Kent and he won't hurt you," she crooned. "Pet her, would you? She'll calm down if you make friends."

Kent stretched a hand toward the small animal, letting her sniff before patting her head. In no time, Frisky squirmed out of Phae's grasp and lay between them, her head resting on Kent's lap.

Phae smiled. "You have a way with her that I didn't expect. Especially after the way you set off practically every dog in Zeke's Bend tonight."

Kent gave Frisky a final pat before continuing the drive home. "I didn't notice much barking after that first house."

"I'm just glad it was a full moon. Most pet owners know that dogs tend to bark more than normal when the moon is full. That's the only thing that saved us. Well, that and my pouch full of dog treats."

"Precisely what are you saying, Phae?"

"I'm saying that while you checked out my good deeds, or whenever you lagged behind, I calmed down all the dogs you'd excited."

He frowned. "I didn't lag behind. I was always right behind you."

In his peripheral vision, he saw Phae shaking her head.

"No you weren't," she said. "You were only able to keep up because I let you. I could have lost you in a second. I only let you follow me because I wanted you to—"

"That's enough," he interrupted, his anger reawakening. "Let's stop talking until we get to your apartment." That will give me time to get myself together again, he thought.

He assumed her silence was assent.

In a few minutes, Phae gave Kent terse directions to Frisky's house, then said nothing else. Kent mutely found his way to the street and stopped the car.

Phae opened her door and picked up Frisky. "I'll be back in a second. Turn off the headlights, would you? It's a big gamble, being out in my own car this time of night."

He complied with her wishes then watched her trot behind a house to his left. It looked familiar, but that didn't surprise him. He'd seen nearly every house in town that night.

Phae jogged back to the car and hopped into the passenger seat. "Hit it, Clyde," she said as she fastened her seat belt.

Kent looked once more at the house where she'd left Frisky. Then he remembered and groaned. "Oh no."

"Don't worry about it. Let's get out of here before anyone sees my car."

He started the engine and pulled out onto the street. "Please tell me there's another dog in the back there. Some dog other than Frisky. A big, hulking, scary dog like a Rottweiler or a pit bull."

"Sorry, Kent."

"This may be the worst night of my entire life."

"It's not that bad," she said in a cajoling way that only irritated Kent more. "I know from experience that when it's dark and you can't see, dogs can sound bigger than they are. Running away like you did is natural. And Frisky probably sounded pretty vicious."

She did, Kent thought. And that only made it worse. What could the silly little dog have done to him? Nibble off a toenail?

Phae sounded thoughtful as she continued. "What I can't get over is that Frisky somehow escaped her pen and managed to track you for so far. I thought I had her calmed down when I left her. She's usually so placid. Hey, that ditch where we found her, was that one of the places where you hid from those cars?"

Kent pulled the car to a careful, calculated stop then turned to look at the chatting ninja.

"Do not say another word." He kept his voice as low and threatening as he could. "Pay close attention to what I'm about to tell you. We are nearly at your apartment. When we get there, you are going to let us in and then you're going to change out of that *Mission Impossible* getup and wash that paint off your face and neck—"

"You can't—"

"Apparently, I've done everything you wanted me to do tonight, so now you will kindly do what I want. After you wash off that junk, you and I are going to have a long discussion. Wait. And take down that Judy Jetson hairdo you've got going on there. Then we'll talk. But until then, not another word. I'm tired, filthy, sweaty and I'm completely out of patience. Please do me a favor. If you really do want to make me feel better, say nothing more and do as I ask."

She crossed her arms over her chest and bit her bottom lip in consternation. Then she nodded and stared out the windshield.

Kent drove the rest of the way in blessed silence.

CHAPTER THIRTEEN

PHAE STRIPPED OFF HER GEAR and stepped into the cool shower. As she re-pinned her hair, she recalled Kent's Judy Jetson dig back in the car. He'd been downright surly.

She relaxed under the soothing spray. The face paint ran off her and swirled in dark clouds at her feet. An ominous sign?

After she finished and dried off, she defiantly dressed in a pair of old sweatpants and a t-shirt. She could hear Sylvie in the back of her head admonishing her for not pulling on something sexy, to soothe the savage beast. Or was that food? Music? Phae couldn't remember.

To hell with that, she thought. If she had to seduce Kent to get him to stop acting like an ass, well then … wait, what exactly was wrong with that line of logic?

She did want him. No, she REALLY wanted him. Sweatpants and t-shirt suddenly seemed like a bad plan.

No. She didn't know what was actually wrong about that line of thought, but it seemed wrong, and at the moment, that was good enough for her. She didn't want Kent if all he was on the lookout for was sex.

"Here goes nothing," she whispered as she headed for the living room.

Kent lay stretched on the sofa, one arm thrown over his face.

"Taking a nap?" Phae asked.

He jerked his arm away and lifted his head. "Good. You're back to normal."

Phae pointed to the empty glass sitting on the coffee table. "I'm glad you got yourself something to drink. Did you find the juice in the fridge?"

Kent shook his head and sat up. "Water's fine."

"I can get you some juice."

"No, just water ... please."

Phae shrugged, picked up his glass and went to the kitchen.

Kent's mood hadn't improved much while she'd been showering. She tried to think of something to make him relax, something that would help him listen calmly to her explanations.

Pasting a smile on her face, she refilled his glass and returned to the living room.

She handed the drink to him then sat in the easy chair. "Are you hungry?"

Kent took a deep drink. "No."

"Want some music?"

He gave her a funny look.

Phae hurried on and surveyed the man's rumpled, filthy clothes. "I have a washer and dryer in the shop. Why don't you take a shower and I'll wash your clothes? You'll feel better once you're clean."

"I don't want to feel better. And I'm not going to hide in your bathroom while I wait for my clothes to dry. All I want is for you to explain why you spend your nights acting like a strange do-gooder ninja."

"I'm trying to be civilized, but you're not helping matters with your attitude. Go take a shower. I'll find something for you to wear while you wait for your clothes. Think of how nice it will be to feel clean again."

He frowned. When he began a serious study of the rim of his glass, Phae knew she had him.

She rose from the chair and walked toward the hallway, hoping Kent would follow. "Come on. Let's find something for you to wear."

He heaved himself up off the sofa and followed her. In her bedroom, Phae opened one drawer after another, trying hard not to think about how close to her bed they were, and how big and close Kent was, standing beside her.

"I know it's in here somewhere," she babbled as she rifled through drawers. "Dad accidentally left behind a pair of sweats after he showered here the last time he visited. We work out together whenever he's here. I saw them a few days ago when I cleaned house. They're in here somewhere. Wait. This is them. Here you go." She held them out triumphantly, convincing herself she wasn't being a rambling twit.

Kent held the gray sweats in front of himself.

"Well," Phae said, "They're a little too short, and a lot too wide, but they have that drawstring. It'll work, don't you think?"

Kent mumbled what she thought was an affirmative.

She tossed him one of her largest t-shirts. "The bathroom's across the hall. Towels are under the sink. Toss your dirty clothes into the hall so I can get them started."

"I don't suppose you know how to remove gum from jeans, do you?"

"Gum? Where? Oh, I see. How did you get gum on your—" She stopped short, noting the dangerous glint in his eyes.

"So? How do you get rid of it?"

"Go take a shower already." She pushed on his shoulder, finding him to be an unmovable goliath of hard muscle.

Without a reply, Kent stalked off and closed the bathroom door.

Phae sighed and tried to remember he was tired and cranky. And didn't he have a right to be a little angry? All of this must be a shock. She certainly knew how shocked she was at having been discovered.

When Kent tossed his clothes into the hall, Phae gathered them up and quickly went to work. She tried using ice to pry the gum off his jeans, but it was too mashed into the fabric to pull off cleanly. She did the best she could.

After shoving everything into the shop washing machine, she relaxed into her easy chair, a tall glass of orange juice in her hand, and waited.

It wasn't long before she heard the water shut off. He'd bathed quickly, not a good sign for her sooth-the-cranky-beast plan.

"Don't be nervous," she told herself. "Be honest. Remember, it's like at the fair. He didn't run away. He's still here."

She propped her feet on the table, sipped her drink and waited. A few short minutes later, Kent came into the living room.

She'd expected to see him wearing the clothes she'd given him, so she wasn't prepared for what she saw.

Kent wore nothing but one of her bath towels wrapped around his hips. She swallowed hard. Day-umm. He looked good. Better than good.

Droplets of water still shimmered on his wide, tanned shoulders. His hair was damp, mussed and spiky in attractive disarray.

Phae tried not to stare at his impressive six pack and bulging biceps as he walked past her, but once he was past, she got a nice long look at his tight butt snuggled under the towel, and his thick, muscular thighs.

She swallowed hard again and had the crazy thought of, "What if he's trying to seduce me the way I should have tried to seduce him?" If so, it was working. She almost laughed out loud.

Kent didn't look at her as he seated himself on the sofa. He picked up his water, took a drink then turned to her. "You were right. I feel better."

"I'm glad. Are you hungry now?"

"No. The first thing I want to know is why you supposedly let me follow you tonight."

"Guess we'll get right down to it, then," she said wryly. "There's no 'supposedly' about it. When I saw you were tailing me, I realized I didn't have any choice. It's not like I could turn around, go home and pretend I'd been out on a midnight walk wearing all that gear."

He didn't smile or respond in any way, so Phae continued stoically. "I noticed you following me almost immediately. When I saw it was you, I knew that you had to have been hiding at my house because there was no way I could have run into you accidentally. Now it's your turn. What made you suspect me?"

"I saw you in your garb last night only a couple of blocks away from here," he said. "As you can see, accidents do happen."

She was surprised, not realizing she'd been recognized. "You were the one in the car?"

He nodded.

"I couldn't see inside it," she said. "But what made you think it was me?"

"It's not important. Suffice it to say I became suspicious as a result of what I saw."

"What did you see?"

"It's not relevant to the discussion."

The more he refused to answer, the more she wanted to know. "It's relevant to me. I can't have people recognizing me out there."

"They wouldn't."

"That makes no sense. You knew it was me, but no one else could?"

He blew out a breath. "Fine. I recognized your butt."

Phae's eyebrows shot up. He couldn't be serious, but she could see that he was. She didn't know if she should be flattered or offended. She opted for flattered and smiled, mostly because he'd been embarrassed to admit it.

"You got your answer," he said brusquely. "Now answer one of mine. Why did you allow me to follow you?"

"I knew if we kept seeing each other, I'd have to tell you about Captain Nice Guy eventually. You simply rushed the process. A lot."

He looked skeptical.

"Honestly. I was going to tell you. I just didn't know when. Everything has moved so fast between us, and I didn't know if I could trust you to keep my secret."

"Uh-huh. Go on."

She tried not to let his ongoing skepticism distract her. "Anyway, when I saw you standing out there tonight, I figured you must have been trying to tail me because you were curious about what I do. I mean, you could have confronted me the second I stepped foot out of my apartment, but you didn't. You followed me and I took that to be a good sign."

"You shouldn't have," Kent said with a frown.

"Obviously. Regardless, I decided the best way to explain what I do was to show you. That's it."

"So you didn't set out to make a fool of me?" he asked, a furrow between his brows.

"No! Why would you think I'd do something like that?"

"In case you haven't noticed, I took quite a beating tonight, Phae."

"You did well," she said softly. "I was being honest when I told you that earlier. And you're not used to the humidity around here, either."

He sipped his water and studied her.

"I know," she continued. "I was a little flippant in the woods. I made a couple of jabs and I'm sorry about that. I was so pumped up, though. My plan at the bar worked perfectly. I was afraid I'd get there too late to sabotage Uncle Leon's truck. That's why I cut through the woods. Everything took longer than I expected tonight."

Kent's mouth formed in the tiniest hint of a smile. "What you mean to say is that I slowed you down."

She returned his smile. "Yeah, but I wasn't going to say it."

"I know you weren't." He slowly shook his head. "Tonight didn't turn out the way I had planned in San Diego. Right now, we should be in bed, sipping wine. Instead, I'm sitting on your couch drinking water."

In a tiny towel, Phae added silently. He was sitting on her couch, drinking water while wearing a very tiny towel and nothing else. That salient detail made all the difference, in her opinion.

"Are you still mad at me?" she dared to ask.

He exhaled. "I'm not sure. I need some time to think about all this."

She hopped up from her chair. "You stay there and think. I'll go check the laundry."

She took her time as she removed the wet clothes from the washing machine and tossed them into the dryer. She couldn't understand how Kent thought she might want to make a fool out of him, but at least it explained why he'd been so upset.

After starting the dryer, she waited in the shop for a few moments to give Kent a little more time to think. She hoped that he'd seen how important her work was.

Tonight, she'd been happier going about her tasks than she'd been in a long time. Knowing Kent was behind her pleased her immensely. She'd longed to have someone to talk with about her work.

Kent was confused, but he'd come around eventually. What was the big deal, anyway? So she liked to help people. He shouldn't have a problem with that, should he?

She took a deep breath and walked back into her apartment. When she entered the living room, Kent looked at her with a wistful expression.

"You're the sexiest woman I've ever seen, Phae Jones," he said, "even in sweatpants and a t-shirt."

CHAPTER FOURTEEN

PHAE HALTED IN THE MIDDLE of the room. Being called sexy was the last thing she'd expected.

Kent patted the cushion beside him. "Come sit by me."

And that quickly, tendrils of sensual fog came wafting in from nowhere and wrapped themselves around Phae, pulling her onto the couch beside the handsome man. One minute she wanted to smack him and the next she wanted to kiss him.

He lifted her hand, lightly stroking her palm. "I want you," he said, almost formally.

A sense of relief washed over her, loosening a tightness in her chest she hadn't realized was there. He was okay. Everything was okay. He'd thought it out and seen that her being Captain Nice Guy was no big deal. He still wanted her.

She looked into his bright blue eyes. "I want you, too."

"We have … issues to work out."

She nodded and trembled when his fingertips passed over the sensitive skin of her inner wrist.

He continued, his voice gone rough, deep. "And I have confidence we'll work them out. Do you?"

She nodded again, entranced by the passion in his gaze as he looked into her eyes. Right at the moment, she was rapidly losing sight of what those issues might be.

"Good," he said. "But we'll do it later, Phae, because I can't wait another instant to be with you."

She sighed in pleasure. "It's about time."

Phae wasn't a shy type, and this proved to be no exception. She reached out and pulled at the towel that was hardly masking the unmistakable bulge between his legs.

He inhaled sharply as she tossed one end aside and finally exposed what she needed so badly to see.

She licked her lips as she took in all that silky, solid length. His cock sprung out, smooth, with a perfectly-shaped swollen head, pointing at the ceiling, growing longer and harder as she studied it.

"Oh …" she sucked in a breath as she realized how large Kent actually was. She ran her fingers down the length of his cock, ticking off inch after inch.

She glanced back up at his face and her insides twisted when she saw the intensity there. Gone was the playful, joking man and the surly, sour man. He'd been replaced by a sex-fueled alpha who was about to take everything he wanted.

A muscle worked in his jaw. "Lose the shirt," he demanded.

She didn't know this voice, this commanding, demanding side. She liked it. No, she more than liked it even when a small part of her thought she shouldn't. She swallowed hard. And pulled off her shirt.

He took it from her and dropped it on the floor. "Now the bra."

Again, she swallowed hard. She reached back, hyper-aware of how the movement thrust her breasts out. She unclasped the bra and let the straps fall down her shoulders, then let the whole thing slide off her arms.

Kent took the bra and dropped it on the floor after the shirt. His gaze burned on her flesh. "Come here," he said.

He lifted her around the waist and pulled her over until she straddled his lap. His rod was hot and hard against the juncture of her thighs. He wrapped one hand around the back of her neck and pulled her head down for a kiss.

It wasn't any old kiss. It was like in the park. It was a claim, a you're-mine-and-you-re-not-going-anywhere kind of kiss. She dug her fingers into his damp hair and opened her mouth. She breathed in deeply, inhaling his essence of clean soap and aroused male.

Their tongues tangled together and Phae did some claiming of her own. They kissed until she was breathless, until she was writhing her hips over his, until their hearts were pounding in shared rhythm.

He broke the kiss and pulled her up higher. She balanced on her knees while he kissed her breasts and sucked her nipples.

She arched her back while his wet, warm mouth worked wonders over her sensitive, tender skin. His teeth raked her nipples and his tongue bathed her.

She throbbed inside, a deep, aching need that threatened to swamp her.

"Oh, Kent," she said, and moaned.

She reached down and stroked his cock, thrilling at the way it jerked in her hand. She ran her thumb over the satiny head and around the edge. He was big, so big.

Kent groaned. "Baby, I've got to have you—now."

To hell with more foreplay. It had been too long. Way too long. "Yes, yes, please," she said.

In a few quick movements, he yanked her pants down to her knees, panties and all, then he pushed her down into a sitting position so he could pull the pants the rest of the way off.

She clung to his wide shoulders for balance and wantonly rubbed her bare ass around on his hard thighs.

Kent smiled at her, a dangerous smile of sexual promise and manly need. He shoved his hand between her legs and speared her with two fingers in a quick, unexpected thrust.

She gasped at the electrifying assault and leaned forward, still straddling him, and mashed her mound against his cock.

It felt huge straining against her stomach, seeming to have grown even more. So big, so wide. For the first time, she wondered if she'd be able to take it all.

She looked into Kent's gleaming eyes. "I don't know. It's so big. I haven't done this in a very long time." She couldn't tell him how long because she didn't want to admit it, even to herself. Three years. What it really true? Three years?

His fingers scissored inside her. "Does this feel good?"

She moaned and rotated her hips. "God, yes."

"You're so wet, Phae. It's hard to hold back."

"I don't want you to," she said, fully adrift again in their shared sea of sensuality.

"Take me inside you. You have to set the pace because I don't trust myself right now." He looked down and pulled his fingers out of her. "I've got to get more of that."

He took her hand and wrapped it around his cock. "Sit up. There. Your pussy is driving me crazy. So hot and wet." He licked one of the fingers that had been inside her. "So sweet. Now, guide my cock to the right place."

She rubbed his cock up and down her slick folds then nestled it at her opening. "Mmm, it feels so good."

"Damn, Phae. Look at that. Look at you. You're going to take all of that inside you, and you're going to love it, aren't you?"

"Yes, oh yes."

"That's my hot girl. Now, push down. Go on now, just to get it inside. Oh hell. That's right. You're so tight. Mmm. Just inside." He sucked in a huge breath and his fingers dug into her hips.

She'd pushed that big cock inside herself until the head disappeared inside her. The great, swollen thing had taken her past comfort, but it was a welcome ache, a rebirth. So good. So right.

"More, Phae," Kent demanded, squeezing her hips and guiding her down. "Take more. Yes, God yes. That's it, baby. So tight. Stretch for me. Stretch. Take it. Just like that."

She moaned, savoring every inch of him that she took inside. Down and down she went taking more and more. Always more.

She hadn't thought she could do it, but Kent held her gaze, his certainty bolstering hers. Pleasure and pain played a sweet melody inside her, and she cherished the pain because it would soon be gone.

"Are you okay?" Kent asked, concern etching his handsome features. "Stop if you have to."

"No, I'm fine." And she lowered herself another inch. She took a deep breath.

"Phae, beautiful Phae," he said, holding her gaze with his own. "Look down at yourself."

She looked between them and realized with a start that she'd done it. She sat fully flush on his lap. She'd taken it all.

"Relax," Kent said, rubbing his big palms up and down her back. "Be still. Wait."

She shuddered and leaned forward against his chest. She was full of him, couldn't be more full. And she realized how much she'd been missing that fullness, marveled she could have gone without it for so long.

How could she have done it? Oh, but the answer was simple. It had never felt like this with other men. Her every nerve was ablaze, quivering, waiting for whatever came next. Her core was on fire with overflowing, unspent desire. Her clitoris pulsed and her breasts tingled.

No, it had never been like this. If it had, she could have never gone without it.

He held her, his arms wrapped tightly around her, and they shuddered and stayed perfectly still. Kent's breathing was ragged and she was grateful for his restraint. So powerful. So fine.

He worked a hand in between them and rubbed his fingers over her clit. Sparks shot through her at the touch.

His breath fell warm and electric on her ear as he whispered, "Don't move. Just feel it. Feel me inside you."

His cock pulsed once, then twice and Phae forgot to breathe. So hard not to move. So hard.

Somehow he knew exactly what she liked, the right pressure and stroke, the right time and direction. Her hips began to jerk without her permission, but Kent held them in place with his free hand.

"Come for me, baby," he said, picking up the pace. "I want you even wetter. I said don't move. Don't. Move."

He bit down gently on her nipple and she dug her fingernails into his back.

She wanted to hold it off, to let it build and build, but the pressure climbed too quickly to check. There was no delaying it, no tease to be had. It was upon her before she knew it.

He circled her clit faster, a little harder, and she began to come.

Her head fell back and she closed her eyes, soaring away on the pleasure. It was glorious and full-bodied. On and on she flew until at long last she heard Kent somewhere in the distance, cursing and groaning as he struggled to hold himself in check.

Knowing he was struggling nudged her away from the peak. It was time to let go.

She grabbed his hair and looked into his eyes. Between gasps and the jolts of her climax, she managed to say, "Fuck me, Kent. Hard."

She'd read of moments of passion where a man unleashed his inner beast and she'd scoffed at the idea. But now, here it was, the real thing, right in front of her.

Kent's face darkened and his grimace changed to a growl of victory. She knew she'd never been as wanted, as desired or as needed, as this man wanted, desired and needed her right then.

He cupped her ass in his hands and in a powerful motion, stood up, lifting her, still impaled on his mighty cock, as if she weighed nothing. She clung to his flexed biceps, wrapped her legs around him and thrilled at the beautiful baseness of the primitive drive guiding them.

He only stood up long enough to turn to the side, then he took her down onto the sofa, onto her back. He loomed over her, pulled his cock out and grabbing her legs behind the knees, shoved her legs open and up nearly all the way to her shoulders.

He stared down at her pussy and nudged his cock against her … once, then twice.

He captured her gaze in his own, and she fell into the fire she found there. Her body quivered in readiness. More. More.

And he said a single word. "Mine."

With a powerful single thrust of his hips, he surged inside her as far as he could go, crushing against the back of her womb. She cried out and raked her fingernails down his back. The force of his entry practically made her teeth rattle.

"Yes, yes," she heard herself saying.

He pulled out all the way, centered himself, then drove his cock into her again. And again. And again. Each time, he growled, "Mine." It was if he was breaching some invisible barrier over and over.

Phae lost all thought, all ability to do anything other than experience passion she'd never known. They cried out together.

And somewhere in the distance she was saying, "Do it. Yes. Hard. Harder."

And he was saying things back to her, things that made her insides quake and her toes curl. Goosebumps covered her skin and peppered her breasts which stung from his nipping. Her lips swelled from his ardent kisses.

She wanted it all, everything he had to give. She reached one climax and was nearing another when Kent went into overdrive.

He pumped inside her hard and fast, his breath a staccato beat in rhythm with this thrusting.

"One more time," he gasped at her.

She knew what he wanted. He wanted her to come one more time, to come with him. Yes. Of course. That's what she wanted, too.

She tightened around him and he lowered his head with a heart-thrilling groan. Faster. Faster. She thrust up against him, meeting him partway, grinding, pressing. The air smelled of sweat and sex.

Again. Tighten and release. Again. Tighten and release. Again. Tighten and release.

Then there was nothing to be done but soar away on a magnificent orgasm that never seemed to end.

And Kent was arching his back, rearing over her, closing his eyes and roaring out his own release.

Mine. Yours. Ours.

They rode the climax wave together. To its very end.

CHAPTER FIFTEEN

IT WAS LIKE A DREAM, Phae thought, lying in Kent's arms on the sofa. She hadn't felt this good in … ever. If she'd known sex could be like that, she'd be a nymphomaniac. She almost giggled at the thought.

Something about this man. What was it? He could be unbelievably irritating, but they had this thing between them that she couldn't deny.

Even now, after the hottest sex of her life, she should have been too tired to move, but Kent's fingertips playing along her spine sent electric buzzes straight to her core.

"Are you okay?" he asked, and not for the first time.

"I said I was."

She couldn't see his face because he spooned her from behind, but she heard the concern in his voice. "I got carried away."

She wanted to smack him for feeling guilty. "You weren't alone. So did I."

"You'll be sore from it."

"I know. I'll like it."

He made an odd rumbling sound. "Damn, woman. Keep talking like that and I'm going to be on you again."

"Okay," she said, smiling when she felt his cock, which was pressed against her rear, twitch in response.

"I can't be this lucky," he said. "You're insatiable."

"And you're a sex fiend," she teased.

He laughed gently. "For you I am."

He pulled her in closer and nuzzled her hair. "Mmm. You smell so good. And it's not only that."

"What is it then?"

"It's the whole package. Well, almost all of it."

Little warning bells in the back of her mind told her not to push this, but she ignored them. "What do you mean? Almost all?"

"It's nothing," he said. "We'll work it out, like we agreed."

"Right. Work it out. You mean, we'll go over the ways in which I'm not the complete package? We'll discuss my failures? Is that what you're getting at?"

"Hey, no, that's not what I mean. Relax." He caressed her shoulder and kissed her ear. "I'm crazy about you, Phae. You know that."

Phae did relax. It was okay. She'd over-reacted. She'd been overcome by a dreadful premonition that this was too good to last, so she'd created a difficulty where there wasn't one.

"You're wonderful," Kent assured her.

"Okay, you don't have to go on and on about it. I wasn't begging for compliments."

He chuckled. "But I love giving you compliments. You deserve them. Did you know you have the best tits I've ever seen?"

"Shut up."

"Nope. And you have these incredible abs. You do work out a ton, don't you? Your body is fucking perfect."

"It is not, Kent."

"It is to me."

"Stop. You're embarrassing me."

"Good. Now let's talk about that ass. Seriously. Best ass ever. And that pussy—"

She grabbed his hand that was cupping her breast and toying with her throbbing nipple. "Seriously. Do not talk about my va-jay."

His laughter was a warm rumble against her back. "You actually are every bit as surly as your family says."

"Whatever," she said, but she smiled and took the sting off it.

She let go of his hand and he returned to idly playing with her captured breast. She floated on the sensations of him pressed down the length of her, of his heavy thigh on top of hers, of her head snuggled under his chin.

He sighed contentedly. "I can't get over it. Tell me, why does a woman as beautiful, smart and all-around wonderful as you are waste your talents performing menial duties for a bunch of people who should handle their own little troubles?"

She flinched, the topic shift like a blow to Phae's senses. "What?"

"You have so much to offer, yet you spend your time sneaking around doing useless, mundane tasks—"

She pulled away from him, twisted around to face him. "Seriously? You're saying this?"

"Yeah. I am. So?"

"So, useless, mundane tasks? You don't know what you're talking about. I help people."

He flinched, appearing to finally realize he'd screwed up. "That came out wrong. I didn't mean it the way it sounded."

It was too late for backing off now. "Then what did you mean?" she asked.

"I wanted to wait to have this conversation later."

"Too late. You've already started it."

"Listen, Phae, I won't lie to you. Ever. If this is going to work, then we have to be honest with each other, and if you want that honesty right now, then I can do that."

"Good. Let's hear it."

"All right then," he said. "It doesn't make sense to me, what you're doing as Captain Nice Guy. The only truly helpful thing I watched you do tonight was preventing your uncle from driving drunk. But instead of simply waiting outside for him like a normal person and offering him a ride home, you played out this over-the-top covert mission scenario. As for the rest of what you did tonight, well …"

Phae went from zero to ninety in a split second. She sprang up, sexual fog utterly disintegrated, her energy reignited by his pompous attitude. "'From what we get, we can make a living; what we give, however, makes a life,'" she quoted.

"What are you talking about?"

She found her t-shirt and pants on the floor, pulled them on rapidly then stood in front of him, hands on her hips. "It's a quote by Arthur Ashe. 'From what we get, we can make a living; what we give, however, makes a life.' Shall I interpret it for you?"

He sat up. "That won't be necessary. You're saying that what you do is noble, that getting dressed up in an absurd outfit and sneaking around town in the middle of the night is a virtuous, fulfilling activity, not the act of a bored, under-challenged—"

"I'm not saying I'm a saint or anything. I like what I do, yes, but that doesn't lessen it. In fact, I think it makes my work better."

"What did you do tonight that was so special and noble?" Kent asked.

"You were there. You saw it." She could hardly believe he was being so dense. "I protected a lot of people tonight from potential harm."

"Would you sit down? You're giving me a headache with that walking back and forth."

She came up short, unaware she'd been pacing. It didn't matter. "So now you're going to give me orders, General Powell? Well, forget it. I think I've had enough of you and it's time for you to leave."

She stalked to the door and yanked it open. With a flourish, she waved outside. Kent propped his feet on the coffee table.

"I'm not going anywhere without my clothes," he said.

"Oh, yes you are. I'll mail your clothes to you. Now get out of my house."

"I'm not leaving like this. If you want me out, you'll have to carry me. So why don't you just shut the door and knock off the tantrum?"

Blood rushed to her face. She slammed the door with enough force to make the glass doors in Grandma Jones' china cabinet shake.

"I am not throwing a tantrum," she said, lowering her voice and trying to calm herself down, not wanting to give him any more ammunition. "I simply don't see the purpose in continuing this conversation when you've obviously made up your mind."

"I haven't made any conclusions about you, other than the obvious one that you're overly sensitive to criticism about your ninja-spy routine. And that makes me wonder about how noble you truly think your actions are."

Phae refused to look at his mocking face. She sat down in the easy chair and stared at the bare wall across from her. "You're trying to goad me into a reaction. It won't work. I've had enough. When your clothes are dry, you've got exactly three minutes to get dressed and get out of my house. In the meanwhile, will you cover yourself with that towel or something? It's hard to have an argument with a buck-naked man."

Kent began to chuckle. She ground her teeth in annoyance, but kept silent.

He got his towel off the floor and tossed it loosely over himself. "You know, Phae, you're not very attractive when you pout."

She wondered if the man had a death wish. "I'm not interested in your opinions of my physical or emotional states."

"I suppose that could be true," he said. "After all, you've never been very concerned about your physical appearance, have you? It's a mystery to me, since I can assure you that I'm a great admirer of your considerable physical attributes, as I've previously noted."

She sniffed and refused to look his way.

He went on. "I'll bet you a hundred dollars that when you tried on that little black dress I gave you, you nearly fainted when you saw how hot you looked."

She swiveled in his direction so quickly that she nearly dislocated her spine. "There's no way you could know that—" she said, stopping the instant she registered Kent's mischievous grin.

"I knew it," he said. "I knew you'd try it on."

Phae crossed her arms over her chest and resumed her study of the far wall.

"I wish I could have seen it," Kent said. "You probably looked hot enough to melt the mirror."

"If you're trying to flatter me, you're going about it in the wrong way."

"I'm not trying to flatter you. I'm trying to remind you that you're a woman. I'd think you'd be aware of it after what we did together, but hell, I don't know. Sometimes I think you've forgotten how womanly you really are."

"I'm aware of my gender, so you can save yourself the trouble."

"It's no trouble, Phae." He exhaled loudly. "You are my pleasure. I don't understand why you won't … oh, I don't know. How do you expect me to respond to this Captain Nice Guy thing? Am I supposed to say it's fine with me if you want to dress up in spy gear and endanger yourself and others in the process?"

"I'm not endangering anyone."

"I still have a knot on my head that proves otherwise."

"Self-induced, Kent. I didn't push you into that pole. And anyway, that was a fluke, a mistake that will never happen again."

Kent studied her for a few moments. "Why did you hide all of those people's car keys in their mailboxes?"

"So their cars won't be stolen."

"I wasn't aware the rate of car thefts had risen so dramatically in Zeke's Bend since my last visit."

"It hasn't, and I like to think I help keep it that way. A car with the keys in it is a temptation. Those people might as well leave a pile of cash sitting unattended in their driveways."

"I see," Kent said. "So you're protecting them from potential criminal activity. And how will these people find their keys tomorrow?"

"The first time I take someone's keys, I leave a note in their car telling them to look in their mailbox. Most of the people I helped tonight are chronically forgetful. They know the routine."

"Has it occurred to you, Phae, that if these people haven't changed their forgetful ways, then they might not be in agreement with your assessment of the situation?"

"You're getting smug. We're not going to continue this conversation if you don't watch the attitude."

"ALL RIGHT," KENT SAID WITH a sigh. "So why do you keep saving these people from themselves?"

"Because they appreciate it. Some nights I find little gifts addressed to me on their car seats. And some people have completely changed their ways and haven't forgotten their keys in months. I can't be out there every night of the week since I do have to sleep. But I go out as often as I can and the people I help appreciate it."

Kent lowered his feet to the floor and leaned forward. "I assume you also check the locks and windows on every house in town for the same reason that you steal their keys."

"Not every house. Just the ones that belong to forgetful people."

"You're a savior to the memory-challenged citizens, then. Oh, and children, too. I shouldn't leave out all the bicycles you saved tonight. And, of course, there was the trash that you so gallantly lugged to the curb."

Phae gave him a hard look.

"Okay, okay," he said, holding up his hands as if in surrender. "I couldn't help myself. Tell my why you went inside that one house. And how did you get on the other side of that wooden fence? It was at least ten feet high and I couldn't see a break in it anywhere."

"I grappled over the fence."

"You what?"

"You heard me."

"Oh, that's too much," he said. "And quit scowling at me. You can't blame me for finding that absurd. You used a grappling device to scale that fence when you could have simply walked into the back yard. Don't tell me you don't see how ridiculous that is."

"I don't see it. I climbed the wall for a reason, so that you wouldn't follow me, you big oaf. You were making so much noise bumbling around that I didn't want you making a commotion while I slipped inside Mrs. Bradford's house."

"And now who's being insulting?" Kent asked, barely containing his anger.

"You started it, buddy."

"I think you should check my clothes and see if they're dry."

"Oh, you can dish it out but you can't take it. That's your problem. And your clothes can wait. First, you're going to hear why I went into that house."

Kent frowned but didn't try to stop her.

"Mrs. Bradford is elderly and had a bad fall three weeks ago. She's been bed bound ever since. Her daughter was caring for her, but I learned today that her daughter had to leave town tonight. Her son was supposed to stay with her and make sure everything was secure before he left. However, Mrs. Bradford's son is the most lazy, worthless human being who ever walked the planet. I went in her house to make sure that everything was okay. And by the way, it wasn't. The state of that unlocked back door should prove it."

"Now, Mr. Kent Holmes," she continued, "this inquiry is over. I hope I can count on your honor to prevent you from telling everyone that I'm Captain Nice Guy. I'll get your laundry."

She rose from her chair and walked out of the room with all the dignity she could muster.

She returned with his steaming clothes in less than a minute and tossed the bundle at Kent who was standing by the hallway, towel wrapped snugly around his hips again.

"They're still a little damp. It's an old dryer and takes a long time. You'll survive, I'm sure," she said.

Without a word and with an unreadable expression, Kent turned and headed to the bathroom.

Phae was waiting in the living room when he returned fully dressed.

He stopped near her. "Thank you for washing my clothes."

"You're welcome. Good night."

"It's not that easy, Phae. I've got a few things to say first and you're going to listen."

She doubted she could carry through with the threat she made to physically haul him out of her house, at least not without slipping a disk or two in her back. She gritted her teeth. "Get it over with."

He loomed over her. "You have a problem, lady. Everything you did tonight, except what you and I just did on that couch, was basically pointless and could have resulted in you being shot as a trespasser, to say nothing of what could have happened two weeks ago when you attacked me in Aunt Eugenia's back yard. Maybe helping out that old woman and keeping Leon off the roads were actual good deeds, but even those two acts could have been handled in a much simpler, straightforward manner."

Phae hated that she had to lean her head back to look him in the eye. He probably planned it that way, she thought with distaste. It was business 101, physically intimidating others to gain the advantage. Well, it would give him no advantage over her.

"Once again, Kent," she said, "you're wrong. I didn't attack you in your aunt's garden. You conveniently took care of that job for me."

She gloated inwardly when she saw him wince. "And by the way, Mrs. Bradford is blind to her son's faults. She would have been insulted if anyone implied that her golden boy wouldn't do right by her. As for Uncle Leon, he wasn't as drunk as he looked. He has a low tolerance for alcohol and his blood level probably was well below the legal limit. My plan wasn't to keep him from driving. I drugged him to keep him from returning home."

Kent's blue eyes widened. "You drugged your uncle?"

"It was only a little something in the beer I left in his truck. I couldn't let him go home, and I had to find some way to fix his truck without him seeing it, so I guess you could say I slipped him a little mickey. He won't sleep for long."

"I can't believe you did that! You can't go around drugging people willy-nilly."

She shrugged and leaned against the door. "I can and I did. And I don't think I'm going to tell you why, so don't ask."

"Ask you why? I don't want or need to know why." He began to pace back and forth in front of her.

"This is absolutely crazy," he ranted. "I can't believe this is happening. I thought, okay, so she's bored and underutilized in this little town. She dresses up and has an adventure or two, adding a little excitement to her otherwise unfulfilling life. We could address that problem. It's a simple matter to find you a more productive avenue to challenge you. But … drugging your uncle … this goes beyond—"

"Shut up!" Phae couldn't take another word from the man. "You're not my judge and jury so quit acting like you are. You didn't have these problems with Captain Nice Guy before you found out it was me. What's your real problem, Kent? Why do you refuse to admit that I'm actually helping people?"

"I don't have the problem. You do. You're intentionally endangering yourself and others and I don't like it. So what if Chicago was too much for you to handle? It doesn't mean you can't still succeed. If you want to challenge yourself, why don't you try starting your own business where you could use that Harvard education and your tenacity in a positive way?"

She couldn't believe he had the nerve to bring up Chicago. He knew nothing, absolutely nothing, but had the nerve to think he had her figured out. "When did you become the expert on what I need to do? You hardly know me. And like you've got so much room to talk. Or have you forgotten that you couldn't handle your own company so you decided to quit and run?"

He glared at her. "That was a low blow, Phae Jones."

"And you know ALL about those, Kent Holmes."

"For your information, I haven't sold Kenrik. Surprised? I haven't had the chance to tell you because I've been too busy chasing you all over town. The company making the offer wants me to stay on after the sale and head up development for a few years. I think I'm going to accept."

"That makes no sense." She couldn't resist another jab. "Why would a billionaire want to work for someone else? That is, *if* you are a billionaire like your aunt says."

He didn't react as she expected, and only shrugged.

"If you're going to take the offer," she said, "why are you in Zeke's Bend?"

"I wanted to talk about the offer with you before I accepted."

"No, you didn't! You wanted me to come back here for a little roll in the hay and then you were going to leave. Don't give me that look. That's why you gave me that trampy dress."

"For the record, I don't have to travel halfway across the country to get laid, Phae. I can get all that I want in Phoenix. You're being unfair."

She didn't doubt that he could have all the women he wanted, but she didn't appreciate his pointing it out. "And your attacks on me were fair?"

"Okay," he said, and held up his hands. "Let's calm down for a second. I gave you that dress because I thought you'd look terrific in it. I have never, ever thought of you as a tramp. God, Phae. I thought you were perfection incarnate."

Phae reached over and opened the front door. "And now you think I'm a crazy woman. There's nothing left to talk about. You'll think whatever you want, and nothing I say will change your mind. Go back to Phoenix and we'll forget any of this ever happened."

Kent stood in silence, staring out the open doorway, nodding his head.

"Please, Kent. Leave."

"Okay, you're right," he said at last. "There's nothing more for us to say. For now. But I wish that we ... never mind. Tonight meant something to me. What we did, making love, it was ... it was—"

"It's over," she said, trying to keep her voice from breaking.

With a final unreadable glance, he said, "Good night, Phae," and he walked into the night.

She closed the door and fought back tears.

He was gone. One minute she had him, was being held in his arms, happier than she'd been perhaps ever. Her body still tingled from his touch. And then the next minute, everything was ruined.

Kent was gone. It was over.

She slowly walked to the china cabinet. She ran her trembling hands over the glistening wood. Her grandmother had so loved this cabinet. She'd never have forgiven herself if she'd harmed it by childishly slamming the front door too hard.

After assuring herself that the cabinet was undamaged, she turned off the lights and went to her bedroom. Exhausted, she flopped on her bed, the darkness comforting her.

The argument with Kent had gone so badly she could hardly believe it happened. Where was the witty, handsome man she'd met in Miss Eugenia's garden? Or the charming, chivalrous man who'd held her hand as he walked her back to the fair? Was that only a week ago?

When she'd seen him trying to hide from her earlier in the night, she'd known that she'd been discovered and that she was going to have a lot of explaining to do. She'd expected Kent to be a little annoyed perhaps, but she'd been certain he'd be reasonable. How could she have been so wrong?

Perhaps the relationship had moved too quickly. They'd made assumptions about one another, particularly Kent. She found it hard to fathom that anyone could consider her a perfect woman.

How did he expect her to live up to that?

She hadn't expected so much from him, merely a little reason. The way he'd attacked her with his unfounded accusations about why she helped people was unforgivable. He was clueless.

All the same, she regretted the cheap shot she'd made about him selling his business. He'd kind of deserved it, though, for the way he'd denigrated her work. He'd made her feel like a loser, a waste of time and space.

She should be thankful he'd left. Kent had proven himself to be over-protective, closed-minded and something of an asshole. And downright wrong. All the rippling muscles and sexy bass voices in the world couldn't change that.

So why couldn't she get past the urge to cry?

She cocooned herself in her blanket. Soon it would be dawn and she wanted to be asleep before the bright morning sunlight found its way through the thin curtains hanging over the room's single small window. She closed her eyes tightly.

Phae would feed her anger and never make such a mistake again. She'd vowed three years ago to never trust a man with power. Her mistake had been to allow Kent to do … what? To make her feel sexy? To make her feel desired? Wanted? To make her say things she wouldn't ordinarily say?

To hurt her?

Yes, he had hurt her.

And maybe that explained why no matter how hard she squeezed her eyes shut, tears still managed to break free and trickle down her cheek and onto her pillow.

Maybe that explained why.

CHAPTER SIXTEEN

PHAE PULLED HER COMPACT CAR into a tight parking space then shut off the engine. She'd been lucky to find a place. Nearly everyone in Zeke's Bend must have been attending this year's Fourth of July celebration at the city park.

Phae didn't ordinarily participate in community activities, but her aunt, Meg, had called and pleaded with her to join the family for a picnic and to watch the town's fireworks display after dark. After the way Meg had punched her husband, Uncle Leon, at the fair, Phae felt she couldn't refuse anything Meg asked.

She dragged herself out of the car and headed toward the mass of people swarming over the park grounds. Nodding and smiling at acquaintances, she tiptoed around picnicking families and scooted and ducked to avoid being bonked by an assortment of balls and frisbees flying through the air.

The Jones group wasn't hard to find. They were always the loudest, most rambunctious family at any gathering. Many of them were involved in a game of touch football. From the way the spectators and participants were cheering and jeering, one might have thought it was the Super Bowl.

She smiled in resignation. It was going to be a long evening.

"Phae-phae! You made it. I'm so glad," Meg called out from behind a row of tables so overloaded with food they sagged in the middles.

Phae waved and walked over. Meg looked pretty in a lightweight, white sundress. Her red-tipped hair sparkled in the sunlight. Phae, as usual, was far less put together than her aunt, wearing a plain shirt and shorts, her hair pulled back in its usual messy ponytail.

Meg gave her a quick hug. "Let's get you some food. Everyone else has already eaten. You know what chow hounds the Jones are. There's plenty left, though. Enough to feed an army as always, and it's a good thing, too. What do you like? How about some of these ribs? I made my sweet slaw, too."

Phae smiled and accepted everything Meg slapped on her plate, at the same time greeting other family members. In no time, she found herself seated on a blanket, two sturdy paper plates in front of her heaped with enough food to feed four.

Assorted relatives chatted to and around her as she attempted to make a dent in the mountain of food. She answered any questions they asked her directly, but otherwise didn't contribute much to the rapid dialogue swirling around her. Thankfully, no one mentioned Kent. The last thing she wanted to think about was that man.

In a way, the hubbub comforted Phae. Since the Fourth of July fell on a Tuesday this year, she and Sylvie had decided to close the beauty shop on Monday to give themselves a long weekend.

Because of this, Phae had hardly left her apartment in the last three days, not much since she and Kent had their fight in the wee hours of Saturday morning.

The hot, early-evening sun warmed her skin while a cool northerly breeze kept the temperature below ninety. Phae wished she could stretch out on the blanket and take a nap, but the noise and confusion made it impossible.

Children squealed and screamed as they raced around the grounds, chasing one another with sparklers and smoke bombs. Firecrackers and bottle rockets popped and zipped, trailing the strong odor of sulphur in their wakes. Tangy gunpowder scent mingled with the odors of fried food and barbecue.

All in all, it felt, smelled and sounded kind of wonderful.

She smiled when she saw Sylvie approaching.

"I've had enough of that ridiculous football game," Sylvie said as she plopped down on the blanket.

"It looks crazy. How many players are on each team? Twenty-five? Thirty?"

"I don't know. How many are there supposed to be?" Sylvie helped herself to a chicken leg from Phae's plate.

"Eleven."

Sylvie took a dainty bite of chicken. "Oh, well, whatever. Dumb game. I hope you don't mind me helping myself."

"No. I can't eat all this." She pushed the second, untouched plate of food toward Sylvie.

"You've got to hand it to the Joneses. We know how to eat. I just ate an hour ago, now here I go again. I don't know how we stay so skinny."

Phae raised an eyebrow. Sylvie had curves on curves, and was damned proud of it, something Phae loved about her. But skinny? The girl was having one of those days.

"Of course," Sylvie waved an ear of corn in the direction of the football players, "not ALL of us do. Some big bellies out there."

Neesa came jogging up, out of breath from the game, and flopped down onto the blanket.

Phae laughed.

"I didn't mean Neesa," Sylvie said. "Girl's the size of a gnat."

Neesa fanned herself with her hand. "Whew! It's too hot to be carrying on like that. Water ... need water." She fluttered her long eyelashes at her cousins.

Phae pulled a bottle from a nearby cooler and tossed it to Neesa, who was about as un-athletic as it was possible to be while still being able to walk. The bottle sailed past her and landed out of reach in the grass.

Sylvie laughed. "Damn, girl, you didn't even come close."

"Whatever," she rolled on her side and gave Phae a needy look. "Try again? Only this time, roll it?"

Phae delivered the next bottle by hand and Neesa opened it and swigged it down greedily.

"I can't believe you were playing football," Phae said to Neesa.

"Ahh!" She recapped her bottle. "Yeah, I know, I probably made an ass out of myself, but it's family, right? Besides, Tonio, Neptune and Jackson begged me to play."

"Yeah," Sylvie muttered, "but not on their team, right?"

"Right. So?"

"They wanted to win."

Phae laughed. "Harsh."

"I don't care," Neesa said. "They were so cute when they were all like, 'Please, Cousin Neesy, please play with us.' What was I supposed to say?"

"You were supposed to tell those cons that you're not falling for their sweet talk, that's what," Sylvie said, handing Neesa a muffin.

"Aw, they're just kids."

Phae was inclined to agree with Sylvie, that those particular three boys were a trio of sharks in the making. But she knew Neesa's soft spot for children, so said nothing. It wouldn't have done any good, anyway.

Sylvie looked around the park. "What we need to do is find you a man, Neesa. Then you can have your own babies and get taken advantage of properly."

Neesa blew out a loud breath. "Not gonna find me a man here. Every man worth having in Zeke's Bend is already taken."

"I guess you're probably right," Sylvie said. "I was lucky to snatch up Alan when I did."

Phae and Neesa shared a quick look. They could do without men like Alan, and wished like hell that Sylvie would clue in and ditch him.

"So where is Dr. Alan today?" Neesa asked.

"Oh, he'll probably be around later. He had some business to take care of first," Sylvie answered, picking at a pile of seven-layer salad.

Phae and Neesa shared another look. Business. Yeah, right. Shady business with a bimbo at a sleazy motel in Rollinsburg. They said nothing, though.

"Hey!" Sylvie grinned at Phae. "Where's that hot piece of billionaire you were smart enough to snatch up right away?"

Phae tried not to flinch but was unsuccessful. She didn't want to answer the question, so she side-stepped it. "He's not a billionaire."

"Miss Eugenia says he is," Neesa teased, "so it must be true."

Phae snorted. "Right."

"Well, even if he's not a billionaire," Sylvie said, "he's probably a millionaire. I sure wouldn't kick a millionaire out of my bed just because he wasn't a billionaire."

"That's right!" Neesa agreed.

Neesa and Sylvie laughed while Phae rolled her eyes.

"That's about the dumbest logic I've ever heard," Phae said. "Not being a billionaire doesn't automatically make you a millionaire. If it did, we'd all be rolling in cash."

"That's not how I meant it," Sylvie said. "You're not following how it is. Miss Eugenia brags about how much money Kent has, and of course, she exaggerates, because that's what aunts and mommas do, they exaggerate. So, it makes sense that Kent's not a billionaire, but he's most definitely a millionaire because … because that's how it works. It's the next step down from billionaire."

Phae had to admit it made a crazy sort of Sylvie-sense. But she wasn't going to say it. "This is a pointless conversation."

"I disagree," Neesa said, eyes twinkling. "If my cousin's going to hook up with a millionaire, then I think there's lots of point in discussing it. By the way, I may need a loan for my farm, you don't suppose you could, you know, drop a bug in someone's ear about that …" she winked at Phae.

Sylvie laughed. "Good one. How about us, Phae? We could use some new equipment in the shop. Some fancy inset lighting would be good to spruce up the place. What do you think?"

"I think you're both losing it today," Phae answered. "Anyway, Kent Holmes wouldn't loan me an ice cube on a hot day, and that's the truth."

Sylvie and Neesa's faces fell.

"What do you mean?" Sylvie asked.

"Did something go wrong?" Neesa asked at the same time.

It was time to fess up. She couldn't keep her breakup a secret forever. "It's over. Kent went back to Phoenix."

"What happened?" Neesa asked, sitting upright, leaning forward in concern.

Sylvie set aside her plate and scooted over to Phae, patting her leg. "He's an ass. You're better off without him."

"She hasn't even told us what happened yet," Neesa said. "Maybe he's not an ass. Not yet, anyway."

"Oh," Phae said, "he's an ass. A total ass."

"I knew it. But if you want," Sylvie said, "I'll tell James to call Kent and tell him to get back here and apologize. What are cousins good for, anyway? I'm sure the fight was all Kent's fault. James will—"

"Don't tell James or anyone else anything, please. It's best left alone," Phae said.

"What happened?" Neesa asked. "Tell us everything."

Sylvie nodded. "Everything." She looked around the park. "You don't see Miss Eugenia, do you? We don't want her to overhear us running down her beloved nephew."

"We're not going to run him down," Phae said. "And I don't want to talk about what happened. It didn't work out. We're too different."

"Hmm," Neesa murmured, her expression concerned.

Sylvie sighed. "It's not a very satisfying breakup if you don't get to rake your ex over the coals. Come on, Phae. What did he do?"

"It doesn't matter. It's over."

"Damn," Neesa said.

Sylvie nodded.

The three sat in silent contemplation for several minutes until they noticed James stepping out of the throng of people still playing football. He was headed their way.

"I think the game's breaking up," Sylvie said. "Here comes James." She waved gaily at their over-sized cousin. "Right here, James!"

"Don't tell him about Kent," Phae hissed quickly. "Don't tell anyone, please, either of you."

Sylvie and Neesa solemnly nodded in agreement.

James sauntered up to the edge of the blanket and glowered down at Neesa. "I thought you said you were going to get me a drink. Instead, I find you over here stuffing your face while I'm nearly dehydrated. So where's my drink?"

Neesa took a big bite of muffin and chewed thoroughly before answering. "Oh, you wanted something to drink? You should have asked."

"I did ask! And you said you'd bring me one. God, women." He stalked over to the cooler beside Phae and pulled out a frosty soft drink.

They watched him down the drink in one go.

"That's disgusting," Sylvie said, her upper lip curling. "You need to learn some manners, Sheriff. You're a public servant and you should think about appearances if you want to get re-elected."

James finished off the can then wiped off his mouth with the back of his hand, earning another reproving frown from Sylvie. "Voters don't care if their sheriff has manners. They only care that he gets the job done. And I get the job done."

The three women rolled their eyes at his macho act, each of them knowing how much he liked to play the tough guy but that he was a softy underneath.

Neesa grinned. "I think the football game has gotten his inner caveman all worked up. Maybe he needs refresher schooling from us, Phae, to put him back in his place."

"Don't start on that again," James said. "If I have to hear one more time about that stupid contest, I'm going to lose it. I'm taking more heat than Kent did for running into Miss Eugenia's laundry pole. Hey, where is Kent, anyway? Haven't seen him in a while. I thought he'd be here with you, Phae."

Before Phae could answer, Neesa leapt up off the blanket and grabbed James' arm. "You know, I do remember promising you a drink now. There's some extra special good stuff over there. Let's go check it out. I'll find something extra refreshing."

James looked suspicious. "What's with the sudden change? What are you up to?"

Sylvie patted Phae's arm and gave her a solidarity nod. She jumped up and grabbed James' other arm. "We aren't up to anything, cousin. We're just feeling bad for giving you such a hard time. Come on now, you remember Aunt Elfleda's extra special lemonade punch, don't you? There's a big bowl of it over there."

James, well remembering that lemonade punch, acquiesced easily. He waved a quick goodbye to Phae as his cousins pulled him away.

Phae knew that Sylvie would never be able to keep her promise not to tell James about Kent. Her inability to resist gossiping was one of the things that made her such a popular hairdresser. She'd be telling James about Phae and Kent splitting up before James' glass was half full of punch.

And then, of course, James would tell everyone else.

Maybe it was just as well, Phae thought with no small dose of resignation. If everyone knew, they probably wouldn't ask her questions about Kent's whereabouts.

She picked up her plates which were still half-laden with food. She felt guilty for wasting so much, but it couldn't be helped. She found a trash bag and deposited the plates. After snatching a cola from a cooler, she hoisted up a vacant lounger and headed for a nearby shade tree. She'd had enough of the blazing sun.

After setting up under the big, shady maple tree, she relaxed and sipped her drink. Several relatives smiled and waved, but no one approached her. The Jones family was accustomed to her idiosyncrasies and would usually leave her to her own devices if that's what she wanted. And today, it was what she wanted—to be surrounded by family yet left to herself, the best of both worlds.

She watched with a smile as five small children tried to climb on Uncle Leon at the same time. The man was a kid magnet. They loved him. No matter how loud or gruff he acted with them, or how much he bellowed that he wanted them to go away and leave him in peace, children still flocked to him. And he loved it.

Meg once told Phae that kids could sense how gentle Leon was under all of his bluster. He and James were a lot alike, and kids were drawn to James, too. Sylvie and Neesa often said they put up with James' and Leon's swaggering only because it wasn't real.

One day, James would make a great dad, same as Leon was, when he and Aunt Meg weren't fighting like cats and dogs, that was.

Phae chuckled as Leon roared like a monster and plucked the children off his stocky body. The kids shrieked with laughter as he rolled them around in the grass. Meg stood nearby, watching the scene with a blissful expression.

Phae set her soda down on the short grass then closed her eyes. She was twenty-eight years old and she'd begun to wonder if she would ever get the chance to be a parent.

She never used to think about children. She believed she had plenty of time to find Mr. Right and settle down to raise a family. But time passed faster with every year and she'd turned twenty-eight before she truly realized it.

So where was Mr. Right? She wanted to have kids while she could still keep up with them.

A picture of Kent with a small, dark-haired child riding on his shoulders popped into her mind. Don't think about him, she warned herself. He wanted someone perfect, and that would never be Phae.

He'd never understand why being Captain Nice Guy was so important to her. So no point in thinking about him. It was over and she should be glad about it.

"Phae, dear, I hope you don't mind my sharing your tree, but I need some shade and this looks like such a pleasant spot," said a familiar voice above her.

She groaned inwardly and opened her eyes. "Hi, Miss Eugenia. Please, join me."

Miss Eugenia unfolded the small, rickety wooden chair she held and primly seated herself.

"That chair doesn't look very comfortable," Phae said. "Why don't you trade with me?"

"No, no dear, don't get up." She fluttered a frail hand. "I can't stand those lounger things. Once I get in, I can't get out again. No, I like my little chair. It suits me fine."

Phae didn't argue with the elderly lady. She did wonder, though, why Miss Eugenia had chosen to sit beside her. Of all the bad luck … and there was no way she could run away without giving offense.

Phae settled into the longer and hoped for the best. Turned out, her hopes weren't met for even a second.

"I'm not going to beat around the proverbial bush, Phae dear," Miss Eugenia said, adjusting her red, white and blue beribboned hat. "You know me, I like to get straight to the point. I want to know what happened between you and my nephew."

Phae wondered why these sorts of things always happened to her. Was she cursed? "I don't know what you mean."

"Don't try that act with me. I taught school my entire life and I know a fibber when I see one."

Phae smiled sheepishly. "I'm sorry. And I'm sorry that Kent went back to Phoenix, but really, it was his decision and I couldn't have stopped him if I wanted to."

"Back to Phoenix? He hasn't gone back to Phoenix. He's barely stepped foot out of his bedroom in the past four days."

CHAPTER SEVENTEEN

PHAE'S HEART PLUMMETED WHAT felt like a foot. "He didn't leave? Is he here?" She frantically scanned the many faces in the park. She had to get out of there before she saw him.

"Calm down, Phae dear. He's not here. I tried to get him to come, but he refused. He said it was too hot and then he practically shut his door in my face. When he was a child, he always begged to get to come to the big Fourth of July celebration at the park. I felt terrible, but I always had to tell him no. It was too dangerous, all these children with firecrackers and things. And then the big fireworks after dark. Oh, the thought of it. He could have been maimed, or worse. Now I want him to come, and he won't. That's how it goes in life."

Phae felt kind of bad for the child Kent, but nearly sighed with relief that the adult Kent hadn't come to the festivities. And her heart still pounded fiercely with the knowledge that he hadn't left town. "I don't see how I can help you."

"He was with you Friday night, wasn't he?" Miss Eugenia asked with an expression that clearly warned she'd brook no more lies.

"I wish I knew how you get your information, Miss Eugenia. Yes, I saw him, but I don't see what that has to do with how I can help."

"It has everything to do with it. Kent woke me up before dawn Saturday morning. Said he was going back to Phoenix and he wanted to say goodbye. I told him to at least wait until the sun came up, but he was insistent that he had to go right away. He tried his best to hide it, but I could see that he was upset. Badly upset."

Phae nodded, but could think of nothing to say. It was hard to know what to believe. After all, Miss Eugenia thought Kent was frail and sickly, and that certainly couldn't have been further from the truth.

"While he went to his room to pack," Miss Eugenia continued, "I went into the kitchen to make him some breakfast. I waited in that kitchen for over an hour and he didn't come down. Finally, I went up to his room to make sure he was okay. I thought maybe he'd fallen and hurt himself or something. But it was worse than that. Oh, Phae dear, when I opened his door and saw him, I just wanted to cry. You should have seen the poor boy." She shook her head and looked at Phae with pity in her pale blue eyes.

"What? What did you see?" Phae asked, mentally kicking herself for not being able to resist asking.

"I've never seen such a sad sight." The older lady sighed wistfully. "Poor Kent was sitting on the edge of his bed with a half-full suitcase beside him. He was slouched over and had his face covered up with his hands. He was the very picture of dejection. He could have been on the cover of the 'Saturday Evening Post.'"

Phae nodded, having no idea what covers of the "Saturday Evening Post" looked like, but not wanting to give Miss Eugenia an excuse to stray from the point as she was prone to do.

"Well," Miss Eugenia continued, "I went over to the poor boy and patted him on the shoulder and asked him to tell me what was wrong. When he looked at me, he had the saddest look I've ever seen in my life. The poor, dear boy. He must have seen how worried I was because he immediately straightened up and apologized for waking me earlier."

She smiled at Phae. "Of course, Kent has always been polite. His parents raised him that way, and I like to think that when he stayed with me, I set a good example. Seems like nobody cares about manners these days, but us older folks know what's important. Manners keep people from being so angry and—oh, I'm sorry. Got distracted."

Phae tried to shrug nonchalantly but was not, unfortunately, a very accomplished actress.

"So Kent apologized and gave me a big hug," Miss Eugenia continued. "He said that maybe he'd stay with me for a while longer. Oh, his pretty eyes were so sad. I asked him again why he was so upset, but all he would say was that he was tired and needed rest. I left the poor boy alone, knowing how sickly he can be. I wouldn't want to push too hard and send him into a decline."

"Of course not," Phae said.

"So, that's how I knew you two must have had a fight. I know you were seeing each other because lots of people told me about you being together at the fair. I wish you would tell me what happened the other night. Did you break up? That's it, isn't it? Oh, my. Tell me what happened."

Phae shook her head. No way was she confiding in Kent's aunt.

"Oh, you young people," Miss Eugenia said with a huff. "You're so closed-mouthed and secretive. Humph. Well, the least you could do is come over to my house and get that boy to clean up. He hasn't shaved or bathed even once, I bet. He's downright disreputable looking. And he won't take his calls either. I know because they're calling on my house phone since he won't answer his pocket cell phone. Kent made me tell them all that he wasn't home. He even made me lie to Sheriff Jones when he dropped by. I was taught you never lie to the law. Couldn't you help me out, Phae dear? I worry he'll ruin his health with these shenanigans."

"I can't help," Phae said quietly. "I'm sorry."

"Poor Kent has never been healthy, and I'm afraid this will take a terrible toll on him. I never scoff at lovesickness. It's a real illness and can lead to more serious conditions like—"

"Lovesickness?"

"Definitely. I've lived on this planet for eighty-one years and I know what I'm talking about. That poor nephew of mine could waste away with it. I'm right to be concerned. Since you won't help me, maybe I should call my brother and tell him to come out—"

"Miss Eugenia!" Sylvie bustled up out of nowhere. "Happy Fourth of July!"

Miss Eugenia scowled at Sylvie then stood and folded her little chair. She turned to Phae. "I have to go now, Phae dear. Think about helping me out and let me know what you decide. Maybe you could come over for tea some time this week and we'll talk more about it."

Sylvie spoke quickly. "I'm sorry, but we're going to be busy this week at the shop. We had to close for two days, so we'll have a backlog to catch up on. We appreciate the invitation, but we have to say no all the same."

Miss Eugenia sniffed loudly and with a brief farewell she walked away.

"You know, Phae," Sylvie said after the elderly lady was out of earshot, "she's been mad at me ever since that day in the shop when I gave her a hard time about Kent bashing his head. She's mad at Neesa, too. Oh well. I guess the old gal will get over it some time."

Sylvie looked closely at Phae's face. "You don't look right. You may be getting heat stroke. Take a drink of that soda."

Phae numbly took a sip. She felt as though she hadn't swallowed since Miss Eugenia had joined her under the maple tree.

"I'm sorry I didn't get over here to rescue you sooner. I was kind of distracted. I take it she told you that Kent hasn't left town."

"How did you know?"

"James told me when we told him what you—oh don't look at me like that. You know how it is. Anyway, he said he stopped at Miss Eugenia's house yesterday to see Kent and she told him that Kent wasn't home, but she kept pointing her finger up in the air. James didn't know what to make of it, so he asked her what she was doing. She shushed him then mouthed something a few times until James figured out she was saying, 'He's upstairs.' James didn't want to get involved so he left. What a funny old lady, huh?"

Phae couldn't help but smile. "I think I'd better go home. Kent might show up and I don't want to have to talk to him or anything."

"That's silly. If he goes out looking for you it would be easier to find you at home than in this crowd. Stay for the fireworks. It'll be dark in an hour or so. Neesa and I won't let anyone bother you, I promise. We'll guard you against all comers. And that's not a gossip promise, so you know I'll be able to keep it."

Phae nodded half-heartedly and even allowed Sylvie and then Neesa to flutter around her for a bit, fetching her a fresh soda and a bowl of homemade strawberry ice cream.

Phae ate the comforting treat and wondered whether or not she should believe what Miss Eugenia told her about Kent's state of mind. Saying that the old woman tended to exaggerate was like saying that the universe was a fairly good-sized place; both were vast understatements.

Besides, it was over between Phae and Kent, so none of this should matter. If Kent had indeed sunk into a depression, then it was probably caused by his disappointment that she'd failed to live up to his unrealistic expectations.

She finished her ice cream then packed up the lounge chair and mingled into the crowd of Joneses, Neesa and Sylvie trailing her like a security detail. She half expected them to be wearing earpieces and to start speaking into their collars.

When darkness finally fell, Phae relaxed and Neesa and Sylvie wandered off. Phae felt safe setting up her lounger in the open field, joining the rest of the spectators in ooh-ing and ahh-ing at the fireworks. Multi-colored balls and sparkles lit the night while crashing booms shook the ground and air.

Someone placed a hand on her shoulder and she turned to see who it was. His face illuminated by the bright flashes of red, blue and gold, Kent stood beside her chair.

He bent down and spoke near her ear. "Can we go somewhere and talk, Phae?"

The bottom dropped out of her stomach when she saw that he hadn't shaved in a good long while. "I don't know," she mumbled, trying to find the strength to deny him.

He reached for her hand and held it firmly in his own, larger one. "Please, Phae, only for a moment. I've got to talk to you."

The look in his eyes was so gentle and soft that she couldn't say no. Against her better judgment, she allowed him to help her up from the chair and to lead her away from the crowd. In no time, she found herself under the maple tree again.

They stood there, the two of them, in uncomfortable silence, their hands hanging loosely at their sides, mutely watching the fireworks through the holes in the tree's canopy.

Phae finally broke the silence. "It seems like you and I are always having conversations in the dark."

The lights from the display cast changing shadows across Kent's face. "I know I said some things to you that I shouldn't have said. I have to tell you how sorry I am. I regretted them even before I could finish packing."

He searched her face, then continued. "I didn't mean it. I was tired and angry and I … I wasn't thinking. I'd never want to hurt you. Never. And I realized later that I had. I'm sorry for that, truly."

She didn't know what to say. She studied his features and thought she saw sincerity there. But how could he say he was sorry and believe that would fix everything?

He wrapped his long fingers around her limp wrists. "I shouldn't have apologized in a hurry like that, but you don't know. I was at home tonight and I was thinking of you, of course, and of what happened. It's all I've thought about for days. Have you been thinking about us, too?"

CHAPTER EIGHTEEN

PHAE GAVE A MINUSCULE NOD.

"You're so beautiful," Kent said. "These pictures of you kept flashing in my head. That little smile of yours right before you opened that present. The way your hair glistened in the moonlight outside the fairgrounds. And those incredible brown eyes of yours that glow with your amazing spirit. And there's dozens of other pictures that have burned themselves into my brain. Like the look on your face, the way your lips trembled when you came for me."

She shuffled her feet. She'd been doing the same, seeing pictures of him in her mind, the way his hair swept back from his forehead, the way he looked at her with those bright blue eyes when she stood naked before him for the first time, his charming smile in Miss Eugenia's back yard. Hell. This line of thought was no good for her resolve.

Kent released her wrists and tenderly stroked the side of her face. She could clearly hear his deep voice even though the booming fireworks continued to explode.

"I lay on my bed hour after hour and these images wouldn't stop coming," he said, "and that's when I knew I had to find you. I can't let this go without fighting for it. I had to tell you these things, so here I am. I've made mistakes, but I want to fix them. Fix us."

He reached behind her head and released the latch on the heavy barrette holding her hair in a low ponytail at the back of her neck. He smiled lovingly as he spread the heavy strands about her shoulders. Phae's heart pounded hard.

He exhaled. "When you weren't at home, I nearly panicked, then I remembered what day it was, and knew you'd be here with your family. I've been running everywhere looking for you. And here you are. You're so lovely, I want to—"

He pulled Phae against his chest then slanted his mouth across hers in a searing kiss. She parted her lips, wrapped her arms around his waist and let herself fall under his spell.

The booming fireworks receded off into the distance; she only had ears for the passionate song playing between her and Kent. She strained against him.

His hold on her waist and neck become more fierce as they sought to get ever closer to one another, as if melding themselves into one body wasn't only possible, but inevitable.

When Kent finally broke the kiss, he held her tightly against his solid chest. She trembled, uncertain but aroused, wanting him as much as ever, if not even more than before.

"You're so incredibly sweet," he said in a shaky voice. "I can't let you go, Phae. I think I'm falling in love with you."

She jerked, thunderstruck by his declaration. In love with her? No, he didn't actually say that. He said he thought he was falling in love with her. Key difference there.

Regardless, did she return the sentiment? Her temples throbbed, she was so confused. Why could she never think clearly when he was nearby? It was irritating. And sexy. Always sexy as hell.

She leaned her head back to look up at him. "I don't want to let you go, either, Kent. But the other night, everything that happened … what was said … I don't see how we can—"

"Shh. We both said things we didn't mean. We'll take it back and forget it ever happened." He smoothed her hair away from her face.

"Can we really do that?"

"Yes, right now. It's forgotten. You?"

"I don't know. I'm confused. I get that way when you hold me."

He bent down, scooping her up in his strong arms like she weighed nothing. She wrapped her own arms around his thick neck as he carried her away, a triumphant smile on his achingly handsome face.

Phae dropped her head on his shoulder. "Everybody's going to see us. What will they think?"

"They'll think I'm taking you home to make wild, passionate love to you. And I don't care what they think about it. Do you?"

"No, can't say I do." She closed her eyes and let him carry her away.

They were probably falling in love, she thought, drifting on thoughts of how safe she felt in his arms, knowing that when he held her, the rest of the world simply didn't matter. Neither the past nor the future had a claim on her. It was all about him and her, together.

So yeah, they were probably falling in love.

Right now, she didn't care if she was making a mistake. She could forget the other night, chalk it up to misunderstanding. He'd said he was sorry, and that should be enough for anyone, shouldn't it?

And his body felt so perfectly right that all she wanted to do was snuggle in closer.

She told him where her car was parked and when they reached it, Kent gently released her, groaning as she slid down the length of his muscled form. He hugged her and caressed her back, both their hearts booming nearly as loudly as the fireworks.

"I think I was going crazy without you," Kent said as he explored the soft planes of her back. "You're all I've thought about since the first moment I saw you. I've got to warn you, Phae. Now that you're in my arms again, I'm not letting you go."

He softly cupped her face. The nearby streetlight shone brightly on his face, revealing a fierce expression as they locked gazes.

"From the moment we met, some part of me knew you're the one," he said. "I know we have issues to work out, but it doesn't matter. We'll work it out because there's nothing else to be done."

She nodded. "We will."

"All that matters," he said, "is that I never lose you. Come to Phoenix with me. I won't sell Kenrik. We'll run it together."

Phae blinked. Her fogged-in brain attempted to make sense of what he'd just said. He wasn't about to ruin everything again, was he? Don't ruin this, please.

"I know this is fast, Phae," he continued, "and I'm not asking you to agree with me right now. We've got time. Once I get you into that bed of yours, we're not getting out again until I've thoroughly explored every square inch of that exquisite body, and that could take weeks. I want you to know my intentions up front. This isn't a brief hookup affair, like you worried about. When I tell you I have feelings for you, I mean it."

She didn't like the direction this one-sided conversation had taken. She moved her hands from his chest, grasped his wrists and began to speak. But he quickly cut her off.

"No. Don't say anything right now. I'm probably scaring you, but I need to assure you that I see a future for us. In time, you'll see that I'm right about Phoenix. You'll be fulfilled and we'll be together. You'll forget about Captain Nice Guy. You can run the business side of Kenrik. It's a huge job that you're well-suited for—"

"Wait a minute." She pulled his hands away from her face. "I'm not sure I understand what you're saying."

She prayed that she'd misunderstood him, but she knew deep down that she hadn't. She almost wished he wouldn't answer so she could fall into bed with him and not think about tomorrow.

As soon as he opened his mouth to speak, she knew that he was, indeed, going to ruin everything … again.

"Look," he said, reaching for her shoulder, "I know you're sensitive about Captain Nice Guy."

Phae recoiled. "I'm not sensitive about it. I thought that you'd taken back all those ugly things you said about it."

"I do and I'm sorry for sneering at what you've been trying to do for this town. But still, Phae, surely you can see it's not normal. I realize you believe that it's important to you, but that's because …well, never mind that. You were meant for greater things and you know it. I want to give you those things."

Phae squeezed her eyes shut and clenched her hands into fists at her sides. She breathed deeply, trying to remain calm, to stem the tidal wave of anger that was threatening to swamp her. When Kent touched her arm, her eyes flew open and she took a step backwards.

"Don't touch me," she snapped.

"Calm down. I'm sorry. I moved too fast. We can talk about this later. Let's get in your car and—"

"I'm not going anywhere with you, let alone to my home and bed. And if you take one more step toward me I'm going to ... well let's say that I'll stop you using any means necessary." She took several deep breaths.

"Okay, I've stopped. Calm down so we can talk about this rationally."

His condescending tone and expression finally accomplished what all of Phae's deep breathing could not. Her anger disappeared, and in its place came an empowering sense of purpose ... cold, unemotional purpose.

"Rational, you say," she said. "After that line of bullshit that you spewed out, you'll have to excuse me if I find it amusing that you now wish to speak rationally."

Kent ran his fingers through his short hair. "I shouldn't have said anything. You weren't ready to hear it. I got carried away."

"I could be a thousand years old and I still wouldn't be ready to accept what you said. The other night you went on about how crazy I am, but the truth is, you're the crazy one." Her voice was low and powerful, smooth from strength of will. "You stood here tonight and solved all my problems, didn't you? In your wisdom, you decided what would be best for me and my life. Aren't you amazing? How did you get so smart? I'd like to know because I am Captain Nice Guy, after all, and I believe it's my job to do the good deeds around here."

Kent sighed. "Look Phae—"

"No. I'm done. You said the other night that all I do for people is little things, nothing important. What you don't understand is that I only do the little things because I would never presume to act on the bigger things. I would never dare to intrude in their lives in such a way, thinking I know what's best for them. And I know these people far better than you know me, Kent. I think before I act. That's the difference between me and you."

He looked her squarely in the eyes. "You drugged your uncle. That's not little."

"Oh yeah?" She raised an eyebrow. "First of all, he's family and I take license with them that I don't with others. Secondly, I dissolved one over-the-counter sleeping pill in a non-alcoholic beer which I then poured into a regular beer bottle. Thirdly and lastly, Uncle Leon is highly susceptible to all drugs, and I didn't want him unconscious, just asleep. Once again, you've made judgments with knowing the full story. That's a habit with you, isn't it?"

Kent's frustration showed clearly on his face. He rubbed his dark, stubbled jaw.

Phae had no intention of backing down. "Socrates once said something to the effect of a man becomes wise when he realizes how little he knows. I guess that makes you an idiot, Kent Holmes. Now, don't start getting angry. I'm not leaving myself out of this. I may not be an idiot since I happen to realize how little I know. And yet, I'm obviously not a candidate for the wisdom hall of fame either. For the record, let's call me a crazy twit, shall we?"

"You're getting carried away, Phae. Let's get out of here. The fireworks won't last much longer and this place is going to be over-run with people any minute."

"Then I'll make this fast." She held up her right hand, palm facing out. "On this day of celebration of our great nation's independence, I'm going to make a declaration of my own."

Kent snorted. "I think I like it better when you're mad."

"Sorry to disappoint. Again. Anyway, back to my declaration. When in the course of human events, it becomes necessary for a person to dissolve the bonds of pure physical attraction which have connected them with one another, and to—"

"What are you talking about?" Kent interrupted.

"That's the opening of the Declaration of Independence, except for that physical attraction part. It means that I'm getting ready to tell you why I'm declaring my independence from you."

"I figured that out, for God's sake. I want to know what you're getting at."

"I want you to know my intentions up front. There's going to be no one night hookup or anything else involving a bedroom between us. When I tell you I'm letting you go, I mean it."

"Your memory's too good. I don't like it."

"Too bad," she replied in an even voice. "So, jumping ahead a bit in the declaration, with necessary changes, I hold these truths to be self-evident that all men and women are created equal, but that I have been endowed with more than my fair share of twit-like behavior. The history of our relationship is a history of repeated nonsense, all having the direct object of you establishing an absolute tyranny over me, Phae Jones, both physically and mentally."

Kent groaned. "This is nuts. I can't believe you think this means anything. I don't want tyranny over you, except maybe in bed, and not even that all the time. I mean, you can tie me up if you want. I won't complain as long as I get to do it back to you."

"You can't distract me with that sort of thing anymore." She propped her hands on her hips then raised her right hand again. "I make a formal vow to you, Kent Holmes. No more will I be a twit who falls willingly into your arms every time you touch me. I'll no longer allow that treacherous sexual fog of yours to hide the fact that you and I are totally incompatible. And no more will I defend my actions, or life choices to you, the idiot, Kent Holmes, who so blindly passes judgment on me."

"Very funny, Phae," he said. "Now let's get serious. We're not incompatible. We wouldn't have such a strong connection if we were."

She waved her hand in his face. "Enough. Here it is, the grand finale. I pledge that any connection between us is to be forthwith and hereafter dissolved. I am now a free and independent woman and grant myself the right to remain such. I pledge to myself, my life, my fortune, and my sacred honor. The end. See ya."

As if on cue, the fireworks launched into an earth-shaking finale of their own. Ignoring the spectacle of light and sound, Phae attempted to brush past Kent but he grabbed her upper arm.

"It's not that easy," Kent shouted over the booms as he tried to maintain his hold. "You can't void our attraction by making a flippant speech. It's real and it won't go away because you're pissed. All I have to do is kiss you and it'll be over. You know it."

As he bent to kiss her, Phae stomped on the insole of his foot with all her strength. He yowled and jumped backward. While he hopped around on his good foot, Phae jumped into her car and locked the door.

She dug the keys out of her pocket, inserted them in the ignition, then rolled her window down about an inch.

Kent hobbled over to the window. "You could have broken my toes."

Phae smiled. "No. If I'd wanted to break your toes, they'd be broken. You'll be fine. Give Miss Eugenia a thrill and let her ice your foot."

"When I get my hands on you ..."

"Don't threaten me. Besides, I'm not completely finished." With her index finger, she wrote on the window.

Kent pulled off his shoe and rubbed his sore insole. "What are you doing?"

"I'm signing my declaration, silly. I've sealed it and there's nothing you can do about it."

Kent grimaced. "If my foot didn't hurt so bad, I'd be laughing my ass off right now."

She shrugged indifferently then started the car. As she backed out of the parking space, she called out, "Don't follow me home, Kent. I won't let you in my house."

He limped over to the moving car and stuck his fingers in the window crack. She considered rolling up the window a little to give him a scare, then toyed with the idea of peeling out and leaving him tottering in the dust. Instead, she pressed on the brake and viewed him with an expression of supreme boredom.

"What do you want now?" she asked. "This is tiresome."

"I wanted to remind you of something," he said. "Have you forgotten that the Declaration of Independence was also a declaration of war?"

"So?"

"So we're at war now, a war of your making. I told you I wasn't going to let you go. You may be crazy and you may be a twit, not that I ever said that, but you are *my* crazy twit, and you can't end this and expect me not to fight for it."

Phae held her finger over the window button, her threat obvious. Kent yanked his fingers out of the crack. She smiled benevolently then finished backing out.

"It's war, Phae," Kent yelled after her as she drove away. "And I'm going to win!"

She rolled her window down all the way, stuck out her arm and waved a queen's wave at the big man who grew smaller and smaller in her rear view mirror. She turned out of the lot just as the last firework faded in the sky.

She laughed out loud at the absurd notion that Kent thought he could win. Never. She finally knew exactly what she was doing, and he didn't stand a chance.

This battle belonged to her, and so would all the others should he dare to follow through on his threat. He'd soon learn that she was an implacable enemy.

If this was war, it was hers to win. No doubt about it.

Chapter Nineteen

TEN MEASLY DAYS LATER, PHAE no longer felt so good about her chances. In fact, she thought as she lethargically scrubbed her Aunt Meg's head, she was downright battle weary. When Kent waged war, he played to win, no matter how low he had to sink to do it.

When the bells on the shop door tinkled, Phae checked the wall clock. Ten o'clock. Oh no. Time for another delivery.

"Come on in, Hal," Sylvie said gaily. "Oooh, tulips! Look, Phae, he sent beautiful tulips today. And at this time of year. Must have cost a fortune."

Phae refused to look, but Meg shoved her hands away then leaned up out of the bowl. Phae quickly wrapped a towel around her dripping head.

"Look at them, Phae-phae. They're simply gorgeous. Where did you find them at this time of year, Hal?"

"Special order, ma'am," the young deliveryman said. "Where would you like me to put them, Miz Jones? I mean, Miz *Phae* Jones."

Phae scowled. "In the dumpster out back."

Sylvie waggled a finger. "Don't be mean to Hal. He's only doing his job. Here, Hal. I'll shove these ones over there so those will fit here. Yes, there you go. Perfect."

Phae's scowl didn't waver as she surveyed her once tidy shop. She'd been receiving two floral arrangements a day since the Fourth of July, one at ten o'clock and one at three. Every stinking day.

Flowers covered the display window, some hanging and some majestically arranged in vases. Baskets upon baskets of flowers covered every other bit of free space in the small room.

If Kent didn't cease and desist soon, Phae wouldn't have any room left for customers.

Sylvie slipped some money to Hal who speedily removed himself from the shop with a mumbled thanks.

"These tulips are my favorite," Meg said. "There must be at least fifty of them. And they're arranged beautifully."

Sylvie sniffed the flowers then glanced over the other floral offerings. "I don't know. They are beautiful, but I think my favorite is still the one with the birds of paradise and all the different orchids. It's so unusual. But those roses in all the pretty colors ... and the mums ... the giant daisies. Oh, I don't know. It's too hard to pick. Which one is your favorite, Phae?"

Phae plopped down into one of the dryer chairs. "None of them. I want them all out of here and the sooner the better." She snapped off a stray branch of baby's breath that had been tickling her ear.

Sylvie ran over and grabbed the twig out of her hand. "Quit defacing the flowers! If you throw these out, I'm going with them. They're beautiful and they shouldn't be wasted." She poked the twig back into its spray.

"Read the card, Sylvie," Meg said.

Phae didn't try to stop her. She'd seen Sylvie snatch the card out of the basket before Hal set it down. Sylvie had done the same thing yesterday and the day before, and so on. Phae had tried to stop her in the beginning but had only managed to pocket a few of them before Sylvie began her interception game. Phae had tired of the fight.

Sylvie smiled and pulled the small card out of her pocket. She read the card silently, giggled, then said, "Oh Meg, this is a good one. It says, 'Roses are red, violets are blue, sugar is sweet, unlike you. I'll take you anyway. Love, Kent.'"

Both women chortled. Phae eyed them disdainfully.

"Yep, pretty good," Meg agreed. "My favorite is the one with all the little red roses shaped into hearts. You know, the one that says, 'Be my crotchety Valentine.'"

"Yeah," Sylvie said, "but I also thought that other one was great, where he wrote, 'Phae, you walk in beauty like a really stormy night.'"

They laughed louder, ignoring Phae's censorious glare.

"And then, the one that went, 'How do I love thee? Let me count the ways ... If you weren't so mean I'd be able to think of something here. Love, Kent.'" Sylvie fanned herself as tears ran down her cheeks. "Oh, he's got you, Phae."

"Enough," Phae said, standing up. "Let's rinse that hair, Aunt Meg."

Meg smiled sympathetically. "I know this is hard on you Phae-phae. And I know you're embarrassed. But you shouldn't be. Everybody thinks it's wonderfully romantic."

"Yeah, and it's good for business. We've been swamped thanks to his antics. How many times have you been in this week, Meg?" Sylvie asked.

"I can answer that," Phae said. "Three."

"Surely not that many," Meg said.

"Well, at least you're getting your hair done. Some of these jokers have only been coming in to get a few laughs at my expense and then they just leave," Phae grumbled.

"Not true," Sylvie said. "We've made more money this week than ever before."

"Whatever," Phae said, lowering Meg back down into the sink. "But if one more corny fool comes in here and places an order for flowers with the old, 'Oh, I thought this was must be a florist,' joke, I won't be held responsible for what I do."

Sylvie sighed as she flipped though her appointment book. "I wonder where Neesa is?"

Phae turned on the water. "Neesa's coming in again? Good Lord. If you trim off any more of her hair, she won't have any left."

"That's what I told her. She said she'd just get a style today." Sylvie wandered to the front door. "She should have been here ten minutes ago. She wanted to be here for the daily delivery, and she's never late. I hope nothing's ... oh ... my ... god ... I ..."

Phae stared at Sylvie who was peering out the small square windows in the door. "What's wrong?"

Sylvie whirled around. "Nothing. I saw Neesa. I think I'm going to see what's been keeping her." And with that, she dashed out the door.

Phae tried to look out the display window, but the mass of flowers made it impossible to see anything. All she could see through the small window in the door was a few heads bobbing around, a common occurrence in the past week. Half the people in Zeke's Bend had strolled by at one point or another to gawk at the flowers.

Phae hurriedly finished rinsing Meg's hair. After tossing her a clean towel, Phae headed out the door, telling Meg she'd be back in a second.

She had a bad feeling as she opened the door, a sensation that only worsened as she realized dozens of people were milling around, spilling off the sidewalk and onto the street.

She craned her neck to see around them. They were circling something. She thought she heard chanting, but the crowd was so loud that she couldn't be certain.

Phae shoved her way past several chuckling adults and into the center of the circle. Her eyes widened.

Three of her teenaged cousins, the most rascally of the Jones clan, Tonio, Neptune and Jackson, were picketing her shop. She blinked. It couldn't be true. Nope. It was. They were actually picketing her shop.

The three teens marched in a circle, holding large signs above their heads as they chanted in unison, "Kent will not relent. Kent will not relent. Kent will not relent."

Phae shook her head in disbelief as her goofy cousins paraded past. They slowed their march and waved their signs in her face. In professionally printed, bold red letters, the signs carried the same message: "Phae Jones Is Unfair to Repentant Suitors."

Tonio broke ranks to tell her quickly, "It's easier than mowing lawns, and it pays good, too."

So much for family loyalty, Phae thought.

She crossed her arms over her chest when the crowd parted and Kent strolled jauntily into view. He wore a light summer suit and a white, styrofoam skimmer hat with a little sign stuck in front that read, "I Won't Relent."

He grinned broadly as he approached. Gallantly sweeping off his hat, he bowed deeply. "Do you surrender, Ms. Jones?"

Phae gave him a dismissive glance then turned back to the shop, pushing her way through the nosy spectators.

Kent called out behind her, "Do you see, ladies and gentlemen, how she refuses my company? Am I wrong to suggest that her treatment of my affections is unfair considering how much time and effort I've spent trying to woo her fair hand? What say you, sir? And you, kind madame? Is she not unfair? If you were me, wouldn't you picket her?"

Phae ignored the responses flying freely from the tittering crowd. She stomped into the shop and headed straight for the phone. Picketing indeed. She'd see about that.

Meg looked at her with concern. "What's wrong? Is someone hurt?"

"Someone's going to be," she answered, "and he's big, dark-haired and annoying as hell. Oh, and he's picketing me, the jerk."

"What?"

Phae punched in 911 on the shop phone. "You heard me. Picketing. It's so stupid."

"Hair be damned. I've got to see this," Meg said, wrapping the towel around her head again and heading for the door.

Phae rolled her eyes and listened to the phone ring. She heard the door jingle, assuming it was caused by Meg leaving.

Then Meg said, "Uh, I think I've changed my mind, Phae-phae. I need to get home. Don't worry about my hair. I'll take care of it and bring your towel back later."

Phae turned in surprise. Meg was tossing her plastic smock on the counter and snatching up her purse. She rushed out the door with hardly a glance back. Then Phae saw why.

Kent stood in front of the window, hands clasped casually behind his back as he admired the flowers.

Phae opened her mouth to speak, but she heard a voice in the phone ask, "911. What's your emergency?"

"Um," Phae struggled to regain her footing. "Um, yes. Hello 911. I'm calling to report illegal assembly in front of a private business. Someone's doing that … to me. I mean, to my business."

Kent softly whistled a tuneless ditty and didn't appear the least concerned that she was calling the cops on him. Phae wanted to smack him.

"Illegal assembly?" the operator asked. "Oh, is that you, Phae?"

Phae recognized the voice then. "Kendra? Is that you?"

Kendra, another one of Phae's many cousins, answered, "Sure, it's me."

"I didn't know you were working in the sheriff's office."

"Only this month. I'm filling in for Freda. She had her baby last night."

Phae sighed. Now was not the time for this sort of thing. "Well, good for her. And you, too, I guess. Anyway, I need you to tell James to get over to my shop. There's an illegal gathering over here."

"A what? Oh, right," Kendra said. "James told me you'd probably call."

"That's not possible."

"It is, though. I've got it written down right here, and he told me to read it to you. He writes that Kent applied for and got all the permits he needs to do everything he's doing. He can assemble, picket, sell souvenirs, dispense refreshments and have a parade."

"What?" Phae screeched, surprising herself that her voice could go so high. "What?" she repeated, deeper and more restrained this time.

"That's all it says, cousin," Kendra said. "Is your billionaire really throwing you a parade? You are so lucky, girl! I mean, damn."

"Oh for God's sake. He's not a billionaire. And he's definitely not mine." She blew out a loud breath. "Say hey to your folks."

"Will do. Later."

Phae ended the call. "There's got to be some kind of law against what you've been doing," she told Kent.

He stopped his annoying whistling and reached into the breast pocket of his lightweight summer blazer. He pulled out several slips of paper and held them out to her.

"What's that?" she asked.

He smiled. "Permits to assemble, have a concession booth, sell trinkets, have a parade. The works."

Phae crammed her phone in her jeans pocket and stalked toward him. "Let me see those."

She snatched the papers and scanned them. As far as she could tell, they were for real. And signed by her Aunt Trinny, the city clerk. What a traitor.

"See? It's all there. I can pretty much do whatever I want," Kent said, brushing past her. He sat in one of the hydraulic chairs.

Phae crumpled up the permits and tossed them at Kent. "Fine. Do what you want. I obviously can't stop you from making complete fools out of both of us."

"I don't want to make a fool out of you, Phae. I want to make love to you. You simply won't oblige me."

Tamping down the butterfly flutters in her belly caused by his seductive tone, she looked at him levelly. "I don't get you. You think I'm a loser and a lunatic, and yet you insist that you want me. How could you want someone you don't respect?"

"I respect you."

"No, you respect who you want me to be, not who I actually am."

"I don't quite follow that. No matter," he said. "Let's chalk this up to chemistry, then. Your atoms are chatting up my atoms, and they must be saying something highly arousing."

"You've got it backwards, science boy. It's your atoms that are doing all the talking, and mine are sick of the chatter."

Kent chuckled, a deep rumbling reverberation. "Maybe I want you because I can't resist a snappy comeback."

"Or maybe you just want me because you can't have me."

"Let's get naked, and after I've had you, you can ask me if I still want you. I bet I will."

"Hilarious. In your dreams."

"That's right," he said quickly. "Every night you're in my dreams. But enough of that. I'm here to arrange a time and place for our peace talks."

"Sorry. Not interested." Phae walked to her work station and began rearranging the products there.

"Too bad, Phae. Here I've made an effort to end this war and all you want to do is continue fighting. Guess this means I'll have to haul out the big guns."

Phae ignored him, hard though it was.

"What?" he asked. "You want to know what the big guns are?"

"I didn't say anything."

"But you wanted to. The big guns is that I've arranged for the local high school band to come serenade you. They're due at two. The director, Quint, assured me they know a number of romantic ditties. He's related to you, isn't he? Cousin twice removed or something. Of course, who isn't related to you in one way or other? Your Aunt Trinny said to tell you hi, by the way."

"Are you going to be here while the band plays?" she asked.

"Of course."

"Good. Because you deserve what's coming to you. I'm sure Quint jumped at the chance to practice in front of a crowd. He can't get one any other way. I'm going to stay in here, where the screeches and whines those teenagers drag out of those tortured instruments will at least be muted. Can't wait to watch those chuckleheads in the crowd run away."

"They're that bad?" Kent frowned. "In that case, let me renew my offer of peace talks with more urgency. If you agree to accompany me to nearby Rollinsburg this evening for a nice dinner and some dancing, I'll call off the band recital and save everyone in Zeke's Bend from unnecessary torture. You can't resist helping the town's citizens, remember? Think of the poor children whose eardrums will be damaged simply because of your blood lust."

Phae dropped into the other chair. "Forget it. I don't want anything to do with you. As for my gossipy friends and neighbors out there, you can bet that as soon as they see that band coming they'll run away like their butts are on fire."

"I bet you're wrong. They can't resist a spectacle, or haven't you noticed?"

She suspected he might be right, but she wasn't going to tell him that. She shrugged.

"Come on," Kent whispered seductively. "Be a good girl and join me for a little wining and dining. I promise I won't say or do anything too promiscuous."

"If you think these tactics are getting you anywhere, you're wrong. Look what you've done to my shop." She waved her hand at the flowers. "It's a mess. And those cards. They're hardly what I'd call romantic."

He waggled an eyebrow. "It's getting to you, isn't it? You love it and you know it. You won't be able to resist me much longer, so why don't you give in now and let me take you?"

"Stop that!" She sprang to her feet. "You're driving me nuts. You don't get it. I've declared my independence and nothing you can do or say will change my mind. You don't respect me or my life. We could sleep together for the next thirty years, but that wouldn't change the basic fact that you think I'm a loser. So stop this crap and find some other poor woman to terrorize."

Kent rose slowly from his chair and began to slowly approach her, a lazy grin on his face. "I accept."

She backed away from him. "What are you talking about?"

"I accept your challenge that we sleep together for the next thirty years. If, at the end of that time, you still think I don't respect you, I'll leave you alone and bother someone else. Let's get started right now." He continued his advance, purposeful, relentless.

Damn. Phae felt herself being drawn into his sexual gaze. She blinked hard and shook herself in an attempt to clear her head. Her retreat was halted when she bumped ungracefully into the back wall.

"Stop it," she said weakly. "You twist my words. Quit looking at me like that."

"Like what?"

"Like you're going to do something … something you shouldn't do."

He placed his hands on the wall on either side of her, effectively trapping her. He leaned down and whispered in her ear. "Like the hat says, darlin', I won't relent."

She shivered at the touch of his warm breath. She struggled to find the will to fight him when he gently nibbled on her earlobe, but found her strength of conviction had made a cowardly escape from the battlefield along with her ability to reason. She was defenseless.

"You smell like a garden of sweet flowers." He nuzzled her neck, his lips and tongue tasting her tenderly.

"It's not me. It's the room," she murmured, trying not to moan.

"Mmm-mmm," was his only response. He licked up the side of her neck.

Phae stared at the ceiling and desperately tried to think of something cutting to say that would break his spell. The only picture that came into her mind was one of Kent, his finely toned body in naked splendor, the smooth skin of his chest glowing in candlelight, his hair glistening, his strong, tanned hands reaching for her.

"You can't resist it, Phae," he said. "You want me. And I want you so badly that I can hardly look at you without imagining you naked underneath me, writhing and moaning, calling my name as I make you come again and again."

He stroked the back of her neck with fingertips that trailed tingles in their wake. "You're shivering. I am too. Let's walk through that door, into your apartment, and I'll give you the kind of pleasure you've only dreamed about. Let me show you how much I want you."

Kissing along her jawline, he inched closer to her lips. "Feel me, Phae. Feel my need." He reached for her hand.

CHAPTER TWENTY

LOCKED IN HIS SENSUAL GAZE, she stood half-boneless as he gently pulled her hand toward his pants. They moaned in unison as she touched him, her hand flat against his rock hardness.

"Five little steps and we'll be in your apartment. Nod, and we'll be there," he said.

She couldn't fight him anymore. The war was over. She'd lost. Screw it. She took a big gulp of air and began to nod.

The bells over the shop door jangled loudly. Kent immediately broke away from Phae, cursing softly under his breath.

It was Sylvie. She looked at them in surprise, then in speculation, then with a glance down at Kent's package, and with a smug little smile. "Oh, sorry, didn't mean to interrupt anything, did we Neesa?"

Neesa peeked around her, and saw the situation for what it was. "Mmm-hmm. So that's how it is? Gotta go."

As they turned to leave, Phae found her voice again. "No, don't!"

Sylvie, Neesa and Kent stared at her, dumbfounded.

"I'm serious," Phae said, shoving Kent toward the door. "He was just leaving, anyway."

"No I wasn't," he said, digging in his heels. "You nodded and I'm holding you to it."

Phae gave up pushing and crossed her arms over her chest. "It was an almost-nod. Doesn't count. Besides, you cheated."

"What are you talking about?"

"I think we should give you two some privacy," Sylvie said, trying to inch her way backwards out the front door.

"If you two leave, I'll never forgive you." Phae looked at Kent. "You fight unfairly, Kent Holmes, and you know it."

"This isn't a game, Phae. This is war. And you know all is fair in love and—"

Phae breezed past him and sat down in a chair. "Leave. Go on. Do your best, or your worst, or your stupidest. Whatever. Bring in a hundred piece orchestra to serenade me for a month. Bankrupt yourself with florist bills. Do whatever you're going to do, but know that it won't work."

"He's a billionaire," Sylvie said, "he could never buy enough flowers to put even a tiny dent in his fortune."

"That's not helpful, Sylvie," Neesa said. "And he's probably not even a billionaire anyway. Why would a billionaire come to Zeke's Bend?"

"Duh. To visit his aunt," Sylvie answered.

During the cousins' exchange, the frustration faded from Kent's handsome features. He gave Phae a sexy little smile, walked over and whispered quietly so only she could hear, "You won't be able to help yourself."

She sighed with feigned boredom. "Until you respect who I am, nothing will change."

"Whatever you say, beautiful." He briskly rose up to full height and strode toward the front door.

Sylvie and Neesa skittered out of his way. Kent opened the door then turned back around to face Phae.

He began a slow and deliberate study of her body, from the top of her head to the tips of her toes. His electric blue eyes sparked with fiery desire. Phae's face burned and her heart beat faster.

"Lucky for you," he said, finishing his lingering perusal, "I find the prize to be worth the cost of the war." He tipped his skimmer hat to Sylvie and Neesa. "Good day, ladies," he drawled. Then with a sexy wink at Phae, he left the shop, bells loudly tinkling behind him.

"Wow," Neesa cried as she stared at the closed door. "Did you see that look, Sylvie? Smokin!"

"I could hardly miss it," Sylvie said. "I'm pretty sure that was his intention."

Neesa rushed over and peered at Phae. She waved her hand in front of Phae's face. "She's a little shell shocked. Think I should slap her? That might snap her out of it."

Sylvie bustled over and studied Phae. "Hey now. I do all the slapping around here."

"Never mind," Neesa said. "I don't think she's fainting. She's overwrought."

Sylvie grinned. "Overwrought from that hell-a sexy man who gave her the once-over. Day-umm. Maybe I should slap her for letting that gorgeous guy go. What's she thinking, Neesa? What are you thinking, Phae? Are you in there? Can you hear me?"

Phae pressed her hands to her hot cheeks.

"Leave her alone," Neesa said to Sylvie. "She knows what she's doing. Probably."

"Sure she does," Sylvie said. "She's ungrateful, that's what. Look at everything this man is doing to get her. If Alan gave me a single, wilted wildflower I think I'd fall over dead from shock. And here she's got all this and—what. Why are you both looking at me like that?"

Phae and Neesa stared at her. This was the first time they'd ever heard Sylvie come close to complaining about how Alan treated her. She always made excuses for him, refusing to see the truth of his callous treatment.

Sylvie raised a hand. "I know, you two. Don't get started on Alan. It's not about him right now. This is about Phae and the billionaire."

Neesa let it go with a shrug. "I'm sure she has reasons for what she's doing. You do have reasons for denying that hot, rich, romantic man, don't you, Phae?"

Phae sighed deeply and looked at them in turn. "I have my reasons. That's all I'm going to say."

Sylvie made a dismissive sound and Neesa walked over to the wall of chairs and sat down.

"Guess that's all we're going to get, Sylvie," Neesa said. "All our support and friendship over the years comes down to her shutting us out when it matters most. And we're supposed to say okay, that's fine. Don't worry about our feelings. You aren't hurting them or anything."

"I think she's gone crazy or something," Sylvie said. "I mean—"

Phae let her ramble on. She felt horrible that she couldn't confide in them about her problems with Kent and what had caused their split. But she simply couldn't do it. If she did, she'd have to tell them about Captain Nice Guy, and she shuddered to imagine what their reactions would be to that thunderbolt.

No, she couldn't confide in them. Not this time.

The bells over the door announced the entry of a pair of their elderly, great aunts, Charmaine and Chelly. Phae wanted to flee when she realized the Jones family matriarch, Aunt Elfleda, was right behind them, ensconced in her electric wheelchair and buzzing dangerously close to Charmaine's frail, bird-like ankles.

Elfleda was something like a great-great-great aunt to Phae, Sylvie and Neesa. They never counted up the "greats," since anything past a couple was like overkill. Aunt Elfleda was ninety-six going on five hundred, and as sharp as a cat's claw.

Phae frowned when she noticed the styrofoam hats perched cockily on their white-haired heads. Little signs on the front above the brim read, "Kent Will Not Relent." They each daintily held small plastic cups in their hands.

Charmaine giggled girlishly as she adjusted her hat in front of one of the shop mirrors. "Isn't it darling? Kent's giving them away free."

Neesa covered her mouth to try to hide her smile, but Sylvie brazenly barked out a laugh.

Phae squeezed her eyes shut and wished herself in another country, or better yet, on another planet.

"And there's a refreshment cart, too," Chelly added. "I've got lemonade. Read the cup, girls. It says, 'Support Your Local Suitor.' Isn't that just the cutest thing?"

Sylvie and Neesa agreed it was.

"Closing your eyes won't make it go away," Sylvie teased Phae. "You might as well give in now. After all, Kent won't relent."

Phae wanted to strangle all four of the tittering women. Miz Elfleda didn't titter; she frowned, deepening the busy network of wrinkles crisscrossing her face.

Elfleda came buzzing up to Phae's chair and tossed her hat onto the counter behind her. "Get a grip on yourself, girl," she said brusquely as she motioned for Phae to remove herself from the chair. "I don't want you ruining my hair today because you're all fired up about that Romeo. I don't care how handsome he is. When you're working on my hair, I don't want you thinking of anything else."

Phae shared a questioning, half-panicked look with Sylvie. They didn't have an appointment on the books for Elfleda. Elfleda always got her hair done at Miss Pearl's Salon, and had done so for at least a hundred and fifty years.

Nonetheless, appointment or no appointment, the trio of cousins helped the family matriarch out of her wheelchair and into the hydraulic chair.

While Elfleda told a wide-eyed Phae in no uncertain terms exactly what she wanted done with the baby-fine, white tufty bits of hair she still had left, Chelly gushed on about the events outside.

"It's like a festival out there," she said. "Workmen have blocked off the street and are setting up all these chairs. There's going to be a concert later today. It's so romantic. I don't know how you can resist him, Phae."

Sylvie and Neesa chimed in to agree but Miz Elfleda cut them all off with a regal wave of her steady hand.

"Leave her alone. She knows what she's about," Elfleda said, surprising everyone in the room.

Phae smiled in gratitude. "Thank you, Aunt Elfleda. You don't know how much I appreciate having someone on my side."

"Don't blame them for their short-sighted ways," the elderly woman said. "They don't have much sense. Few women do when it comes to dealing with handsome men."

"I do get a little silly around the lookers," Chelly said.

"Mmhm, it's the truth," Charmaine added.

Elfleda scowled the two ladies into silence. "Listen up. Any smart woman knows you have to keep a man dangling. The honeymoon's over soon enough, so you might as well get what you can while the getting's good."

Sylvie snickered, Neesa hid another smile behind her hand, and Chelly and Charmaine nodded sagely, as if they'd said it themselves. Phae looked heavenward for strength.

"It's especially true of rich men," Elfleda continued. "If you're going to land a millionaire, you—"

"He's not a millionaire, Aunt. He's a *billionaire*," Sylvie said.

Elfleda scoffed loudly. "Humph. Of course he's not a billionaire. That's ridiculous. That silly twit Eugenia always exaggerates. But even so, he's sure to be a millionaire."

"That's what I said!" Sylvie exclaimed.

"No you didn't, girl," Elfleda said. "You just said he was a billionaire. I'm old, but I know what's what. Can't pull the wool over my eyes, youngster." She reached out and grabbed Phae's arm in a shockingly tight grip. "You, stay tough until he starts handing out jewelry with big rocks, like diamonds and rubies. You can go ahead and let him kiss you a few times, give him a little taste so he gets all hot and bothered, but don't let him feel you up. Not yet, not until you get some of the good stuff."

Phae's jaw dropped. "Aunt Elfleda! I'm not trying to clean the man out. I simply want him to leave me alone."

"Are you serious?"

Phae nodded.

Elfleda looked at Sylvie and Neesa, both of whom gave a we-can't-believe-it-either-but-it's-true nod.

Elfleda made a strange dismissive sound, half-snort and half-plastic-click from snapping her dentures shut. She dismissed Phae with a wave. "Well then, there's nothing left to say. Load me up in my chair. Can't be getting my hair cut by a simpleton. A stubborn … well, I'm a lady and won't finish that. Load me up!"

Everyone bustled around, getting the old woman back into her wheelchair. Neesa tried to smooth the blanket over her legs and got smacked on her hand for the favor. Elfleda seriously had her dander up.

Charmaine and Chelly cowered behind the chair as Elfleda roared off toward the door. Sylvie held it open, standing to the side, afraid of being run over.

Elfleda screeched to a halt and gave Phae a hard final look. "Didn't you go to a fancy school out east?"

Phae could only nod.

"Humph. And I thought you were supposed to be smart. Your parents ought to demand their tuition money back."

With that parting shot, she whirred out the door, Charmaine and Chelly rushing behind, sending a final, apologetic glance at the three cousins.

"Damn," Sylvie said as she closed the door.

"Damned straight," Neesa said. "That was—"

They heard a roar from outside.

"Oh what the hell now?" Phae asked.

Sylvie peeped out the window. "Jugglers. And clowns. In the street. With a donkey cart."

Phae took a deep breath and threw her hands in the air.

This was turning out to be a very, very long day.

CHAPTER TWENTY-ONE

As PHAE WAITED UNDERCOVER behind Trapper's Tavern, she reflected that the day had indeed been long and exhausting. At two o'clock sharp, the high school band had assembled on the street outside the shop and begun the most horrendous love song concert in the history of time.

She'd hoped that most of the music, if she could call it that, would be muffled since she was inside, but one flimsy wall proved scant protection against the cringe-worthy caterwauling. Phae thought she might never heal from the damage of the band's tragic rendition of "Let's Get It On." Somewhere in heaven, Marvin Gaye wept.

Kent had been correct, however, about the spectators not leaving. The crowd grew steadily throughout the endless concert, which actually lasted less than an hour. Kent must have pulled some strings because by three o'clock, the band was replaced by the excellent high school choir, which helped to staunch the bleeding from everyone's ear drums.

Phae couldn't help but be proud of herself for how well she'd handled the situation. She'd remained calm and not lost her temper as person after person entered her shop and cut loose with one corny joke after another.

As for her tiny slip-up in Kent's arms earlier in the day, she'd never denied that she found him attractive. She wouldn't waste her time worrying about one failure. Next time, she'd be better prepared for his assault, if there were a next time.

The country music inside Trapper's Tavern fell silent. Phae peeked around the corner of the building. As usual, only Leon's and the owner's vehicles remained in the parking lot. Once again, Phae had counted on her uncle's pattern of being the last to leave as a crucial part of her night's plan.

Only a thin sliver of moonlight hung in the black sky, meaning she was forced to rely heavily on her faulty night-vision monocle. She should have thrown the thing away, she thought as she flicked the plastic casing to bring it into focus. At least she wasn't trying to plant a garden tonight, she thought wryly.

True to his routine, Leon stayed behind after the owner departed. Phae had been amused to note that her uncle had checked to make sure his truck would start before he yelled goodbye.

"Here we go, kitty," she whispered to the small animal she held in her arms.

With a great, heaving push, she shoved a big piece of tin roofing onto some metal cans, unleashing a tremendous racket in the quiet countryside. She struggled to hold onto the startled cat.

Phae smiled when she heard Leon turn off his truck.

She quickly pitched a rock onto the tin roofing. Shortly, she heard footsteps crunching in the gravel parking lot.

When she saw the glow of Leon's bouncing flashlight, she ducked around the back of the building.

"Hey!" Leon called out, rounding the side of the bar. "What's going on back here?"

He clanked around among the junk for a few moments then muttered something about animals.

Phae waited until she was certain he'd decided to return to his truck. Crossing her fingers that she'd be heard over the chirping crickets, cicadas, tree frogs and other night singers, she called out to Leon in a deep, eerie voice, "Leeeonnn Jooooonessss."

"Huh? Who is that?"

On silent feet, Phae dashed to the other side of the building, rounding the edge just as Leon and his flashlight turned the corner at the back of the bar.

"Whoever you are, you get on out here right now," he demanded.

"Leeeonnn Joooooonessss."

"I don't know what you think you're up to," Leon grumbled as he stomped loudly through the undergrowth.

Phae raced to the front of the building then leaned around the corner. Leon's flashlight bobbed brighter as he approached the side. She took a deep breath.

"MEOWRRRR!" she yelled as she dropped the frantic cat on the ground, waving her arms and flailing her feet to get the cat to run to the rear of the building.

"What the —" Leon yelled.

Like a shot, the cat streaked away, straight past the beam of Leon's flashlight.

"What the—" Leon yelled again.

Nearly as quick as the cat, Phae sped to Leon's truck. If he hadn't reacted as she expected him to, the keys wouldn't be in the truck and her plan would be dead in the water.

She jumped inside the truck and saw the keys in the ignition. She did a quick fist pump in celebration, then started the truck, flipped on the headlights and slammed the gears into reverse.

Spewing gravel, she roared out onto the road, focusing the headlights on the corner of the bar where she expected her infuriated uncle to appear momentarily. She rolled down her window.

"Hey! You!" Leon shouted as he rounded the corner. "Get out of there! What do you think you're doing?"

Phae revved the motor and began to back down the road.

Leon chased after her. "You come back here! Get out of my truck!" His face was bright red in the glare of the headlights.

"Come and get me," Phae murmured as she maintained a steady distance between them.

Just as she'd planned, Leon followed the retreating truck. Glancing between the windshield and the back window, Phae managed to keep her eyes on both the road and her livid uncle. Now, as long as no other cars came along, everything would be perfect.

That was part of the problem in her business, Phae thought as she eased the truck down the road. Too much of her success depended on luck. Sure, she could be pretty certain that no cars would be out here at this hour, but she couldn't be positive. Luck was required, like with the keys being in the truck and the cat running the right way.

She idled in the road while she waited for her uncle to gain more ground. The last thing she wanted was for him to give up. Luck. It had been absent all day at work, but it was definitely on her side tonight.

She yanked off the hot, itchy mask and tossed it onto the seat beside her. She daubed her sweaty brow with her shirtsleeve. It seemed summer would never be over. It was so much easier to do her work in cooler weather.

As Leon came closer, she could see the poor man was gasping for air, even though they'd gone less than half a mile. They still had a way to go before Phae could stop. Her uncle was more out of shape than she'd imagined.

She slowly depressed the accelerator and resumed the odd car chase/retreat.

Luck. A strange thing. One never knew when it would come and when it would—

Phae gasped out loud and her heart jumped in her chest when the passenger door flew open.

CHAPTER TWENTY-TWO

KENT NEARLY LAUGHED WHEN he saw Phae's startled expression. Her hands flew upward to cover the dome light.

"Shut the door!" she hissed.

Kent grinned and hopped into the truck, slamming the door behind him.

She gunned the truck's engine, jerking Kent toward the windshield as they were propelled backward.

"I can't believe you did that," she said. "Leon might have seen us!"

"Plus, I nearly scared you to death. Right?"

Kent could make out Phae's fierce expression in the soft glow of the dashboard lights. He was glad she'd not worn that awful face paint tonight. She was painfully beautiful.

"You didn't scare me to death," she said. "But I'm seriously pissed. You have no idea how much trouble I'd be in if he saw me."

"He didn't see you. Those headlights are so bright he's running blind."

Her face relaxed slightly. "I hope you're right. But still—what are you doing out here?"

"I overheard one of your relatives gossiping today about whether Leon would go out drinking tonight. It wasn't hard to guess where I would find you." He glanced out the windshield. "You should probably slow up. You don't want to give the guy a heart attack."

Phae stopped the truck and looked at Kent.

She opened her mouth to speak, then quickly snapped it shut again. She slowly shook her head before finally saying, "You know, I almost told you to get out of the truck, but I realized it would be a waste of time. I must be getting to know you better."

He smiled. "You're right. I'm not going anywhere that you don't go."

She propped an elbow on the steering wheel and rested her cheek on her elegant, slender hand. "Get on with it. Tell me why you're here."

"Your acceptance of this situation is a surprise. Can't you throw in a little name-calling to put me at ease?"

"Don't tempt me. I've had a long, exhausting day, thanks to you and right when things were looking up, you popped back in and nearly ruined everything. So back off and tell me why you're here, though I think I can guess why."

"You do?"

"Yeah. You're trying to sabotage my operation."

"No I'm not. I thought about what you said in the shop and decided to give it a try. I'm here to learn how to respect your work."

She leaned back against her door and crossed her arms over her chest. "Sure you are. And I'm out for a little country drive."

"I'm telling the truth. I want you to teach me about being Captain Nice Guy."

He knew she was skeptical, but had he seen a flicker of hope sparkle in the corner of those big brown eyes? Maybe it was wishful thinking on his part.

She looked out the windshield, watching her uncle struggle to catch up. She began slowly backing down the road again.

"So?" Kent asked. "Are you going to teach me about your work or not?"

She divided her attention between her uncle and the road. "No, I'm not. And I have no problem telling you why. You've already made your mind up about me and nothing I tell you could change that."

"You have a point," he admitted. "That's why I don't want you to tell me much, except about what you're doing with your uncle. I want you to show me what you do as the captain. Maybe if I experience it firsthand, I can understand it better."

Phae reached into a pocket on her belt, pulled out something pink, then flung it out the window. Kent squinted to make out the small object on the pavement.

"What is that?" he asked.

"Rabbit's foot."

"And?"

Phae didn't answer.

"Why did you pitch a rabbit's foot into the road?" he tried again.

"Actually, it's a fake rabbit's foot. The one on Uncle Leon's keychain here is real. It's disgusting. I can't believe he carries this nasty thing around." She stopped the truck some distance from the foot.

"So what's it all about?" Kent asked the lovely lady who had more attention for the road than for him.

"Uncle Leon looked tired and I thought he might give up," she said. "Now be quiet and watch. That's what you wanted, wasn't it? To learn by being shown?"

Kent shrugged. What was it about this woman that made him put up with her no-nonsense, often surly attitude? It drove him wild for some reason he couldn't explain. She ignited an itch inside him that he couldn't scratch without her.

Although they were a good distance from Leon, Kent knew that the headlights provided adequate light for Leon to see the rabbit's foot on the ground. He wasn't surprised when Leon bent over and picked it up.

Leon waved his fist in the air and began to shout. Kent couldn't make out the words exactly, but the gist was clear. Uncle Leon didn't like that foot, and he was downright pissed to find it in the road.

Leon began running.

Phae stomped on the accelerator. Kent barely had time to brace himself to avoid being pitched into the windshield.

"Listen carefully," Phae said calmly as they sped backwards down the highway. "Shortly, we'll be on the other side of this rise. There's a turnout there. I'll be stopping the truck and leaving a few things behind for Uncle Leon to discover when he finally gets here. I want you to get out of the truck as soon as I stop and head for those trees on the right. You didn't bring your car out here, did you?"

"No."

"Good, because we'll be walking back tonight. Now let me repeat. When I stop the truck, you will get out immediately and head for the woods. Wait for me there."

She swerved the truck over into a small turnout and stomped on the brakes. "Go—now."

"Wait a second," he said, watching her dig in a pouch. "What are you doing?"

She blew out an exasperated breath. "I knew you wouldn't do what I asked you to do."

"I can't help it. I want to watch."

"Fine," she said curtly and handed him the end of a weighty string of rabbits' feet. "Tie this end to the sun visor."

Kent opened his door so the dome light would come on. He inspected his end of the cord. "What's this all about?"

Phae tied her end to the visor on the driver's side. "Please don't hassle me with questions right now. We've got to hurry."

He shrugged and tied up his end of fake feet.

She pulled a piece of paper and a small roll of tape from her belt. After taping the note to the steering wheel, she turned off the engine and mashed on the emergency flashers button.

"Let's go," she told him.

He leaned in to read the note. "What's it say?"

"You stay and read it if you want. I'm getting out of here." Phae snatched up a mask on the seat that he hadn't noticed before, then she hopped out of the truck.

Kent watched in surprise as she flung Leon's keys into the darkness then ran off and disappeared into the night.

Rapidly, he scanned the note she'd left for her uncle. He smiled as he read: "Your keys are in the ditch. I'd wish you luck in finding them, but all the rabbits' feet in the world won't protect you from me. The fates frown on those who drink and drive."

Kent jumped out of the passenger's side, leaped over the ditch and headed into the woods. He'd not gone far when Phae appeared from nowhere and grabbed his arm.

"Shh, he's coming."

Kent peered through the trees. Sure enough, Leon had cleared the rise and was limping his way to the truck. He warily approached the deserted vehicle, scanning the surroundings before getting into the cab. He ran his fingers over the rabbits' feet then pulled the note off the steering wheel.

Kent expected Leon to be outraged by the note, but instead it seemed the man shrunk. Even with the distance separating them, Kent watched Leon's head swivel rapidly left and right, trying to see into the pitch blackness.

Phae whispered, "Hold my hand and walk slowly. All these bugs buzzing out here can only cover so much noise, so be careful. I'll lead."

Though he would have liked to stay a while longer to see if Leon could find his keys, he allowed her to pull him deeper into the woods.

Before long, she picked up the pace until they were walking at normal speed. The darkness was nearly complete in the heavily forested area. Kent stumbled.

"Sorry." Phae grabbed his arm. "I'll slow down."

"How can you see out here?"

"Well," she mumbled, "I have this night-vision thing."

"You do? Cool. Let me see it."

She released his hand. "It's on this mask. Usually I have it on a strap, but tonight I thought it would be safest if I wore a mask. You'll have to put it on to see through the monocle."

Finally, he had an explanation for that weird strap she'd been wearing the night he trailed her. "The mask must be what made you sound muffled," he said as he fumbled with the hard cardboard object Phae had pushed against his chest.

The monocle gave the mask some heft. He figured out which way was up and pulled the mask on and adjusted the elastic band.

"I don't see anything," he said, wiggling the monocle over his right eye.

"It's kind of blinky. Give it a flick or two and it will come on."

He flicked the side of the plastic casing. Suddenly, the forest around him came into view in shades of green.

He squinted in an attempt to correct the blurriness. "Am I doing something wrong? It's out of focus."

He couldn't make out Phae's features, but he could see that she had her arms crossed over her chest. Not a good sign. It would be best to tread carefully unless he wanted to find himself stranded in the dark forest.

"Look, it's not very good, but it serves its purpose well enough," she said in a defensive tone.

"I can see how it would."

It was kind of fascinating, he thought as he turned in a slow circle. Details were blurred nearly beyond recognition and because you could only see through one eye, everything was flattened. But other than those two defects, Kent realized such a gadget could come in extremely handy on a night like this.

"Can I have it back now?" Phae asked, extending toward him what Kent decided must be her arm, though the resolution was so poor it might have been a tentacle had he not known better.

He pulled the mask off and managed the handoff without mishap.

Phae must have been using the monocle in his aunt's garden that night, he thought. No wonder she'd done such a lousy job.

Still, it could have been worse if she hadn't been using the gadget. But then again, if she hadn't had the monocle she probably wouldn't have attempted to plant the garden on such a dark night and Kent wouldn't have nearly knocked his brains out on that stupid pole.

Further still, if she hadn't done such terrible work in the garden and felt guilty about mistaking him for a robber, she probably never would have offered to come and fix the mess. And Kent might never have met her.

He grinned. Thinking in circles never helped anything.

"What's wrong with you?" Phae asked.

"Nothing." He groped in the dark for her hand.

She began to slowly lead him through the forest again. "We'll be out of this soon. You'll be able to see well enough to maneuver on your own once we're on cleared ground."

"Does that mean you won't hold my hand anymore?"

"Yep."

"You're a hard woman, Phae Jones."

"Don't talk. Just concentrate on walking and not falling."

They carefully picked their way through the woods. When they came to a clearing, she slid her hand from his grasp.

"Do you think your uncle found his keys yet?" Kent asked, stepping around a clump of rocks.

"I don't know. Maybe. He had a flashlight."

"Tell me about what you did tonight, Phae. I swear I won't pass judgment," he said with all the sincerity at his command.

"Okay, but one cheap shot and I'm gone. And that means you'll have to find your own way home. Understand?"

Kent was growing weary of her threats and demands. The things a man had to do to get a woman these days. It was probably better back in the old days when you slung the woman you wanted onto your horse and rode off into the sunset.

He nearly laughed out loud when he thought of Phae, dressed in a frilly western dress, slung over his horse's rump and cussing up blue streak, threatening to unman him the second they stopped galloping. That was his Phae all right.

And he liked it, dammit. He liked her, in fact. Maybe even more than liked. Probably.

"I won't break my promise," he said, "so get on with it."

"Off to a good start already. But remember that I warned you."

He didn't respond.

"Okay. You asked for it. It's a long story but I'll try to keep it simple."

"I think I can handle something complicated. I'm not stupid."

"I didn't mean it that way," she said. "Damn. Touchy. Anyway, this all goes back to last year when we had a big flood."

"Your uncle drinks because of a flood that happened last year?"

"Sort of," she said. "Not really. Anyway, there's a river, not much more than a creek actually, a small tributary, but it's called a river, and it runs along the edge of Uncle Leon's property. After the flood, the river changed course, and it moved about ten feet into Leon's neighbor's property."

Kent stepped over a hole.

Phae clucked her tongue. "Be careful. Don't twist an ankle. I can't carry you out of here."

He had another urge to pick her up and carry her off, but resisted it. "Why didn't you stash your car tonight like last time?"

"I needed the exercise. You not up to a hike? I'm trying to take it easy on you."

God, she was competitive. He grinned. "I'm fine, thank you very much."

"So anyway," Phae continued, "the river moving led to a feud between Leon and his neighbor, George Slinker. According to the original deeds, the property line between the two is determined to be the center of the river bed. It quickly turned into an ugly fight, mostly on George's side. They've been in court multiple times and keep going back for more."

"Who's been winning in court?" Kent asked.

"Leon. The last judge told George that maybe he'd get lucky and one day another flood would give him back his ten feet and then some, but until then, he was shit out of luck."

Kent grinned. "Did he actually say 'shit out of luck?'"

"Yep."

"I'd like to meet that judge."

"Not in his courtroom, I promise you."

"So what does the river and feuds have to do with Leon drinking?"

"That's another long part of the story." Phae sidestepped a large rock with agile grace that made Kent's lower half clench.

"Well, it's a long walk."

"Okay. So Uncle Leon and Aunt Meg have been married like three years. It's a second marriage for both of them, and they brought baggage with them. Uncle Leon's first wife was something of a harpy who complained about everything he did, or at least, about everything he did that she didn't tell him to do. And Aunt Meg's first husband was a drinker and a cheater who couldn't hold down a job."

"Lovely."

"I know. Oh, and Leon doesn't have any kids from his first marriage, but now he has three. He adopted Meg's two daughters and about a year and a half ago, Leon and Meg had a son together."

"And they lived happily ever after, flood feud not included," Kent quipped.

"You'd think," Phae said, "but much as I love them, Leon and Meg are stubborn as anything and they've let their pasts get in the way of a good thing."

"Stubborn people? In the Jones family? That's weird."

"Funny." Her teeth flashed bright white in the faint light. "To make a long story shortish, after the feud started between Uncle Leon and George Slinker, Leon began going out to Trapper's Tavern once in a while and drinking with the local boys. He said he was there to drum up local support for his court case."

"Did it work?"

"Yeah, with the boozers who hang out at Trapper's. But that didn't matter. My Aunt Meg couldn't stand it and didn't want Leon turning into her ex-husband. Because she complained, and loudly, Leon said he wouldn't be told what to do, and accused Meg of being like *his* ex. And so they both dug in their heels."

"Seriously?" Kent asked.

"Seriously. Sometimes people make no sense. Meg is nothing like Leon's first wife, and he knows it. He knows she has good reason for being afraid, too, with her past. But then, Meg knows Uncle Leon is nothing like her ex, and almost always nurses a single beer when he's out. Honestly, I don't think Leon even wants to go to the bar anymore, except he won't let Meg win."

"Do they fight about this all the time?"

"That's the thing. They don't. Once a week, Leon has to make his stupid point by going to Trapper's, and once a week, he comes home smelling like beer and he and Aunt Meg have big, loud arguments."

"Wow. And they have kids ..."

"Exactly. The kids seem to know it's mostly bluster, I think most of the time. It never lasts long because Leon and Meg are really crazy about each other and make up right away. Uncle Leon's loud even when he's not in a fight. Still, most of us wish they'd quit it because we can't be positive it's not hurting those kids."

"Couples fight sometimes. I've never known one that didn't," Kent said.

"Me either. My own parents got into it from time to time, and I remember being scared by it, but they always worked it out. If anything, I learned you can fight with someone and still love them, and you can work out your difficulties eventually."

"Huh," Kent said. "It's like you're making the point I've been trying to make with you."

"I'm not talking about us."

"Too bad." Kent thought about what she'd said. "So that's why you're trying to scare your uncle away from drinking at Trapper's Tavern? For Leon's and Meg's kids?"

"Yeah. That's why."

"It's a good reason."

Her response was warm and gentle. "Thanks."

They walked in silence for a few moments before Phae said, "But there's another reason, too."

"You don't want him drinking and driving?"

"Sure. But that's not it. I told you about George Slinker. He's mad that the court cases aren't going his way, and he can be a real asshole when he wants to be. So, when Leon and Meg get into these fights, I guess George must be able to hear them. We think he waits for Leon to come home and sneaks around his house to see if they start fighting. We can't be sure. But however George learns about the arguing, he always calls the sheriff's office and demands that someone come investigate."

"Huh."

"I know. And James has to have his deputies go out there because, well, that's how it is, family or no. Lately, it isn't good enough for George to call the cops. Not long ago, George reported Meg and Leon to child services."

Kent skidded to a halt. "You're joking."

"I'm not."

"Did they investigate?"

"Yep. Sent out a social worker and everything. But they didn't pursue anything. With what those people see all the time, they aren't going to spend their limited resources pursuing a couple with well-cared-for kids and a penchant for the occasional loud argument."

"That must be a relief," Kent said, walking on.

"Yeah, except George wasn't finished. He has a sister-in-law who works in family services. And even though no one there wants to pursue anything against Leon and Meg, George's sister-in-law won't let it go, and she's pretty high up in the food chain. She made it clear that if Meg and Leon don't quit fighting, she'll take action against them."

"That's not fair. Surely Meg and Leon wouldn't push it to that point."

"Yeah, that's what you'd think. But like I said, they're stubborn, and they don't think they're doing anything wrong. They don't take the threats seriously, Kent. They think that because they're Joneses living in Zeke's Bend they're untouchable."

"Are they right?"

"Maybe about some things, but not this. This is state level action. They could be in serious trouble, and those kids would be the ones to pay the price."

Kent was disgusted. "Someone needs to talk sense into them. Meg, Leon, George, the social services woman, all of them."

"Believe me, we've tried over and over."

"Is George serious? He'd actually have their children taken away because of a feud over ten feet of land? He must be a piece of work."

"He can be a hothead," Phae answered, "But this is above and beyond. His wife, Amy, is a sweet woman, and she's tried to get him to realize that he's pushed it too far. It's a mess, Kent, and there's not a Jones in Zeke's Bend who can figure out how to fix it."

"Except you," he said, experiencing a strange sense of pride that she was brave enough to step up and try to do something to fix the seemingly unfixable. "You're doing something."

"I'm trying. Do you know how to climb a barbed wire fence?"

"I hope that question is rhetorical."

"Nope," she answered. "There's one right up here. And there will be another one before we hit the city limits. Can you handle it?"

He bristled. "Of course."

A few moments later, Kent wished he hadn't spoken so soon. He poked his finger through the big hole in his blue jeans. If he didn't quit tromping all over the countryside, he was going to run out of pants.

"You did pretty good," she said pleasantly as they continued their trek, "for a city boy."

"I did spend my summers here, you know."

"Apparently James didn't teach you about barbed wire fences."

"Most of the time, Aunt Eugenia wouldn't let me leave her yard."

Phae laughed, a silvery, bell-like sound that made Kent happy.

When he couldn't think of anything to make her laugh again, he said, "Back to Meg and Leon. Do you really think their kids aren't affected by those fights?"

"All I know for sure is that whenever anyone asks the girls about it, they shrug and say they've gotten used to it. After their former lives with an out-of-control alcoholic, it probably doesn't seem too terrible. Besides, those girls are loud themselves. In fact, lots of the Joneses are loud, even the adopted ones."

"And fiery. You Joneses are a fiery lot." Didn't he know it?

"Can't argue with you. And some of us are crazy superstitious, Uncle Leon being one of the worst. Black cats, walking under ladders, spilled salt, full moons, on and on. You saw how he was with that rabbit's foot. He believes that nasty thing brings him luck."

"Do you think he'll believe that it actually was 'Fate' who stole his truck tonight? He can't be that gullible. Fate left him a note? I don't know."

"He looked pretty scared to me," Phae said, "but I'm not certain, either."

"If he's still looking for those keys, I bet he's anything but scared right now."

"You're probably right. But it's all I've got. I'm pretty sure he won't call Meg to bring him a spare set."

"Yeah. Doubt that would go over well the way things are."

"I figured it would be a lot easier to scare Uncle Leon out of visiting that bar than it would be to try something with Aunt Meg. I couldn't fool her for a moment, about anything."

Kent laughed, recalling something at the bar. "I just realized why you meowed at your uncle back there. Black cat?"

"Yep. It lives at a farm up the road. Let's say I borrowed him for an adventure. Uncle Leon hates black cats. And that note you read? I wrote it in disappearing ink."

"He's got to realize it's a put on."

"Maybe," she said. "But all I want to put in his head is that whenever he goes out drinking, he's going to be unlucky. He can attribute that bad luck to anything he wants, cats, fate, kids pulling a prank, whatever. As long as he knows he'll have bad luck, I'm counting on that to do the trick."

"And the trick is …"

"I think he'd love to have an excuse to quit going out, but he can't give in because of what happened with his first wife. I'm giving him the excuse he needs, so he can do what Meg wants without doing it because she demands it. He'll do it because of other reasons."

Kent admired her way of thinking. "That's very wise."

She mumbled a modest thanks.

They tramped over the hilly countryside in companionable silence for a while. Kent took deep breaths of the heavy, muggy air. He was becoming accustomed to the humidity, though he doubted he'd ever come to like it.

He made a better show of climbing over the second barbed wire fence, taking more time and making it to the other side unscathed in person and pants.

Phae rewarded him with a friendly smack on his back and a, "I'll make a country boy out of you yet."

Not much farther and he realized they were close to town.

"That was fast," he said, looking at the glow of a familiar convenience store which sat on the edge of the city limits.

Phae stood close to him, the bulky mask dangling from her fingertips. "It's my shortcut." She glanced around the area. "We should split up now so we won't attract notice. You know where we are, don't you?"

"Yes, but I was hoping we could go back to your place and you could start my lessons. Why don't we split up here and rendezvous back at your house?"

Phae shook her head. In the shadowy light, he could make out her expression. She actually looked tender. "It's not a good idea. I do what I do because I care about these people. I know who they are. I can't teach you about that."

"I care about people."

"I'm sure you do. But you can't know what all of this means to me and I can't explain it in ten easy lessons. I can't show it to you either. You'd have to find it out for yourself. Besides, we have more problems than this one. You could be taking that job in Phoenix and I'm not leaving Zeke's Bend, Kent. This is my home, and I love it. We should cut our losses and part as friends."

Kent knew she was right about the Phoenix part, though he didn't want to admit it. He'd have to make a decision about the future of his company soon.

"If you won't help me learn how to be Captain Nice Guy," he said, "then I guess I'll have to teach myself."

"You won't listen to reason, will you? Well, whatever. You do love a good spectacle, if this past week and a half is anything to judge by. But don't expect me to change my mind about us."

"Come on, Phae. You can't fool me. A part of you loved everything today. And if we hadn't been interrupted by your cousins, we wouldn't even be having this conversation. We'd still be in bed, which is where we should have been all along."

She gave an un-ladylike snort. "I won't fight with you. You do what you're going to do and I'll do what I'm going to do. One word of advice, though. If you're serious about helping people, then you'd better learn how to get around without making so much noise. I don't want to feel guilty because you wound up getting chewed on by a dog or shot by an overzealous homeowner."

He desperately wanted to say, "That's exactly what I worry about happening to you," but he kept his big mouth shut for once. Instead, he said, "Thanks for the vote of confidence. And I have a word of advice for you, also. This is the second time you've refused my truce offers. If you thought it's been bad so far, wait until Monday. My advice is that you shouldn't refuse my third offer. I'm not giving up."

Phae smiled. "Fine, then may the best woman win."

"That's 'man,'" Kent called out to her as she jogged away. "May the best *man* win!"

She responded with the same little wave she'd used at the park on Independence Day. He watched her lope away, her long legs stretching gracefully. Even in baggy pants, she had the best pair of legs he'd ever seen.

He vowed that he would make her come around. She was softening toward him, though he couldn't say precisely how he knew that. Perhaps it was that she sensed he truly was sorry for over-reacting the other day, and he truly did want to know why she had to be a secret do-gooder ninja.

He turned for home, thinking of Phae in the moonlight.

CHAPTER TWENTY-THREE

PHAE TOSSED THE BAG OF warm food onto her kitchen table then pulled out her cell. She found Miss Eugenia's number.

"He'd better be there," she said, tapping her foot, ticked that Kent hadn't returned her last calls or texts.

She found it hard to believe that only a few days before, she'd been softening toward him. Kind of. A little. The jerk.

The phone rang five excruciating times before it was answered. "Hello? Miss Eugenia?" Phae asked. "Yes, this is Phae Jones ... uh-huh ... uh-huh ... yes, you too. Listen, Miss Eugenia, ... no, wait ... look, I just need to talk to ..."

Phae stifled a sigh as she listened to the old woman rattle on and on. "Please, ma'am. I'd like to speak to Kent ... please ... Yes, I know he's trying hard, but this matter is between him and me and ... uh-huh ... uh-huh ... Trust me, Kent is not going to waste away from hunger ... really ... no, he'll be fine."

She gritted her teeth. "Look, I'm sorry to interrupt you, but I need to speak to Kent ... Yes, right now ... I'm sorry this has been hard on you ... uh-huh ... arthritis, so sorry ... I can only imagine how painful, but Miss Eugenia ... yes, ma'am ... I really want to talk to Kent—now!"

She tapped her nails on the table as she waited for Kent to come on the line. She glanced at her watch. Almost six. Kent answered the phone, finally.

"It's me. Phae."

"So I heard," Kent said.

"What's with ducking my calls and texts?"

"Been busy. Sorry."

"I'm aware you've been busy. That's what I'm calling about. If you don't get over to my apartment in five minutes, I'm going to come hunt you down."

"Hell, darlin' you know you only had to ask."

"Enough. Five minutes."

She ended the call, refusing to acknowledge that the infuriating man had been laughing.

"Stupid man," she muttered as she stalked to the spare bedroom and climbed onto the elliptical machine. "He has his nerve!"

Her legs pumped furiously as she tried to relieve the tension that had built up over the course of another trying day. When Kent had warned her last week that his efforts to win her were only going to get worse, he hadn't been making an empty threat.

Her legs began to burn and she welcomed it. She increased her speed.

One way or another, she had to make the man stop. She couldn't take any more of his antics now that he'd gone too far.

She worked out at breakneck speed until she heard a jaunty knock, which only upped her blood pressure. She snatched up a towel and headed to the front.

She yanked the door open. "Get in here," she told a grinning, casual Kent.

He strolled into the room, carrying a paper sack under his arm.

"You'd better listen up," she said as she closed the door. "We're going to have a talk about your behavior and then—"

"Wait. You haven't seen what I brought." Kent reached into the bag and pulled out a bottle of wine and a knife and fork. "See? I came prepared. Where's the chow?"

"I did not invite you for dinner and you know it. And who brings their own silverware? Stop acting like—"

"Oh, it's in the kitchen, of course. I can't wait." And off to the kitchen he went.

Phae rushed behind him. "We aren't eating together. We're doing nothing but discussing your behavior."

Kent shrugged and pulled out two wineglasses, more silverware and two plates from his bag. He ignored Phae as he set the table.

"You can't do this, Kent. You can't steamroll over me. I won't have it."

"Do you have any napkins? I forgot to bring any." He opened a few cabinets. "Never mind. I found some."

He finished setting the table then opened the bag Phae had dumped there earlier. "Hey! What's this?" He pulled out a white cardboard box. "This isn't homemade. This came from a restaurant. What's the deal? She knew she was supposed to make it from scratch."

"Great Aunt Charmaine has better things to do than fix my meals. Like for instance, she can sit around in her rocking chair being freaking elderly, for God's sake!"

"Hey, she volunteered," Kent said. "Oh well. I guess it'll have to do. I think we're ready to eat."

Phae watched in disgust as Kent pulled the cork out of the wine bottle with one easy twist. He filled their glasses and held one out to her.

She shook her head. "Absolutely not."

"Suit yourself. But this is a great wine." He began to scoop food onto both plates.

He took a bite of lasagna. "Not bad, considering where it came from. Sit down. Eat."

"Nope. Not in the mood." Phae pulled open the freezer door. She gestured to the foil-wrapped containers stacked in wobbly piles. "See? It's all filled up. Nothing but lasagna. I've got it coming out of my ears thanks to you."

"You should have eaten it all. That's why I had it sent to you."

"Yes, I'm aware of that. But lasagna for lunch and lasagna for supper isn't exactly a balanced diet. Would you knock it off already?"

He took a huge bite of garlic bread and chewed with a thoughtful expression. "I don't know, Phae. For some reason, I don't feel like knocking it off. Besides, lasagna is my favorite. You know that. That's why I send it to you—so you'll think of me when you're tasting something good."

She hated her body for the tingle his last words sent zooming through her lower half. She slammed the freezer door then slumped into the other chair. "It's impossible to have a rational conversation with you."

"I can't help it if I'm excited you've finally invited me back over to your house."

"See? That's what I'm talking about. I didn't invite you. I ordered you."

"Semantics. Besides, I'm a good guy. Surely all of my goodwill ambassadors have proven that."

She leaned forward, palms flat on the table on either side of her plate. "You've got to stop this. I can't take it anymore. All day people come into the shop, interrupting my business, spouting your praises to high heaven, and it's all nonsense, stuff you've obviously had them memorize."

"I did not. I simply asked if they wouldn't mind telling you what they thought about me. And that's what they've done, expressed their honest opinions."

"Yeah, sure they have. And all of these women you've hired to cook for me have done it out of the goodness of their hearts."

"It's true. Folks around here like me. I'm kind of flattered by it. The only people I've had to pay are those extortionist teenage cousins of yours who handle the picketing and concession stand. And the florist, of course. And the candy shop. Did you get those pecan turtles, by the way? They're delicious."

"Just eat up, laughing boy. And you'd better listen, too, because I'm having my say and you're not going to stop me."

He shrugged and reached for his glass. "Speak on, fair lady."

"Listen, the flowers, the picketing, the concerts, the food, the testimonials, blah blah blah, it's going to send me over the edge."

"You're right, about part of that. I was thinking it over and obviously, you're not a flowers and candy kind of woman. My bad. I'm on it, though. Don't worry."

He threw her off her tirade for a moment with his admission, but only for a moment. "Good," she said. "That's something anyway. But the bigger issue is this latest stunt. It's got to come to a halt. Immediately. I won't have you making a laughingstock out of Captain Nice Guy."

"What are you talking about?"

"Don't play dumb with me. I know you've been out at night deliberately trying to ruin my reputation, well, the captain's reputation."

He dropped his fork on his plate, eyes flashing. "I have not! I've been trying to be the captain as best I can. If I'm not very good at it, you've only got yourself to blame."

"Not very good at it? Come on. In the last two days you've been sighted at least a dozen times. And those are only the ones that people have been talking about in the shop. I can't even guess how many others have seen you but aren't telling anyone about it."

"I admitted I'm not very good at this sneaky, do-gooder ninja thing yet. And I'm pretty sure all the dogs in town are out to get me. Honestly. I tried that dog treat trick of yours, but only that one little dog, can't remember her name … Fluffy? Feisty? Only she'll let me get near her."

Phae rubbed her temples with her palms. "I don't know what to believe. Some of the stories I've heard—"

"What did you hear? Did you hear about the lady who nearly knocked me silly with her broom before I could tell her who I was? She was a lot stronger than she looked."

"I heard. And I heard about you losing a chunk of your pants to the Webster's dalmatian and about how your ladder smashed a hole in Mrs. Humphrey's French doors."

Kent held out a hand. "I want you to know that I went back later that night and left a big pile of cash in her mailbox so she could have those doors fixed."

"I know that, too. But that doesn't mean you can keep doing this. I mean, you can't count on every man with a shotgun being able to control himself when you hold up your hands and yell, 'Don't shoot!

It's me—Captain Nice Guy!' Unbelievable. At least five people have nearly had heart attacks because of your antics."

Kent sighed. "I know. It's dangerous out there."

She could hear what he wasn't saying. "I agree, but only for you, not for me. In all the years I've been doing this, I've never been closely sighted by anyone except you. And you saw how fast I got away from you. Look, Kent, you seem to be sincere when you say you're not screwing up on purpose."

"Good, because I am sincere, and I'm not doing it on purpose to make a fool out of you … or the captain … whichever."

"Okay, but you've got to stop right now, before you or somebody else gets hurt. I'm not joking around. It's a serious situation."

He leaned back in his chair, slowly sipped at his wine. "Maybe I should buy myself a bullet-proof vest."

"And dog-proof pants?"

"Do they make those?"

"I was kidding."

"Too bad." He set his glass on the table. "Tell me something. Do I look like I'm in good physical shape?"

Phae rolled her eyes. "Oh come on."

"Seriously. I look physically fit, right?"

"You know you do. That's why you wear those tight shirts, to show off your muscles and … whatever."

He grinned. "Nice to know you're looking. But I do try. I'm not compulsive about working out, but I try to stay in shape. So I don't get it. I'm fit and I usually get along well with animals. I've read my fair share of spy books and seen a lot of movies with ninjas and so on. All that, and I can't pull off being Captain Nice Guy. It's inexplicable."

Phae couldn't help herself; she laughed. "You thought it'd be a walk in the park, didn't you?"

"Kind of. Maybe. I definitely didn't think it would be this hard."

"Don't feel bad. You need practice, not books and movies. I didn't step foot into anyone's yard until I'd spent months out in the woods alone, practicing how to move soundlessly. My defense lessons helped me learn self-control and discipline. In my workouts, I focus on core strength."

"Trust me, I'm well aware of how fit you are." Kent gave her a sizzling look.

"Yeah, so, do we agree that you should stop trying to imitate me?"

"No. Even though I'm not good at it yet, I like it."

"Then go practice in the woods and stay out of people's yards."

He shrugged. "You may be right. I was thinking that already. Also, I've been thinking that just because I'm no good at sneaking around yet, that doesn't mean I couldn't help you plan your capers."

"Capers? What movies did you say you've been watching? Were they silent or talkies?"

"I don't know what else to call it. So what do you think? I could help with the Meg and Leon problem. I have some good ideas."

Phae nearly groaned. "Please. Don't. Stay away from that one."

Kent poured himself another glass of wine. "I heard they've been at each other's throats lately, worse than before."

She finally picked up her own glass and took a healthy swallow. "Yeah. And it's all my fault. Uncle Leon blames Aunt Meg for what happened at the bar last week."

"So I heard."

"He actually believes that Meg took his truck and did the rest of it. It's unbelievable. I tried to tell him that it was Captain Nice Guy who did it, but he won't listen. He insists it was Meg's way of trying to run his life. They've had a couple of big fights and I guess George Slinker's sister-in-law is really putting up a stink about it down at family services."

"So what are you going to do?"

"I don't know. I'm almost afraid to try anything now. I thought I could try one more time at the tavern and put on a big show, prove to him that it's the captain and not Meg who's been harassing him."

"That sounds risky. Why don't you tell him the truth?" he asked.

"I told you. I tried and he wouldn't listen."

"No. I mean tell him that you're the captain and that you're the one who pulled that trick on him last week."

"No way." Phae took another drink. "The situation isn't that desperate."

"Not yet."

She chewed on a piece of cold garlic bread. "I'll think of something soon."

"Maybe I could help," Kent said.

Phae looked down at the bread and the half-empty glass of wine. Damn. She'd been consorting with the enemy. She tossed the bread onto her plate. "I don't want your help, Kent. I appreciate that you're going to stop trying to be like the captain. Now, if you'd stop all the other foolishness, my life would be complete."

"No it wouldn't. You need me, even if I'm only an irritation right now. I remind you there's a bigger world out there and that you should be part of it. Only with me will your life be complete."

Where did that come from? What could possibly make him think she'd be incomplete without him? Absurd. Something thudded in her belly. It didn't mean anything, she told herself.

Kent pulled another package from his paper bag. This one was gift-wrapped.

He pushed it across the table. "Remember how I said I'd finally figured out that you aren't a flowers and candy kind of girl? Well, I think this might be more to your liking."

She eyed the gift. "Don't tell me. It's a pair of thong underwear to match that obscene dress you got me."

"Nah. That'd be a gift for me. Go on. Open it. I promise you'll like it."

Phae knew she should refuse, but she couldn't resist. Something about the combination of eagerness and confidence in Kent's expression made it impossible to push the present away unopened.

She lifted the lid and peered inside. "What is it?"

"Guess."

She pulled out a gizmo that consisted of some type of heavy suction cups strung together on a cord. "I'm afraid to guess."

He waggled an eyebrow. "You have a dirty mind, Phae Jones."

"It's not my mind I'm worried about, buddy." She pondered the strange straps and suction cups. "I have no idea what this is."

Kent stood up and took the device from her. "Here. I'll show you. I'll put it on the fridge because it might mark up your walls."

He stuck his hand through one of the straps then pushed the suction cup against the refrigerator. "See? Look how it holds. It's incredibly strong and won't release until you push this button here. See? Then it pops right off."

"Okay. I see."

"No you don't. Look, these two go on your hands and these two go on your feet. Do you get it now?"

She chuckled at the sight of Kent decked out in the strange contraption, the suction cups on his palms and toes, the straps dangling. "No. I don't get it. It's the funniest looking—"

"Watch me." He raised his arms and feet up and down. "Do you see now? It's for climbing. With this thing, you can climb straight up a sheer face wall. Of course, the wall has to be smooth. But think about it. With this thing, you could head up the side of a building like you were Spiderwoman."

Phae itched to try. "Let me see it."

He handed over the device. Phae slipped the straps over her hands and Kent helped her with her feet.

She shoved a toe cup against the fridge. "I can't believe this. I'm pulling as hard as I can, but it won't budge. Do you think this thing would really hold me?"

"I know it will, but don't try it on the fridge. You'll probably pull it over on yourself."

She popped the cups off and on for a while, practicing the process until she was comfortable with it. She glanced into the living room and eyed the bare walls.

"You don't really think these cups would mark up the paint, do you?" she asked.

"I do. I've got all these circles on the walls of my room at Aunt Eugenia's house to prove it."

Phae grinned. She realized that he was standing next to the table with his paper bag in his arms. "Oh, you've cleaned everything up. When did you do that?"

"While you were experimenting. I'm all packed and ready to go. I went ahead and threw away the rest of the lasagna."

"Thanks. So you're leaving, then?"

"I don't want to wear out my welcome and I promised myself I'd be on my best behavior. So I guess this is goodnight."

She stood aside and he passed by her. "Yeah. Goodnight."

He stopped at the front door and said, "Before I go, I was wondering if you'd mind if I called you once in a while. Just to chat and maybe get some advice about the best way to practice. Would you mind?"

Once again, Phae did the exact opposite of what she knew she should do. "No. I don't mind," she said. "And thanks for this climbing gizmo. I really like it."

Kent smiled, his straight white teeth like a flash of sunshine. "You're welcome. I'm glad you like it. Oh, how do you feel about Mexican?"

"Mexico?"

"No, not Mexico, Mexican. As in food. You know, salsa, guacamole, enchiladas …"

She groaned. "Oh no."

"Just thought I'd ask," he said with a wink. "Goodnight, Phae. I'll call you tomorrow." He closed the door behind him.

Phae shook her head. She'd been so strong, and now this. Dammit. How dare he start acting like a gentleman? He was wearing her down.

She glanced at the cups on her hands and then checked her watch. It was still too early to go out. She fiddled with the straps and thought about her Uncle Carston's big concrete silo.

She could hardly wait until midnight.

CHAPTER TWENTY-FOUR

IT TOOK HER LESS THAN A WEEK to become an expert using the climbing device. She also mastered the other gifts Kent had left sitting on her back porch every evening.

Her favorites were the long-range listening device and the shiny new pair of night vision glasses. It had gotten so she could hardly wait for nightfall to head out with her new equipment.

It was difficult to focus at work, too, because she couldn't stop daydreaming about her new toys and wondering what Kent might surprise her with next.

After another long day of waiting, she was on the verge of locking up the shop when James walked in. He glanced around at all the flowers, boxes of candy, balloons and stuffed animals.

"Still at it, is he?" James asked, seating himself in one of the hydraulic chairs.

Phae nodded, picking up a huge box of assorted chocolates and offering it to her cousin. He seemed extra large in this setting, his size magnified by his stiffly-pressed uniform, his huge, shiny black shoes and massive belt complete with gun holster and large radio. Every so often, a spurt of chatter would blare from the radio.

He waved off the box of chocolates. "No thanks, Phae."

"Oh come on. Help me out. There's enough candy in here to feed a small nation for a week."

James smiled and accepted the box. He plucked out a piece of chocolate and popped it into his mouth. "Not bad," he said when he'd finished chewing.

"He has good taste in candy, I'll give him that much. And I just got my evening meal delivery if you want something more solid."

"What is it today?"

"Chinese. Aunt Charmaine made it."

He looked dubious. "Aunt Charmaine knows how to make Chinese food?"

"No. I checked it out. Looks like she cut up some fried chicken strips and waffles and stuffed it all into a couple of those white boxes you get from Chinese takeout. And there's a couple slices of sweet potato pie in there with handwritten fortunes stuck on them."

"Damn. In that case, yeah I'll have some."

Phae found the bag and set it on her workstation. "Have it all. Take it home for supper. I don't have any room left in my refrigerator."

James picked up the bag, opened it, took a long sniff then shut his eyes in ecstasy. "Admit it, Kent's not so bad."

"If you came to sing his praises, save your breath. I've heard it all. Trust me."

He set the bag back on the counter. "No, that's not why I'm here, though I admit he's tried more than once to get me to fall into line with everyone else. I thought he'd gone as far as he could when he started that picket line a while back, but he proved me wrong."

"Yeah, he's a bundle of surprises."

James picked out another piece of candy. "Kent can be impulsive sometimes, but I know he's serious about you or I wouldn't put up with everything he's been pulling. Now don't get mad at me, Phae. Wipe that look off your face or it might freeze that way."

"Gee, thanks Grandma Jones."

"Well, she was right about a lot of things, and that's one of them. Anyway, he didn't put me up to saying this, but you should know that he's never done anything like this before, not that I know of anyway."

Phae studied her fingernails.

James perused the chocolate box again. "He's always had this idea that his perfect woman was out there waiting for him and that when he met her, he'd marry her and that would be that. I guess his parents' marriage worked that way. I've always told him it wouldn't be that easy, but Kent ... he's kind of stubborn."

She snorted.

"But he means well," James continued, "most of the time. And he's one of the few truly honest people on this planet. That counts for a lot, with me anyway. Don't hold out on him for too long, Phae. The poor guy is suffering."

"You've sure changed your tune since the fair," she said, nonplussed.

"Doesn't matter. Man can change his mind if he wants. But I didn't come here to talk about him. Is Sylvie gone already?"

"Yeah."

"Good. I want to talk to you about Uncle Leon and Aunt Meg."

Phae nearly winced. "What about them?"

"They're in big trouble. Don't tell me you haven't heard."

"I did. I even went and tried to talk to them about it, but they won't listen."

"Nancy Carter down at Family Services called me today. I guess the Slinker woman won't let it go and Nancy says if Leon and Meg have one more blowout, they won't be able to stop Slinker from stepping in."

"What? I didn't hear that."

"She called me today."

"Did they have another big fight?" she asked, panicked. "When?"

"Last night. It was the biggest yet. I had to go out there and try to stop it, but it didn't do any good. Meg is still furious that Leon won't believe she didn't pull that trick on him at Trapper's Tavern a while back. And you know Leon; he won't back down. These fights used to blow over by the next morning, but this one never ends."

"This is horrible."

"I tried to tell them that it was most likely Captain Nice Guy who played that trick."

"I told him that, too. And Meg."

James took off his hat and ran the back of his hand over his brow. "They don't listen. They're headed for a showdown on this thing, and I don't know how to stop it. Any suggestions?"

"Have you told them what Nancy said?"

"Yes, but they don't take it seriously. Meg says that George's wife wouldn't let her husband be involved in something so terrible. And Leon says he's a Jones and family services wouldn't dare touch any of them, what with half the office being related in some way or other. He's wrong about that, I think. Nancy says it's serious."

Phae had never felt so helpless. And guilty. "Do you think the social worker will follow through?"

"I do. Those Slinkers' brothers think they have something to prove. And there's nothing more dangerous than that."

"Send Aunt Elfleda after Meg and Leon. She'll set them straight."

"This may shock you, but Aunt Elfleda refuses to get involved. She said you can't protect fools from themselves." He put the lid back on the candy. "My only thought left is that maybe Captain Nice Guy will come up with something. He's always there when we need him. He may be our last chance."

Phae wanted to cry she was so frustrated.

James stood up, handed her the box of candy and picked up the bag of faux-Chinese food. "Guess I'll head on home. Thanks for the supper."

"You can thank Kent, and Aunt Charmaine."

She followed him to the door to lock up after him.

"See you, Phae. Be careful," he said then strolled toward his patrol car.

Phae called goodbye, locked the door then headed to her apartment. She no sooner stepped inside than her cell began to vibrate in her pocket. She pulled it out. It was Kent.

A wave of relief flooded her. She would tell him about Meg and Leon, see what he thought, maybe get some suggestions or feedback on what she should do, if she should even dare to try.

Suddenly, the impossible seemed possible. Maybe she could solve this problem after all, with Kent's help.

The thought rattled her. She was taken aback. Without realizing it, she'd come to enjoy Kent's calls and to look forward to them. Strange.

How long had it been since she'd had someone to confide in, someone she could trust with her secrets? No one since her grandmother died.

Kent. A confidant. Who'd have thought?

She answered his call with a smile.

THREE DAYS LATER, PHAE WASN'T smiling anymore. She collapsed into her easy chair and covered her face with her hands. How had everything gone so terribly wrong?

She'd come up with an elaborate plan to end Leon's trips to the tavern once and for all, and had it all set to go tonight, but she'd never gotten the chance to put the plan into action. Luck wasn't with her tonight, and Leon had left the bar early, blowing everything.

She thought about the night two weeks before when she'd taunted Kent that the best woman would win their contest. She'd certainly proven that she was nobody's best woman. She was a meddler and a fool and had probably ruined her aunt's and uncle's lives.

She jerked when someone pounded on her door. She glanced at her watch. It was two a.m.

"Phae! Let me in!"

She raced to the door, jerked it open, then rushed into Kent's strong arms.

"Everything is going to be okay," he murmured as he smoothed her hair.

Holding her tightly, he eased his way into the room, closing the door with his foot.

Phae struggled to hold back tears. "I've messed up so terribly. Everything I tried only made it worse, and now the worst thing possible has happened. Oh, Kent, you were right all along. I never should have messed with anyone's lives. I should have let them handle their own problems."

He gently shushed her and led her to the sofa. He picked up the night-vision glasses she'd tossed on the cushion earlier.

"Hey," he softly teased, "you should take better care of these things. Don't you like them? Where's the case?"

"I love them. And you should take them back. I won't be needing them anymore. I'm never going to meddle in anyone's life ever again."

"You just feel that way right now. I can make you feel better."

She took a deep breath and gazed into his gorgeous blue eyes. "I'm so glad you're here. I needed you. I completely failed with Meg and Leon. I was just at their house. Oh, Kent, something awful has—"

"Shh. Things aren't as bad as they seem. Trust me, I—"

A car door slammed outside. Kent raised his eyebrows and looked at Phae questioningly.

"I don't know," Phae whispered.

Someone banged on the front door hard enough to make the frame shake.

"Let me in, Phae! I know you're awake. You've gone too far this time. Open this door before I break it down. You hear me? I'll break it down!"

"It's James," Phae said. "Don't let him in. My clothes! I've got to change so he doesn't see me in this."

"You're okay. Nothing suspicious about dressing like a beatnik from the fifties."

"What?"

"You know, black turtleneck and slacks. Whatever. Be thankful you didn't put on that black paint tonight. Where's your tool belt?"

She pointed toward her bedroom. Kent leaped up off the sofa, grabbed the night vision glasses then dashed down the hall.

In a moment, he strode back into the living room, sent Phae a fortifying look, then opened the front door.

James barged inside, every part of him testifying to his fury. "What are you doing here?" he demanded, glaring at Kent.

Kent closed the door and leaned against it. "I might ask you the same question."

James ran his hand over his head then turned to Phae, who sat glued to the sofa. "Tell him to leave. I've got some things to say and I don't think you want him hearing it."

"Leave her alone." Kent walked over and placed a reassuring hand on her shoulder.

Phae stared open-mouthed at her livid cousin. "I don't want him to leave. What's going on? Why are you here?"

"Fine," James said, "have it your way. I want you to get over to Meg's and Leon's right now and tell them everything you've done to ruin their lives."

Tears burned at the back of Phae's eyes. "I don't understand."

"Dammit, Phae! Family services took their kids tonight and Meg and Leon deserve to know who made it happen."

"Whoa!" Kent interjected. "You need to back the hell off. Phae didn't make this happen. Their stubbornness and refusal to see reason is why their kids were taken. And the situation isn't as bad as you—"

James' glare burned into Phae. "It wouldn't have been so bad if someone hadn't meddled where she didn't belong. And those poor kids would be sleeping in their own beds right now instead of being shuttled to a foster home and scared half to death."

That did it. Phae burst into tears. It was too much. James was right. She was to blame. The more she'd tried to fix Leon's and Meg's issues, the worse it had gotten. She'd destroyed their family.

She was the worst person who ever lived.

Kent bent down, scooped her up, then sat back down with her cradled on his lap. "It's okay, baby. James doesn't know his ass from a hole in the ground. Shut up, James. So help me God, if you say another word, I'll …"

Phae buried her face on Kent's shoulder. She didn't deserve his comfort, or his defense, but she needed it more than anything.

"You don't know everything, Kent," James said. "And it's time you did. Phae is Captain Nice Guy."

He said it like he was dropping a bomb on the room, and when it didn't go off, he was at a loss to continue. Phae cried quietly and Kent held her tightly, murmuring she had nothing to blame herself for.

"I said, Phae is Captain Nice Guy. Do you understand what I'm saying?" James demanded.

"Obviously," Kent answered. "What I'd like to know is how you know."

"Me too," Phae said with a sniffle.

"How do *you* know?" James asked.

"I figured it out," Kent said. "Your turn."

James finally stopped looming over them and sat down in the easy chair. "I've known all along. Grandma Jones told me years ago."

Phae sat up straight, stunned. Her grandmother had told James? Why would she do that? Phae had trusted her to keep the secret and she'd been betrayed.

She hardly registered that Kent and James were talking.

"I don't see how you could have figured it out," James said.

"And I don't see what difference it makes," Kent said. "If you'd shut up for a second I could tell you—"

Phae found her voice finally. "James, how could Grandma have told you about me? Did she tell you about Chicago, too? She told you all my secrets, didn't she?"

"I don't know anything about Chicago. She told me about your night-time activities long before the paper started calling you Captain Nice Guy. Grandma wanted to protect you, to make sure that I or one of my deputies didn't shoot you some night thinking you were a criminal."

"Grandma didn't trust me to be good at this?" she asked.

"Unbelievable. That's what you take away from it." James' upper lip curled. "It had nothing to do with trust and everything to do with people who love you trying to protect you."

"I don't know what to think," Phae said.

"I know what to think," Kent said. "Your grandmother loved you and didn't want you hurt, so she protected you the best way she knew. The same thing you did for Meg and Leon. Isn't that right, James? Family protects family."

James blew out a loud breath. "Dammit."

"I really did try, James. I'm so sorry I messed it all up. When you told me I was the last chance, I did everything I could think of, I swear. I just wasn't good enough," Phae said, quickly sinking back into devastation.

"What did he tell you, Phae?" Kent asked. "About being the last chance?"

"I put a bug in her ear a few days ago, that's all," James said. "I stopped by to let her know what was happening and hint that maybe Captain Nice Guy would come up with something to save the day."

Kent's chest swelled. "What the hell? You go to her, put that kind of pressure on her, and then come over here yelling and blaming her when it doesn't go down how you wanted? That's a load of crap."

James looked like he wanted to say something, but his mouth snapped shut. He looked at Phae, then at Kent, then he looked down at his hands. He appeared to be thinking.

Finally, his massive shoulders slumped. He looked back up at them. "You're right. I don't know what I was thinking. I shouldn't have blamed you, Phae. I'm so mad that this happened, but I shouldn't have taken it out on you. You tried to help and I can't fault you for that."

Phae shook her head. "No, you're right. It is my fault. The only thing to do is go over and confess that I'm Captain Nice Guy. I've been the one trying to keep Leon away from the tavern. It should end the worst of the fight, anyway."

"I don't know if it would help," James said, sounding bleak. "Maybe we should leave it alone."

"I can't believe the kids are gone," Phae said.

"Me either."

Kent sighed. "You Joneses. You're good people and I'm lucky to know you. But you're terrible listeners."

"We are," Phae said.

James nodded morosely.

Kent sighed again, slipped his hand into his pocket and pulled out his phone. "Hold on. I've got a message." He listened for a while, then with a smile, he stuck the phone back in his pocket.

He patted Phae's back and dried her tears with his fingertips. "Let's go, beautiful. There's something you need to see."

She didn't know what he was getting at, and she wasn't in a place to try to figure it out. "I can't, Kent. I need to go to Meg's and Leon's and try to do something. Even if it's too late."

"It's not too late," Kent assured her. "Do you trust me?"

Her instinct was to immediately say yes, but she took a few seconds to think about it, to make sure she'd gotten it right. She had. "I do."

His face lit up, so handsome and bright it made her heart ache. She didn't feel worthy of him tonight.

"Then believe me when I say everything is fine. Now let's go and see what needs to be seen."

Phae glanced over at James who was eyeing Kent with a speculative expression.

"What's this about?" James asked.

"It's a surprise," Kent said. He gently lifted Phae off his lap and set her on her feet, then he stood himself. "We'll go in my car. You follow us, James. I promise, you won't be disappointed."

Chapter Twenty-Five

PHAE STOOD ON THE HILL THAT faced Leon's and Meg's property. Kent and James flanked her on either side. She could hardly believe what she saw.

Massive floodlights lit the area below, turning night into brilliant day. Four massive earthmoving machines slowly crept across the landscape, trolling the banks of the river that separated Leon's property from the Slinkers' property. Dump trucks and other smaller vehicles dashed around the site like insects in a behemoth's wake.

"What the hell is happening down there?" James asked.

Kent rocked on his heels, pleased. "They're moving the river. Well, it's more like a creek, but a big creek. And they're going to move it."

Phae gawked at him. "You're kidding."

"Nope."

"Why the hell are you moving the river, Holmes?" James asked.

"I'm not moving it. They are. Or more accurately, your Great-Great-Great-whatever-Aunt Elfleda is moving it."

James snorted. "She doesn't have that kind of money."

"She may have a benefactor, an anonymous benefactor as far as everyone knows, everyone but us and Elfleda," Kent said.

Phae immediately saw the brilliance of the scheme. The pieces fell into place and she beamed at Kent. "I get it. You're brilliant!"

"Oh, I don't know if I'd go that far."

James looked at Phae questioningly.

"Elfleda steamrolled over Leon and George Slinker," Phae said. "I bet she told them she was going to fix the situation and they were going to shut the hell up and get out of her way. The river's going back to where it was before the flood, isn't it?"

"That's my clever lady," Kent said, wrapping an arm around her shoulders. "The river goes back to where it was and in exchange, George Slinker drops the lawsuits and calls off his sister-in-law."

"Is that Aunt Elfleda down there?" James asked, pointing at the brightly lit front porch of Leon's house.

Phae squinted and could barely make out the tiny body ensconced in the big wheelchair, her fluffy white hair a halo around her head. "Yep. That's her. Up and kicking at this time of night."

"What about the kids?" James asked. "Where are they?"

"They should be here any minute," Kent answered. "The message I got at Phae's house was that they were being bundled up and would be heading home soon."

James waved an arm at the unprecedented scenario playing out below them. "Couldn't this construction have waited until morning?"

"That was Elfleda's idea," Kent said. "She said having all those big machines behind her when she confronted them would make it more real, intimidate and convince them that she meant business. She was right. I hid nearby in the shadows when the confrontation happened. Slinker agreed quickly, and it's no wonder. His wife looked outraged enough to leave him when she learned that Leon's and Meg's kids had been taken because of her husband and sister-in-law. Truth is, she may have been enough to get Slinker to back down all on her own, without moving the river."

"Maybe, but who could be sure? You did the smart thing," Phae said.

"I don't know," Kent said. "Elfleda and I planned this together, and we meant it to only be a last ditch plan in case Meg and Leon didn't straighten up. Neither of us thought it would actually go so far as the children being taken. If we hadn't waited, we could have saved those kids a lot of fear tonight, and saved all of you a lot of heartache."

"You're smart as hell," James said, "but you're not a fortune teller. I think everything may have happened exactly the way it should, especially for Meg and Leon. If they aren't honest, if they don't put their old fears behind them and help each other heal, then there's no hope for them as a family. I think this scare with their kids is going to show them what's really important."

Phae hoped he was right, and deep inside, she took some of his words to heart for herself. Honesty. Putting her old fears behind her. Healing. Knowing what was important. She realized, she was guilty of the same sins as her aunt and uncle.

Kent squeezed her shoulder. "Look." He nodded toward Leon's house.

She watched a car pull in the driveway. Two small figures jumped out of the back seat and ran toward the porch, while two larger figures ran down from the porch to sweep the little ones into their arms. A woman stepped out of the car holding a baby and walked up to the reunited family.

The kids were home where they belonged.

Phae looked up at Kent and saw that he hadn't been watching the scene down below. He'd been watching her reaction. In the reflected light of the work site below, she easily read the tenderness in his expression.

She felt light, like sweet spring air. She laughed, pulled away from Kent, spread her arms, twirled and waved at the scene below. "You are one crazy, crazy man. I can't believe you did something this huge, this over-the-top, this amazing. Look down there. It's nuts and all kinds of wonderful!"

"If I'd known it would make you laugh like this, I'd have done it even bigger and crazier, with helicopters maybe, whatever it took," he said, laughing with her and catching her up in his arms again.

A tingle spread through her.

Fear. Honesty. Healing.

It was time. Time to stop holding everything in. Time to let go and take a chance.

She wrapped her arms around his neck and he squeezed her around her waist.

She looked deeply into his dear eyes and risked everything. "I probably love you, Kent Holmes."

She knew what he'd say before he said it; it was written on his handsome face.

"I probably love you, too, Phae Jones," he said, his voice low and edged with powerful emotion.

"You're going to kiss me, aren't you?"

"Damned straight I am."

Phae only halfway heard James speaking from somewhere far away.

"Uh, think I'll be heading down to the site and make sure everything stays in order down there. See you two … later."

Phae and Kent remained wrapped in one another, gazing into each other's eyes.

"I thought he'd never leave," Kent said.

"Who?"

Kent grinned. "Did I say I love you?"

"Probably. You can say it again if you want."

"I already did."

"Shut up and kiss me."

"Your wish is my command, beautiful," he said, and his lips descended on hers.

And he stole her breath away.

"KEEP YOUR EYES SHUT," KENT said, guiding her with an arm around her shoulders.

Phae walked easily on the smooth, level ground, trusting he wouldn't let her fall. "Where are we going?"

"It's a surprise."

"I don't know if I can take another surprise tonight. My eyes are still dazzled from the lights at Meg's and Leon's."

"Just a few more seconds. It'll be worth it, I promise."

"I believe you," Phae said with a laugh. "I'd be a fool not to. After the surprise can we go back to my apartment and finish what we started with that kiss?"

"Actually, I'd planned to take you home to my place."

"No way I'm going to Miss Eugenia's house, Kent. You've got to be kidding."

"I wasn't talking about Aunt Eugenia's house. I said I wanted to take you to my place." He stopped walking and let her go. "You can open your eyes."

Phae opened her eyes and blinked. They were standing in front of the old Belleterre Mansion. Not far from the old downtown area of Zeke's Bend, the home had been empty for as long as she could remember. It sat tucked away in the middle of a huge lot, surrounded entirely by wrought iron fences and stone plinths, shielded by dozens upon dozens of trees, many of them century oaks.

It was a spectacular example of Victorian architecture, and Phae had always admired it, though she'd only been inside the fence a few times in her life. Tonight, there were lights on inside the house and spotlights along the exterior edges showing off the lovely, but faded and decaying woodwork.

"What do you think of it?" Kent asked.

"I've always liked this house. But why are we here? No one's home, I can promise you. It's been empty forever."

"It's my house now. I bought it," Kent said, watching her closely.

"You bought the Belleterre Mansion? What for?"

"To live in."

"But, you've got that job in Phoenix."

He shook his head. "Nah. I turned them down. Told them I got a better offer. You, by the way, are the better offer."

242

Phae didn't know what to say. "You're moving here? Permanently?"

"If you don't mind."

"Of course I don't mind. I'm just ... what about your company?"

"I sold it. Goodbye Phoenix. I am now, officially, a citizen of Zeke's Bend."

Phae's heart beat a jerky rhythm and her brain struggled to figure out what all this meant for them as a couple. Should she make assumptions? They said they loved each other, and now there was a house, too? Damn.

"Come on inside," he said. "I can't wait to show it off."

He took her hand and pulled her to the front door. She followed him in a daze, hardly listening to him talk about the renovation work he had planned and how he was going to semi-modernize the interior while keeping the exterior true to its age all the way down to the gingerbread trim.

The mansion was huge, though most of the rooms were small, as was the style of the times when it was built, with tall, narrow windows and high ceilings. Wallpaper was peeling from most of the walls and the wooden floors were scarred and in need of refinishing.

The kitchen hadn't had its fixtures or appliances updated in the last fifty years, and the bathrooms were stained with age and the brass fittings tarnished and/or broken.

She couldn't imagine the amount of work it would take to rebuild the place; it was staggering. But to hear Kent talk about what he was going to do with it, it seemed it would be the work of a moment. His enthusiasm was catching.

On the second floor, after a quick look into the rooms there, he led her to one with a pair of exquisitely carved wooden doors.

"The master suite," he said, reaching for the knobs. He pushed the doors open.

Phae gasped. This was no rundown suite. Obviously, Kent had put some people to work recently. How had he kept this quiet? She was shocked she hadn't heard about the house being bought and worked on.

The suite was a large room, and she wondered how many walls were taken out to get it that size. The creamy, textured walls were romantically lit by dimmed sconces and a large light fixture in the center of the room.

A fireplace drew the eye right away with its elegantly lined polished mantle. There were several antique bureaus and an exquisite wardrobe, too. The wood was rich and almost velvety looking. Several overstuffed chairs near the fireplace looked invitingly cozy.

The room was eclectic in style, and warm in all ways, from paint to paper to fabric to flooring. The massive four-poster bed sat like an emperor in the room, the bedding in shades of pale greens, plush and begging to be touched.

The air was redolent with a spicy, light floral blend. An air conditioner purred in one of the windows, keeping the room comfortable and relieving the humidity.

"I was able to get a little work done already, but central air will take some time," Kent said. "The window unit works for now. What do you think of it?"

"It's beautiful. So lovely."

"Not half as lovely as you," he said, moving in beside her and taking her hand. "Everything here was inspired by you."

"It's perfect." She didn't want to say how moved she was and how much at home she felt from the moment she entered the house. It would be awkward.

Their gazes fell on the four-poster bed at the same time. Phae's face warmed up and she looked down when Kent turned back to her.

"You know what I want, Phae," he said. "If you're not ready for this, tell me now. I don't want to pressure you."

She ran her fingertips over his cropped black hair and down his manly jaw. "I've never done this before."

He raised a brow. "I've been dreaming about you and me on that couch of yours for what seems like forever, so I have to ask, are you confused about never having done this before?"

She smiled. "No. I mean, I've never had sex with a man I'm in love with. You'll be my first."

"Really?"

"Really. I've never been in love, and I've never said 'I love you' either."

"I'm honored," he said. "I've never said it either."

"Come on. 'I love you' is the first line guys learn as horny teenagers."

"I learned it. I just never used it."

They smiled.

Phae reached behind her head and unclipped her hair. She spread it over her shoulders and let it fall in ringlets, free and wild around her face.

Kent watched her every movement with a gleam in his eyes. She reached to stroke his face.

With a deep groan, Kent swept her into his arms. She held on tightly and kissed him fiercely as he carried her to the bed, letting go reluctantly when he lowered her onto the soft mattress.

Holding her breath, she lay still, every nerve in her body tingling while Kent pulled his shirt over his head. She wanted to touch the tanned smoothness of his skin glowing in the soft light, but he nudged her hand away.

He sat on the edge of the bed, hungrily studying the length of her body. He reached down and, one a time, removed her shoes and socks with aching tenderness, caressing her feet and running his hands up her ankles.

She sucked in a deep breath when he pulled her shirt over her head, gently lifting her in the process to pull it free.

One more time, she reached for him.

"Please, Phae, don't touch me," he said, pushing her back down onto the mattress. "I won't be able to hold back if you do, and I don't want to rush. You have no idea how long I've wanted to see you like this. I'm taking my sweet time."

With a delicate touch that belied his great strength, he smoothed his hands over her neck, shoulders and arms. He skimmed fingertips over the tops of her lacy bra cups, a feathery touch across the upper curve of her breasts that made her shiver.

"Your skin glows in the light," he said, almost in wonder. "So smooth. Like silk."

Phae gave herself over to his gaze and his touch. She dug her fingers into the soft bedding to keep from touching him.

He tugged gently on her pants, unbuttoning and unzipping, then slowly pulled them down over her hips and off her legs. He dropped them aside, his gaze centered on the tiny strip of fabric covering her mound.

"Damn," he muttered, and traced a tingling line around the edges of her panties.

Like before, she'd never been so certain of the depths of a man's passion as she was of Kent's.

Tears pooled in her eyes as she witnessed his desire. He made her feel perfect, new, untouched and undamaged. He stroked the length of her inner thighs, making her moan.

She had to touch him. She couldn't hold back.

When he dipped a finger under the elastic at the top of her panties, she reached down and clasped her hands over his.

"I want you so bad," she said. And she pushed his hand the rest of the way under her panties, pressing her hips upward, leading his fingers down to her dripping folds. "Feel that. It's for you."

Kent's expression went from tender to animal in a split second. He groaned and his eyes flashed.

"Hell," he said in that wonderfully deep voice that made her stomach flutter. "I should have known I wouldn't be able to wait."

CHAPTER TWENTY-SIX

PHAE SAT UP AND CLUNG TO HIS shoulders, kissing him across his neck and jawline. He smelled and tasted so good, salty and spicy, like a man should. Like her man should.

He unclasped her bra and the lacy lingerie went sailing away. He fell on her breasts with lips and tongue, teeth and fingertips, squeezing, pulling and nipping.

Phae threw her head back and pulled him closer, ever closer. She savored the growls she got as a reward for raking her nails across his strong back.

Her skin was on fire, and her insides purred, demanding she let him in. She reached for the hard bulge straining against his jeans.

Kent grabbed her wrist and pulled her back. "No."

She tried again but he jumped off the bed and held out his hand to stop her.

"Don't move, Phae," he said. "I want to see your breasts while I get these damned pants off. Hold them up for me. Arch your back. God, you've got beautiful breasts. Show them to me."

Marveling at how free she felt, she cupped her breasts and ran her thumbs over pebbled nipples which were still damp from his kisses.

"Spread your knees," he demanded, unzipping his pants slowly, his gaze moving rapidly over her. "I want to see those wet panties. All for me, you said. All that sweet goodness is just for me."

"Only you," she repeated, her own gaze on his package, waiting with bated breath while he shoved down his jeans and boxers at the same time.

She licked her lips and her heart thudded when his cock sprung free. So big. She'd thought often about how big and beautiful he was, late at night, alone in her cold bed.

Now here he was, larger than she remembered. And like the last time they were together, she had a moment's pause, a split-second's worry that she might not be able to take it all.

He held his cock and stroked up and down the mighty length. "This is all for you, beautiful," he said. "Tell me that you want it."

"You know I do." She swallowed hard as he stroked himself again. "I want to do that."

A feral grin turned up one corner of his sexy lips. "No, this is how it's going to work. I'm going to spread those sweet thighs and take you until you scream and then I'm going to turn you over and take you from behind until you scream again. Hard. It's going to be hard. Because that's how you like it. Tell me. Tell me that's how you like it."

"I do," she said, her voice trembling with need. "I do like it that way. Tonight."

"And so do I. And when you think you can't take anymore, I'll give you more."

Something lodged itself high in her throat. She wanted him so badly she couldn't breathe.

"You think you can handle that?" he asked.

She nodded. "Yes. Do it now."

"Take off those panties then, and spread those sweet thighs."

She slipped her panties over her hips, wriggling slowly from side to side, willfully enticing a man who needed no further enticements. She did it anyway, because she couldn't resist the power of turning his blue sky eyes dark and stormy. Out of lust. For her.

"Damn, Phae," he said, watching the slow slide of the panties down her thighs.

And then he pounced. One moment she was in command of herself and him, and the next moment he was on her. Her panties were gone in an instant, yanked off by an alpha male who'd taken charge of her and of the moment.

He pushed her down on her back and pulled her to the edge of the bed where he stood, a Viking raider, muscles bulging, flexing, black hair catching the light in flashes.

He grabbed her legs and lifted until her ankles rested on his broad shoulders and her butt was against the edge of the mattress. He captured her gaze with his own and grabbed the tops of her thighs.

Then he drove into her, one swift and rough push. He buried himself inside her and she cried out, "Yes! Ahh!"

So he did it again. And again. Filling her to overflowing, making her toss her head from side to side. Her world was only him, only the way he made her feel, only the pounding of his cock and the grunts of his exhalations and he took her where she wanted to go, her ears filled with the sex sounds of wet on wet.

It didn't take long before her first release exploded inside her. She cried his name and dug her heels into his shoulders, rising up to give as good as she got. Every time she reached for him he pushed her back down, so she stretched her arms over her head and grasped at the bedding.

"Scream for me. That's it, baby. Scream for me," he told her between quick breaths as he pumped inside her.

She cried out and barely crested the peak of her climax when Kent grabbed her ankles and pushed her up farther on the bed.

"Turn over," he demanded. "On your knees."

He helped her turn over. "God, that ass." He ran his hands over her cheeks and kneaded her softness. He groaned.

Phae hung her head, half worn out from the intense orgasm that continued to pulse inside her. She ached to be filled again.

She didn't have to wait. Kent grabbed her hips, nestled at her opening then pushed inside. Deep, so deep. Phae's head jerked up and she welcomed him into her with a moan.

He took her hard and steady, sometimes bending down over her and giving her sharp love bites on her shoulders and neck. A few times he swatted her rear and laughed long and low when she asked for more.

"I can't get enough of you," he told her, grinding up against her soft backside. "You're so hot and wet. So slick. Mmm, Phae. My love."

And with those words, she exploded again, her front half collapsing onto the mattress, sending her rear even higher into the air in unconscious surrender. Were those her cries or his? Was his agony of pleasure as sweet as hers?

Her breasts shook against the bedding and sweat dripped down the sides of her face. He pumped inside her with a ferocity that might have been frightening had it not been Kent—had it not been the man she loved and trusted.

Then he climaxed, too, his release blasting inside her and driving her even higher. Her body was ablaze with sensation, every nerve ending screaming release. Kent seemed to be everywhere at once, in and around her, holding her, telling her he loved her.

They collapsed together, both of them gulping air. Phae thought her heart might pound out of her body. Aftershocks throbbed inside her.

How long did they lay there? She'd never be able to recall. She'd only remember that when he rolled off her he took her in his arms and they lay wrapped in one another. He smoothed her hair and kissed her temples and she palmed the contours of his muscular form.

Before long, he was ready for her again. But this time, in contrast to before, the ferocity was replaced with tenderness, the greedy need with slow and sultry desire.

She rode him, taking him deeply with tantalizing, prolonged strokes. He held her there, buried inside her, pulling her down to kiss her, sweetly exploring.

He touched her with reverence, devotion, with such care she thought she might float away on the exquisite lightness of his caresses.

Slow, deep, ardent and passionate. They concluded with a mutual release so intimate and trusting, she whispered his name while tears trickled down her cheeks. He kissed them away.

So this was what it meant to be with a man she loved. A man who loved her.

He'd been worth the wait.

KENT PULLED PHAE BACK AGAINST his chest as he relaxed into the sloping back of the deep, claw-footed bath tub. The warm water soothed his muscles, muscles worn out in the very best of causes.

He softly kissed Phae's hair. She'd insisted on pinning it up, and though he liked it best down, he didn't much mind. He nuzzled her and inhaled her sweet scent, like sunshine and spring.

She snuggled in his arms, melting into him perfectly. "I think we forgot something."

A condom, he realized with a start. They'd forgotten their first time, too, though they hadn't talked about it, everything had gone wrong so quickly afterward that there had been no time to discuss it.

"Do you mind?" he asked, realizing the idea of a pregnant Phae filled him with a sense of euphoria.

She turned her head and smiled up at him. "No."

"Me either." He hugged her tightly. "We could have made a baby just now."

She lay her head back against his chest. "It's not likely. I don't think we should worry about it."

She looked so trusting and beautiful as she reclined against him, so peaceful. His insides turned over. She was his now. Now and hopefully forever.

"You know why I sold Kenrik and bought this house, don't you?" he asked.

"I don't want to presume anything," she answered evenly, but he could detect a hint of what she wanted to hear.

And he was happy to give it to her. "I did it because you said you'll never leave Zeke's Bend."

"I hoped that was what you would say."

"There was no help for it."

She pushed an escaped, damp lock of hair behind her adorable ear. "Are you sure this is what you want to do? For yourself, and not only for me?"

"Of course I'm sure," he said.

Some water splashed over the edge of the tub as she sat up and twisted to look at him. "It's just that you can be impulsive sometimes and I want to make sure you've thought this out."

He tried not to stare at her generous breasts that were glistening wetly in front of him, her nipples perky and hard, begging to be licked. "Of course I'm sure," he managed to say.

"Small towns aren't for everyone, Kent. I know that." Her breasts bobbed slightly as she breathed.

Kent grunted as he took her by the shoulders and turned her back around, sending more water onto the tile floor. He wrapped his arms around her, resuming their former position.

"If we're going to have a discussion, I think it's best if we stay like this," he said to the slippery woman struggling against him. "And you'd better quit sliding against me like that, too."

Phae abruptly stilled. "I only want to make sure that you know what you're doing."

He smiled with satisfaction when she leaned back against him. Her breasts were firm against his forearms, and he shifted his arms slightly, revealing the tops of her breasts that were only half-covered by the water. Her dusky nipples remained enticingly pert. He slipped his hands under her breasts and ran his fingers over the perky buds.

She trembled. "I thought we were supposed to be having a conversation. I can't think while you're doing that."

He squeezed her, pushing the perfect globes up out of the water. He couldn't believe how he wanted her again already. He couldn't get enough, it seemed.

But they did need to talk so he needed to get a grip. But not on her. Groaning, he released her breasts.

"Cover yourself, woman," he said brusquely.

Phae crossed her arms over her chest, hiding her tempting breasts from his view. Too bad, he thought, but it had to be done.

He took a deep breath. "I completed the sale of Kenrik quite a while ago, but I didn't tell you because we weren't in the right place for it yet."

"So you sold your business before you knew I'd take you back?"

"I did. After everything that happened between us, the way you made me feel, our connection, I could never have packed up and gone back to Phoenix. Even if I couldn't have you, ultimately, I couldn't imagine leaving you. It was an easy decision, in the end."

"We are pretty incredible together," she said, her voice easy with pleasure. "You want to do it again?"

"You know I do," Kent said. "Have I mentioned that I like insatiable women?"

She smiled and sighed happily. "Lucky for me."

"So here's my plan. I've got the renovations underway here but I'll stay on at Aunt Eugenia's unless I get a better offer," he said.

"That wasn't a slick hint at all," she said.

"I never thought I was slick. I make up for it by being tenacious."

"You are definitely that."

"I think I may start a new business. And Phae, I'd like us to do it together."

She stiffened in his arms.

"Don't overreact," he said gently. "I'm not making demands like before. I only want you to know what I'm thinking and what I'd like us to do. It's not what we have to do, okay? Besides, I hope you're finally willing to admit that hairdressing isn't a sacred calling for you."

"Well, no it isn't, but I'm not as terrible at it as some people think."

"Of course you're not. So this new business is something we can talk about later. It can be anything we want it to be, Phae. Think about it."

"I take that to mean you got a good price when you sold Kenrik."

"I did. Thanks to you. My refusal to give them a firm answer made them raise their bid several times. My bank accounts thank you. Though I didn't want to brag."

She laughed lightly. "Sure you didn't."

"Well, maybe a little. You can't blame me for wanting to impress the woman of my dreams."

"I've never been the woman of any man's dreams before," she whispered.

"You are now. And one other thing. I want to officially say that I changed my mind about Captain Nice Guy. I still think it's dangerous, but I respect how much you've trained for it, and how good you are at it. I trust you, you know that, don't you?"

She nodded. "Now, yes. But I'm not as sure about being the captain as I was before. I've always accepted that by trying to help someone, I might not always do the best thing. No one's perfect. But after what happened with Leon and Meg, I don't know if the risk is worth it."

He smoothed her hair. "Give it some time."

"I don't think time will help, Kent. I think I should quit."

"No, you shouldn't quit."

"There you go again, telling me what to do."

"Expressing an opinion isn't telling you what to do," he said.

Phae sat up and turned to look at him. "Let's not talk about this right now. I want to feel good for a while."

"I want that, too," he said. And he did want it, but he couldn't ignore what she'd said. This wasn't right and he needed to reach inside her, not let her push him away every time he questioned her.

"I'm glad," she said. "Kiss me."

"I will in a moment. First, give me an actual good reason for you to quit helping people."

"I did."

"No you didn't. It sounded to me like things have gotten hard, and there have been some consequences you'll have to deal with, and instead of working them out, you want to run away. Do you always do that? Quit when things get hard?"

He hated to see her frown, but there was no help for it. He had to get through to her. He couldn't imagine a future with a quitter.

"Phae, is that why you left Chicago? Because it was too hard?" he asked.

She reacted as vehemently as he'd expected. She pushed away from him, sloshing a great wave of water over the side of the tub.

She crossed her arms over her chest and gave him a hard look. "I'm not a quitter. I told you why I left Chicago and now you're throwing it in my face."

"No I'm not. I want the truth about what happened, and I know you haven't given it to me. You say you trust me, but you continue to hide."

"I don't want to talk about this. You're going to ruin everything." She struggled to untangle herself from his legs so she could get out of the tub.

"I am not. And you're staying put." He grabbed her shoulders and held her tightly. "I'm not accusing you of lying, but I know you didn't tell me the whole truth that night at the fair. I knew it then and I know it even more now. You've never told anyone but your grandmother, so why would you have trusted me with it when you'd only known me for a week? And while we're at it, I'd like to know how your grandmother fits into everything."

Phae grabbed the sides of the tub. "I've told you as much as you need to know."

"To hell with that. You owe me the truth."

"I don't owe you anything."

CHAPTER TWENTY-SEVEN

IN FRUSTRATION, KENT RELEASED her shoulders. "Fine. But maybe you owe it to yourself to talk about it, get over it and move the hell on."

With that, he climbed out of the tub. The floor was half-flooded so he had to fight for footing. Grabbing some towels, he wrapped one around his waist, threw the rest on the floor, then stomped out of the bathroom and into the bedroom, ignoring the curses coming from the angry woman in the tub.

He fumed silently as he poured himself a shot of bourbon from the small table. She said she didn't owe him anything. The more he thought about it, the angrier he got. They loved each other. She said she loved him. If that didn't gain her trust and confidence, what would?

He stomped to the armoire and pulled out a pair of bathrobes. He pulled one on and when Phae came charging out of the bathroom, struggling to pin a towel around herself, he tossed her the other robe.

She stepped aside and let it fall to the floor. "I don't need that," she said, looking around the room. "I'm finding my clothes and then I'm leaving."

Kent's stomach churned. "You've got to be kidding."

She snatched up her pants. "I'm not. You blew it."

Something snapped inside him, something he couldn't name but which changed everything. He'd had enough. "It's easy for you, isn't it? Things get a little tough, things are said that you don't like, and you cut and run. It's all you've done since I met you. You act like you're tougher than nails, but you're actually soft as putty."

"Shut up," she said, pulling on the pants under her towel. "You don't know me."

"Maybe I didn't, but I'm getting a handle on it now. I would, since I'm the one who's done all the work in this relationship. All you do is quit whenever you're disagreed with. If that's what it means when you say you love me, then I don't want that kind of love. And Phae, it's not the kind of love I've offered you."

She had bent over to pick up her shirt, but she stopped and sat down on the floor. She didn't say anything for the longest time. When she covered her face with her hands, Kent had to struggle not to go comfort her.

He took another great gulp of bourbon, and focused on the way it scalded his throat. "Go on. Get your clothes on and leave. I'm not running after you anymore. If I'm not who you want, then there's no point."

Phae didn't move. Kent set his drink on a shelf and vigorously rubbed his hair with a towel before tossing it over the armoire door.

"I told you to go ahead and leave. You don't owe me anything."

Phae slowly pulled on her shirt then lifted her head. His jaw clenched when he saw a tear fall down her silken cheek.

"I do owe you, Kent," she said so quietly he could hardly hear. "I'm sorry. I've been on my own for so long, I've forgotten how to be part of something else. Something more, like us. And I'm afraid of what you'll think of me …"

Her voice trailed off when Kent walked up to her.

He held out his hand. "Trust me, Phae. Trust us."

She thought about it, then nodded and took his hand. He helped her up and led her to the plush settee. They sat side-by-side. He didn't let go of her hand.

"Do you want a drink?" he asked, lifting her chin and pushing a lock of hair off her face.

She shook her head, her beautiful brown eyes shining with unshed tears.

Kent's heart ached for her, but backing down now wouldn't do either of them any good. "Tell me why you quit your job in Chicago."

She looked away. "You're going to think I'm stupid."

"I won't. You're the loveliest, most passionate and smartest woman I've ever met. Just take a deep breath and tell me."

She inhaled, exhaled, then looked him squarely in the eye. "I didn't want to quit my job. I was forced into it."

"How?"

She glanced away then back to him again. "Sexual harassment."

"You had to quit because someone sexually harassed you? That's illegal."

"No. I sexually harassed someone else."

Before he could stop himself, he barked out a laugh. "Ridiculous! You'd never do such a thing. Damn, you'd never have to. You're joking."

"I'm not joking, Kent," she said in a deadened tone. "It's part of my official work record at Fullerton."

He stared at her. "You're serious."

She nodded mutely and turned her gaze on her hands resting on her knees.

"I think we could both use a drink," he said and headed to the small table where he refilled his glass and poured a fresh one for Phae.

She accepted the drink, took a large gulp then coughed loudly. He patted her back.

"Sorry," she mumbled once she'd caught her breath. "Not used to the hard stuff anymore."

"It's okay. I like that in a woman."

She set her drink aside. "It wasn't true, about the harassment. I didn't sexually harass anyone."

Kent sat back down beside her. "Of course you didn't. Why don't you start at the beginning?"

She settled into the corner of the settee, looking resigned, tired and frightened all at the same time. "It was a big deal to get signed on to Fullerton straight out of college. And getting that job meant my parents' investment in Harvard and their sacrifices had been worth it. I'd made the big time. You can't imagine how it was. Everyone in the family was so proud, and they counted on me to succeed. All the Joneses."

Kent hated to think of the pressure she must have felt. His own parents and aunt thought everything Kent did was perfect, whether he failed or succeeded didn't matter to them.

"I had no idea what I was getting into when I took that job," she continued. "I was still a small-town girl, even after Harvard, and I was mixed in with these big-city sharks. I don't think I ever stood a chance, but I didn't know it at the time. All I knew was I had to do whatever it took to succeed. I worked day and night and though I had a few small setbacks, I advanced quickly."

She reached for her glass and took a small sip of the strong liquor. "Then I made a fatal mistake. I slept with my boss."

Though he knew it was foolish, Kent's hackles rose at the thought of innocent Phae in the hands of her worldlier, probably depraved, boss. Not that he had any real reason to think the guy was depraved, but whatever.

"What's his name?" he asked on an impulse.

She cast a sideways glance over the top of her glass. "It hardly matters. The sex wasn't any good, by the way. It may not have been his fault, I suppose. I was only with him because I was lonely and homesick and overwhelmed by the job."

"I can understand that," he said.

"I suppose, but it was so stupid. We'd gone on a sales trip to New York. Our last night at the hotel, I drank a little too much. I was on a high because the trip had been successful and was a huge coup, and I wanted to share that happiness with someone else. I'd been so unhappy for so long, and I finally had a reason to celebrate. Unfortunately, I celebrated with my boss."

She adjusted herself on the settee, turned more toward Kent. "He was a vice-president and had always been nice, showing me the ropes, giving me advice. I thought he liked me."

Kent lightly touched her leg, hoping to dispel some of her forlorn air.

She shook her head as if she could shake away the bad memories. "What can I say? I'm an idiot. We flew back to Chicago the next day. He was really sweet on the plane and I thought I'd found someone to care for, so I didn't even mind that the sex was lousy. Sex wasn't what I was after, anyway. He dropped me off at my apartment and kissed me goodbye. He said he'd see me at work the next day."

"When I showed up at work the next morning," she said, "I ran straight to his office and jumped into his chair with him. He acted flustered and put out and kept saying that what I was doing wasn't necessary. That's exactly how he said it, 'Phae, this isn't necessary.' He told me to go see my new office. Before I could ask him what he was talking about, he shoved me out of the room and practically shut the door in my face."

Her upper lip curled. "I actually asked his secretary about a new office, and she gave me the strangest look before telling me to go to the regional director's office. As I headed that way, I noticed people giving me odd looks. Some would stare and whisper as I passed. It was bizarre and made me nervous. I hadn't noticed them acting this way when I entered the building, but then, I'd been so stupidly happy, I wasn't paying attention."

"I quickly found out that I'd been promoted," she said. "The ex-director was in the office boxing up his belongings when I arrived. He told me, in a nasty tone, that our jobs had been switched. He'd been demoted and I'd been promoted, and he'd been left with the task of telling me. It was outrageous, but there wasn't anything I could do about it. The guy was livid, and who could blame him? He sneered when he left and made a few filthy comments I'd rather not repeat. To summarize, he called me a whore who was sleeping her way to the top."

A profound anger was growing inside Kent. He attempted to contain it for Phae's sake, but it clawed at the edges of his restraint.

Phae ran her tapered finger around the brim of her glass. "I can't stand admitting it, but like a fool, I ran crying to my boss. I told him I didn't understand what was happening, that I hadn't slept with him to get a promotion and that I liked and wanted to be with him. Guess what he said?"

Kent could only grunt a negative reply.

"He told me to back off, to quit pretending to be innocent. He said I'd known 'the score' as he called it. I'd been rewarded and that was that. If he wanted to sleep with me again, he'd let me know, and in the meantime, I needed to keep my mouth shut. After all, he had a wife and children to protect."

Kent couldn't contain himself anymore. He leaped off the settee and began pacing the room, trying to walk off his anger.

"You're mad at me," Phae whispered.

"Not at you, Phae. I'm—"

"I swear, Kent. I didn't know he was married. He didn't wear a ring and he had no pictures on his desk, and in the time I'd known him he'd never mentioned a family. I think back on it now and I wonder if he wasn't lying, making up a convenient excuse to get rid of me. Maybe that's wishful thinking. But don't you think that someone in the office would have mentioned meeting his wife and kids? Wouldn't he have a picture somewhere? I don't know, and the worst part is, I'll never know the truth. I'm afraid to know it. Thinking that I'm an adulterer makes me want to throw up."

"Don't think about it," he said. "There's no point. The man lied either way. He's slime. Tell me his name and I'll ruin him faster than you can blink."

CHAPTER TWENTY-EIGHT

PHAE DID BLINK, SEVERAL TIMES, stared at him and blinked. "What are you talking about?"

He shouldn't have said that, he realized. He'd put her off her confession. "Never mind. I hate that you were treated that way. Go on."

"The story gets worse," she said with a bleak look. "You might want to sit down."

He wasn't sure he could handle any more. "No, let me pace. It'll be better that way."

Phae sighed. "Suit yourself. That day went by in a blur. It was a nightmare that I sleepwalked through. I buried myself in figuring out my new job. Before I knew it, it was almost midnight. When I realized how late it was and how silent the building had become, I started to leave, but I never made it out of my office. The ex-director was standing in my doorway."

Kent stopped pacing, his heart taking a dive in his chest.

"He'd been drinking heavily," she said. "He called me some more filthy names and started coming toward me. Though his voice was slurred, I could understand it. He believed that since he got demoted, he ought to get a little something from the slut who'd stolen his job."

Kent realized his hands had tightened into fists. He shoved them behind his back so she wouldn't see. He could hardly breathe. "Did he … hurt you?"

"He attacked me, threw me down on my desk, touched me …" her eyes went glassy. "I couldn't get away, no matter how hard I fought, how hard I tried. He was too strong. And he wasn't even a big guy, or a fit guy. But he was too much for me. I couldn't get away. All I could do was scream."

Kent wanted to charge from the room and track down the bastard, rip him to pieces, shred his very soul. But Phae needed him to calm down and listen to her, he reminded himself. His body taut, he said, "I'm sorry, Phae. You don't have to talk about this anymore. I didn't realize—"

"No, it's okay," she said, her eyes clearing. "He didn't rape me. It was close, though. I got lucky when a security guard showed up. The guard stood in the doorway, coughed a few times, and when the ex-director heard it, he jumped off me and ran out of the room, trying to zip his pants as he ran."

She continued. "I lay there for a few minutes, catching my breath and trying to get myself together. When I was together enough to leave, and had straightened myself up, the guard escorted me to my car."

"Did you call the police?" Kent asked.

"The guard suggested it, but I told him no, it was all my fault. That's what I believed. I'd caused it to happen because I'd stolen the guy's job. If I hadn't done that, he never would have gotten drunk and been angry enough to attack me. All my fault. That's how I saw it."

Kent went to her then, sat beside her and tried to comfort her.

"No, Kent," she said, pushing away his arm. "If you do that I'll break down. Just let me finish and get it over with."

Kent collapsed back on his side of the settee and willed himself to be still and patient. Phae was here, alive and healthy. She was fine. That was the past, and this was now. But his heart broke for her.

She took another small sip of her drink. "I didn't sleep much, and after too much thinking, I went to work the next morning determined to force my boss into returning the ex-director to his former job and me to mine."

"But I didn't get the chance," she continued. "Security met me at the door and I was immediately ushered to my boss's office. I was shocked to see the ex-director in there, too. I sat down and my boss proceeded to inform me that the ex-director had leveled a sexual harassment charge against me. I'd supposedly attacked him in my office the night before."

"I can't believe they could be so ... so ...." Kent said. "I don't have the words for it."

"Yeah, well, I was such a big fool. It's hard to talk about this and have any dignity left."

"Screw dignity," Kent said. "That's nothing between us. And you weren't a fool."

"I was." She smoothed her palm over her thigh. "I'd never bothered to learn the rules of the game. I'd left myself ignorant and unprepared. My arguments were nothing to them. They cut them down before I could begin them. The bottom line was, it was my word against the ex-director's word, and he'd been with the company ten years longer than me, so who would they believe?"

She laughed in an ironic way. "They even had signed testimony from the security guard stating that I'd admitted the encounter was my fault. My boss told me I was finished at Fullerton, that they wouldn't pursue civil or criminal charges against me if I'd quit right then and go on my way. If I didn't quit, I'd be fired."

Kent emptied his glass in a long draught. "Did you fight them?"

"I didn't see there being anything left to fight for. Either way, I'd lost my job. I quit, signed a few papers and then was escorted out of the building by a couple of guards who'd already boxed up my things. That was the most humiliating walk of my life. I still burn when I think about it."

Although he figured she'd resist, he leaned over and hugged her tightly anyway. "I don't blame you for leaving Chicago, Phae. Anyone in your position would have."

"But I didn't leave Chicago, not right away. I couldn't come back home a failure; I had to find another job. And I tried, Kent, I really did. I tried so hard, day after day, week after week, month after month. It was nothing but rejection after rejection. I couldn't even get a part time job at the corner coffee shop to make a little money to keep me going while looking for something better. It was devastating."

He couldn't imagine dealing with such constant rejection. He suspected, though, that he knew the cause of it. "Your boss had blackballed you, hadn't he?"

She pulled back and looked up at him. "Yeah. How'd you know that? I didn't figure it out until an old schoolmate of mine told me after an interview that they'd checked my work history and called Fullerton and they didn't have anything good to say about me. Lies, all of it. That I was abrasive, didn't work well with others, had a bad attitude, left work early. You name it, if it was bad, I was it."

"It makes sense. Your boss couldn't have you making a success of yourself elsewhere and creating a name for yourself. You might one day come back to haunt him, so to speak."

"Yeah, I think that's exactly it. Wish I would have figured it out back then so I wouldn't have wasted so much time. When I learned what was happening, I dropped Fullerton from my resume, hoping that would help, but with that big gap in my work history, no one was interested. And by that point, I'd already applied to every company worth applying to. I was done. Finished. Out of funds and energy. He beat me. I had to come home. A loser and fool."

"You weren't a fool," he said. "Or a loser. Those two men, however, are bastards."

"Like I said, I didn't educate myself. I let them walk all over me. Because I quit, I didn't even try to get severance pay or unemployment. I used up all my savings and ran up my credit cards trying to find a job I'd been blackballed from. Grandma Jones had to wire me bus money so I could get home. I couldn't have been more ashamed."

"You weren't to blame, no matter what you say." Kent studied her. "But you don't sound angry about it. I think I'm angrier than you are."

"It happened three years ago," she said. "I've had to accept what happened, and most of what I'm left with is embarrassment. Sometimes I think maybe there was a reason for it beyond my stupidity. I hope there was, anyway."

With the first hint of emotion she'd shown in a while, she said, "Grandma Jones sure was mad about it, mad at them, like you. After I cried for almost a whole night, she came to me with a piece of paper. She didn't say a word, just handed it to me. On one side of the paper were all these quotes. Grandma believed wisdom could be found in the past. I still have that paper. Mostly, they were about having the strength to fight when all the odds are against you, and that the fight is more important than the victory."

"At first," she continued, "I thought she wanted me to go back to Chicago, and there was no way I could do that. But she pointed to the bottom of the page. Do you remember the quote I told you by Arthur Ashe?"

He nodded. "Sure. What we give, makes a life."

"Pretty close." She stood up and walked over to the bed. "Grandma always had a plan, and while I'd been crying, she'd made one for me. On the back of the paper was a list of occupations complete with addresses and phone numbers."

With a wistful expression, Phae sat on the edge of the bed. "I'll always remember the way she looked at me while she explained everything. She was so fierce, but in a protective way. I miss her so much."

Kent went to her and took her hand.

"I'm okay," she said. "Grandma's plan was the life you see me living today. She had me pick a job from the list of occupations that I thought I could live with. They were all jobs with what she called a high gossip potential, like police dispatcher, social worker and waitress. Obviously, I picked hairdresser. And to make sure I never had another close call with an evil man, there were phone numbers for different defense and martial arts classes."

"Are you telling me that being Captain Nice Guy was your grandmother's idea?" Kent asked.

"That's right, though we didn't call it that. That was some joker at the paper's idea. Grandma certainly didn't make fun of it. She told me that if I learned how to fight for others, then I'd learn how to fight for myself. At first, my heart wasn't in it, but it finally became important to me. I care about these people now and can't imagine not being in their lives, even though it's in a silent helper kind of way."

She thought for a moment, then said, "When Grandma died, she left me the building downtown where I have my shop and apartment, along with her china cabinet and some money. In a sealed letter she left with her will, she wrote that the shop was for my livelihood for now, and that every time I looked at the china cabinet I was to remember to fight for what I believed in, and she said I should save the money to start the business of my heart when I was healed and ready."

Kent sat beside her. "She must have loved you a great deal. She even made sure James would keep an eye out for you."

"That was a surprise. I can't believe James knew about me all along."

"I'm sorry I never got a chance to meet your grandmother."

"Me too. She would have liked you. Or more to the point, she would have liked to butt heads with you."

"I get the feeling that I wouldn't have had a chance of winning. I've had a hard enough time with you."

She dropped back on the bed, her hands behind her head, and stared up at the ceiling. "I'm not the same person I was three years ago. Not even close. I used to be such a pushover and now I'm not. I can say no when it's important now. Grandma Jones did that for me."

He leaned over and tenderly stroked her cheek. "No. You did that for yourself. Your grandmother only nudged you in the right direction."

She smiled. "Maybe you're right." Her smile fell almost instantly. "After everything I've told you, what do you think … of me? I mean, I've been so—"

Unable to resist any longer, he stretched beside her and gathered her into his arms. "You're a strong, brave woman. I don't deserve you, Phae Jones. I'm sorry about what happened in Chicago, and how I accused you of being a quitter."

"Don't be sorry. I have been a quitter, and I think if you hadn't made me realize it, I would have walked out of this house and made the biggest mistake of my life. You know what? I actually feel better after telling you everything. It's been this huge ball of shame and guilt and regret that's been rotting in my stomach. Maybe it's gone now. I feel lighter. Freer."

An incredulous expression washed over her features. "It is, Kent. I think it's gone. I can't believe it. Do you think it will still be gone tomorrow?"

He watched silently as Phae unconsciously rubbed her stomach. Without thinking about it, he said, "I love you, Phae Jones. No probably about it."

She looked up at him, her big brown eyes wide and trusting. "And I love you. I love you for not giving up on me."

They held one another, savoring the novelty of being intimate, being together. He was a lucky man, he thought, to have won such a woman.

She pushed her hand under his robe and ran fingertips over his chest, sending electric tendrils out over his skin. His body responded instantly. He wanted her ... always and all the time.

He looked at her smile and smiled in return.

"So are you finally un-declaring your independence from me?" he asked.

She raked a fingernail down his abs and made him shudder. "I guess so. And that means you won the war after all."

"I'll need your complete and total surrender, you know," he said, tugging up the hem of her shirt. "And I'll require some war damages. Let's start with you relinquishing all rights to your clothing. I think that's fair."

She took in a quick breath as he peeled the shirt over her head and hungrily eyed her bare breasts. "A little heavy-handed, but I accept."

He flicked his tongue over her nipple, pleased when it hardened right away. "And you'll have to serve some time under house arrest. In bed. Not allowed out of it ... ever."

She laughed. "Idiot. I have to work, you know. And eat. And have a life."

"You don't need to work. I'm rich, remember?"

"You're not *that* rich, I'm sure." She cupped his cock and balls and he thought his head might fly off his shoulders.

"The hell I'm not." He pulled her hand away, flipped her onto her back and pinned both her hands over her head. "I'm a billionaire."

She laughed and laughed. "That was a good one," she said finally.

He gently bit her nipple and enjoyed her gasp. "I'm a billionaire, Phae. If you don't believe it now, you'll believe it when we're married."

"Who said anything about getting married?"

"I just did. Marry me, Phae, and help me figure out what to do with all this damned money."

She struggled and tried to get free from his hold, but he held firm. "You know I can make you let me go, right? I mean, I have three years of training and all."

He licked around the circumference of her high, round breast. "I know, but you won't because you don't want to hurt me. Besides, I'll let you go if that's what you really want."

"It's not what I want."

"Thank God."

She sighed and her chest rose and fell rapidly as he worked his hips against hers. "Are you really a billionaire?"

"Yep. The sale of Kenrik pushed my bottom line over the top."

"Do you really want to marry me?"

"Damned straight. And you're going to say yes because you know I'll get my way in the end. Remember, Kent won't relent."

She groaned. "That's so corny. But I love you anyway."

"And you'll marry me." He kissed her neck and licked at her ear lobe making her tremble.

"Oh, yes. I'll marry you ... as long as you don't tell anyone else that you're a billionaire. We'd never hear the end of it."

He grinned at the woman who had become the most dear thing to him in the world. "It's a deal. You can't back out now."

"Kiss me," she demanded.

Yep, he thought. Those were demands he could live with ... for the rest of his life.

EPILOGUE

Three months later

PHAE WATCHED AS THE BURLY moving man hauled out the last piece of exercise equipment from her old home. The room seemed bigger now that it was empty. She walked slowly through the rest of the rooms, checking to be certain she hadn't missed anything.

The only sad part about moving was that there hadn't been all that much to move. She was leaving the old furniture, so the living room didn't look much different from before, except for the absence of Grandma Jones' china cabinet.

She fondly touched the worn-out sofa. She understood now why she'd never bothered to decorate this home: it had never actually been a home. It had been a way station, a place to rest until her real life began. Somewhere deep inside she'd known this all along.

She smiled at Kent when he stepped inside the apartment, sunlight streaming through the door, sparkling in his jet black hair.

"Is that everything?" he asked, surveying the room.

"That's it."

Kent yelled out to the worker to head over to Belleterre, then said to Phae, "Ready to go get incorporated?"

"Yeah, but let's walk. It's a beautiful day for November," Phae said as she took his hand. "And the office is just on the square."

"A stroll with my lovely wife? I think I can handle that. Do you want a few moments to say goodbye to the old place?"

She didn't bother with a final glance. "No. I'm done here."

She locked the front door then followed Kent into the beauty shop. Sylvie, looking dejected, sat in one of the hydraulic chairs.

"It's so weird without you, Phae," she said with a little sigh. "I'm going to miss you."

"We'll only be on our honeymoon for a month. That's not so long," Kent assured her.

"It's not that," Sylvie said. "I wouldn't want Phae to give up a trip to Europe for anything. No, it's that it'll never be the same here, now that she's not working here anymore."

"Aw, Sylvie," Phae said, patting her shoulder. "I'm going to miss you, too."

"It sure will be lonely." Sylvie looked around the small salon as if it were the size of a deserted football field. "All empty and lonely."

Phae grinned at her dramatics. "You're so full of it. Neesa told me that Aunt Meg's gonna graduate beauty school soon and when she gets her license, she'll be joining you here."

"Neesa's such a blabbermouth," Sylvie said. "But yes, it's true. Meg's been on that toot all this time about not being so dependent on men, or some other such nonsense. She sounded like you, Phae."

Phae and Kent gave one another a meaningful glance.

Sylvie fluffed her hair in front of the big mirror. "I don't know why so many women have such a problem about men supporting them. Oh well, at least I'll have some company before I go out of business from losing all of your regulars, Phae."

"I looked at the books last week and you're doing fine. It's not like my part was ever that profitable anyway. I mostly worked on family and older ladies who couldn't see well enough to know I sucked."

"Don't believe her, Kent," Sylvie said. "She was pretty good, actually. Not everybody has a flair for it, but she did okay. It's different with me. I get this sort of weird feeling when I'm working with hair. It's kind of supernatural. By the way, Phae, I absolutely love what you've been doing with your hair these days. All kind of wild and curly. Big hair suits you."

"Thanks. I think."

"She does it for me," Kent said, pulling her in close and nuzzling at her hair. "I think it's sexy as hell."

Sylvie laughed and Phae shoved at Kent's chest. "Stop that!"

"It's so cute. Newlyweds. Hey, aren't you two supposed to be heading out today? Can't believe you didn't go on your honeymoon right after your wedding," Sylvie said.

"It's only been a week. We had a few details to settle with the house and stuff," Phae said. "We'll have a big housewarming party when we get back. The house should be completely done by then."

"Good deal. I'll be there. Have fun on your trip. And be safe," Sylvie said.

They bid their farewells and Phae got a pang when the little bell over the door jingled as they left her shop. No, it wasn't her shop anymore. It was Sylvie's.

Phae and Kent walked toward the square.

"Are you nervous?" he asked.

"No. It's going to be great."

"We'll be helping a lot of people."

A thrill of excitement shot through her. "And having fun doing it."

"I'm still not convinced we can keep this a secret. Setting up facilities to train people to be Captain Nice Guys will be hard enough. Getting the right candidates who'll keep the secret … I don't know."

"I've got lots of ideas for that," Phae assured him, confident they'd pull it off. "Imagine it. Someday, I hope every town in the state has their own do-gooder ninja."

"I wish you'd quit bringing it up that I called you that."

"And I wish you weren't so good at sneaking up on me. You've become a real expert."

"All the better to seduce you, my dear."

"You should knock that off," she teased.

He coughed and sputtered, clutched his chest. "Stop seducing you? I think you've killed me finally. We've only been married a week and you're kicking me out of your bedroom."

Phae rolled her eyes. "It's not the seduction part I mind. It's the sneaking. You make me feel ... well ... like I'm losing my skills. You've sexed all the edge out of me."

He laughed loudly. "You're a hard woman, Phae Holmes." He pulled her into a gap between two buildings and began kissing her neck.

She giggled when he nibbled her earlobe. His every touch made her tingle, but she was particularly sensitive on the ear. "Stop it. People will see."

"I don't care. And you said you didn't mind me seducing you."

"Oh ... my," she moaned as he licked around the edge of her ear. "I can't remember what I was complaining about."

A loud voice boomed near them. "Okay you two kids. Break it up. There's a law against this kind of behavior in these parts."

Phae sprung away from Kent and looked around to see James watching them with a twinkle in his eye.

Kent gave James a sour look. "You have the worst timing, friend."

James pointed at Kent. "Don't you forget it. It's time you cleaned up your act and behaved like a respectable old married man."

"Never."

James shrugged then joined the pair as they resumed their walk.

"Are you ready to be Captain Nice Guy while we're gone?" Phae asked. "I don't want you screwing up my legacy."

"I think I can handle putting cutesy notes on bicycles and checking for keys in cars," he said in a gruff voice. "Don't know why you've had me working out so much. I'm so sore I can hardly move."

Phae tried not to smile but couldn't help herself. "Poor baby. I do appreciate it, though. It would have been suspicious if Captain Nice Guy had disappeared at the same time I went on my honeymoon. Aren't you having a little bit of fun?"

"I guess. But I prefer using my badge to help people."

Kent slapped his old friend on the back. "It's harder sneaking around than you thought it would be, isn't it? I know from experience."

"I'll be glad when you're home and we can get back to normal life. Well, if you can call a woman running around at night pretending to be a superhero normal." He held up his hands in a defensive gesture. "Now don't go getting riled up, Phae. I'm just joking with you."

"You'd best look out, James," Kent said. "I've had her softened up for months now and I don't want you ruining it."

Phae ignored the pair of them.

"So where are you two heading?" James asked.

"We're off to the lawyer's office to sign the incorporation paperwork for our new company," Kent answered.

"And what will this company do?"

"Design software," Phae lied easily. "But don't ask what kind. Kent hasn't decided yet. He won't settle on an idea."

"That's not true and you know it," Kent said. "The truth is that you're insatiable. I tell you, James, your cousin is so greedy, she won't let me out of bed long enough to get any work done."

"On that note, which I didn't want to hear by the way," James said, "I need to be getting back to the office. Have a safe trip and check in now and again so we know you're safe."

"We will," they assured him. Phae knew she'd definitely keep in touch because she'd want to know if he was doing her job correctly or not.

After they parted from James, Phae remembered something she'd read online.

"I meant to tell you," she said, "I saw on a news site last night that my old boss at Fullerton has been indicted on charges of fraud and mishandling the company's retirement funds. Pretty wild, huh?"

"Interesting," Kent said, sounding way too casual for Phae's liking.

"The ex-director I knew was also arrested, as an accomplice."

"Is that so?"

"I thought you might have heard about it."

"Not that I recall."

"Not that you recall?" She stopped and gave him a hard look. "Come on."

Kent looked in the opposite direction, craning his neck to see nothing worth seeing. "I don't see why you'd say that. I'll admit I'm not sorry they've been caught."

"I'm not sorry either," Phae said. "You figured out who they were, and you went after them, didn't you? I know you did, so don't try to hide it. There's one thing I have to know, though—you didn't set them up, right?"

Kent turned to her and blew out a breath. "I won't apologize for it. They had it coming, both of them, the bastards. But no, I didn't set them up. They were totally crooked and my investigators had no problem finding enough dirt to bury them three times over. They were bad men, Phae, to more people than you."

She felt a surge of pride. She leaned up and kissed him on the cheek. "And you are a good man, Kent. The best man I've known."

He beamed down at her. "I was afraid you'd be mad, so I didn't tell you."

"I'm not mad. I'm relieved. I've always felt guilty that they might be hurting other women, and I didn't stop them. I'm glad. Thank you, Kent, for defending my honor."

"It was my pleasure, Ma'am," he drawled.

They walked along for a bit until Kent broke the silence. "So, my lovely wife, any last minute doubts? Once we cross this street we'll be at the lawyer's office."

"No. Except the name. I keep worrying CNG, Ltd. will be too obvious."

Kent shook his head. "No way. No one around here will even know it's us, let alone make the connection to Captain Nice Guy."

"You're right. I've got last minute jitters, I guess."

"Like you had before our wedding?"

"I didn't have jitters, Kent. I've never been more sure about anything than I was about marrying you."

They shared an intimate look.

"Same here," he said.

"I will say, though," Phae said, "I had a moment's concern when Miss Eugenia called me the night before and talked my ear off about everything I need to know to keep you alive: vinegar head wraps, garlic rubs, calming teas and infusions, all sorts of smelly stuff I'll have to put up with if you're going to survive the winter."

"You're a saint," Kent said, squeezing her gently.

They started across the street.

"Speaking of saints," he said as he reached into his pocket. "I happened to run across this little thing while we were moving the last of your stuff today. I don't suppose you could bless me by wearing this tonight on our honeymoon, could you?"

"What is it?" Phae peered closely at the black wad of fabric crumpled in his hand. "Oh, you're kidding me. It's that slutty little black dress you got me, isn't it? Forget it, buddy. I'm not wearing that thing."

"Come on. It's not that bad. Be a nice girl, Phae."

She snatched the dress and crammed it into her handbag. "No way. You knew I wasn't a nice girl when you married me, so live with it."

They stopped in front of the lawyer's office. "True. You're pretty testy and crotchety." He leaned in and whispered near her ear. "And when you're in bed, when you're soft and hot as hell, you aren't nice there, either."

She shivered as his warm breath caressed her. "Neither are you."

"Just how I like it. I wouldn't have you any other way."

He pulled back, drawing his sexy fog with him. He gestured at the door. "After you, Mrs. Holmes."

She stopped beside him and stood on tiptoe to whisper in his ear. "I may not be a saint," she said, "but I could be a fortune teller."

He raised an eyebrow in speculation.

She gave him a sexy wink. "I think I see a little black dress in your near future."

She loved to make her man groan.

MIA'S OTHER BOOKS

Don't miss Sylvie's story in the second book of the *Fabulous Jones Girls* series: *Two Heirs for the Billionaire:*

Sometimes, one night can last a lifetime

There were three things Sylvie Jones didn't expect to happen when she took a weekend trip to Chicago:

1. Finally kicking her boyfriend, Alan, to the curb (he *seriously* deserved it).

2. Meeting a sexy and wealthy stranger named Heath, and being mistaken for a paid escort.

3. Not correcting Heath's error and … a little of *this* and a whole lot of *that* later, Sylvie's taking an airplane flight of shame all the way back home (she isn't really ashamed—the night was too incredible for that).

None of these three unexpected events might have changed her life if it weren't for two more surprises which arrive nine months later—twins, Jadyn and Quentyn! Sylvie doesn't know for sure who their father is, but who cares. Her children are all hers and she can raise them all by herself.

This might have been the end of the matter, except for one final thing: Heath. He can't forget the incredible night he spent with a special lady in Chicago. He'd seek her out, but he doesn't know her name. She dashed off like Cinderella, not even leaving a shoe behind as a clue to her true identity.

He vows to find her. And Heath Collins, reclusive billionaire, always gets what he wants, no matter how long it takes. Getting the lady *and* twin baby boys, however, may be more than he bargained for.

ALL ABOUT MIA

Mia Caldwell has been fantasizing about stories of "Happily-Ever-After" since she was a little girl, and now that she's all grown up her "Happily-Ever-After" stories have taken a steamier turn!

After graduating from college Mia still wasn't quite sure what she wanted to do with her life. Bored with her day job as an administrative assistant for a non-profit, she started writing stories on the side and sharing them with her friends. They gave her the push she needed to share them with you!

She lives in New York with two rascally cats named Link and Zelda, eats too much chocolate and Chinese take-out, and goes on way too many blind dates. She's still waiting for Mr. Right, but in the meantime she'll keep dreaming up the perfect man!

Made in the USA
Columbia, SC
26 June 2017